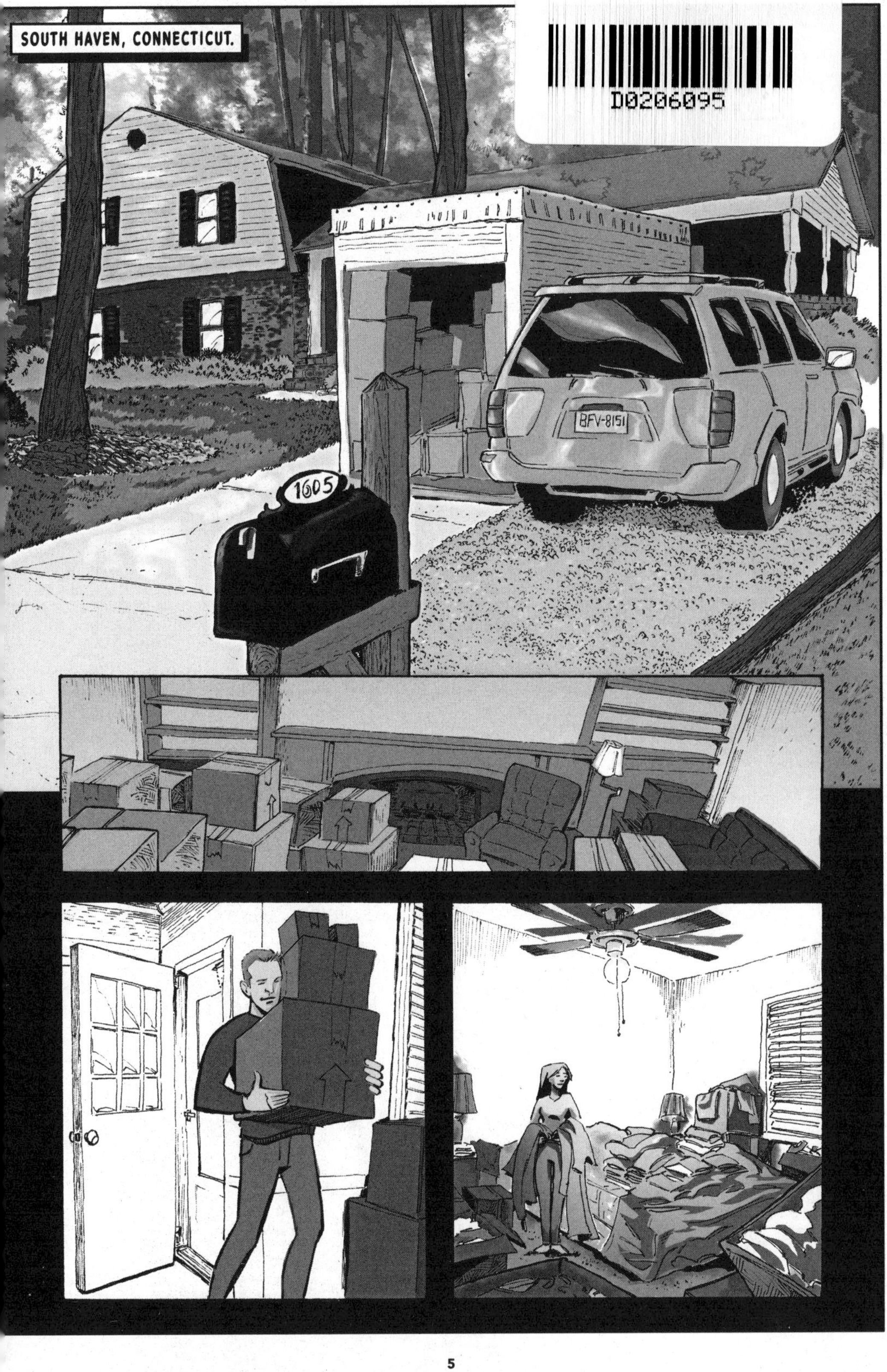
SOUTH HAVEN, CONNECTICUT.
1605
BFV-8151

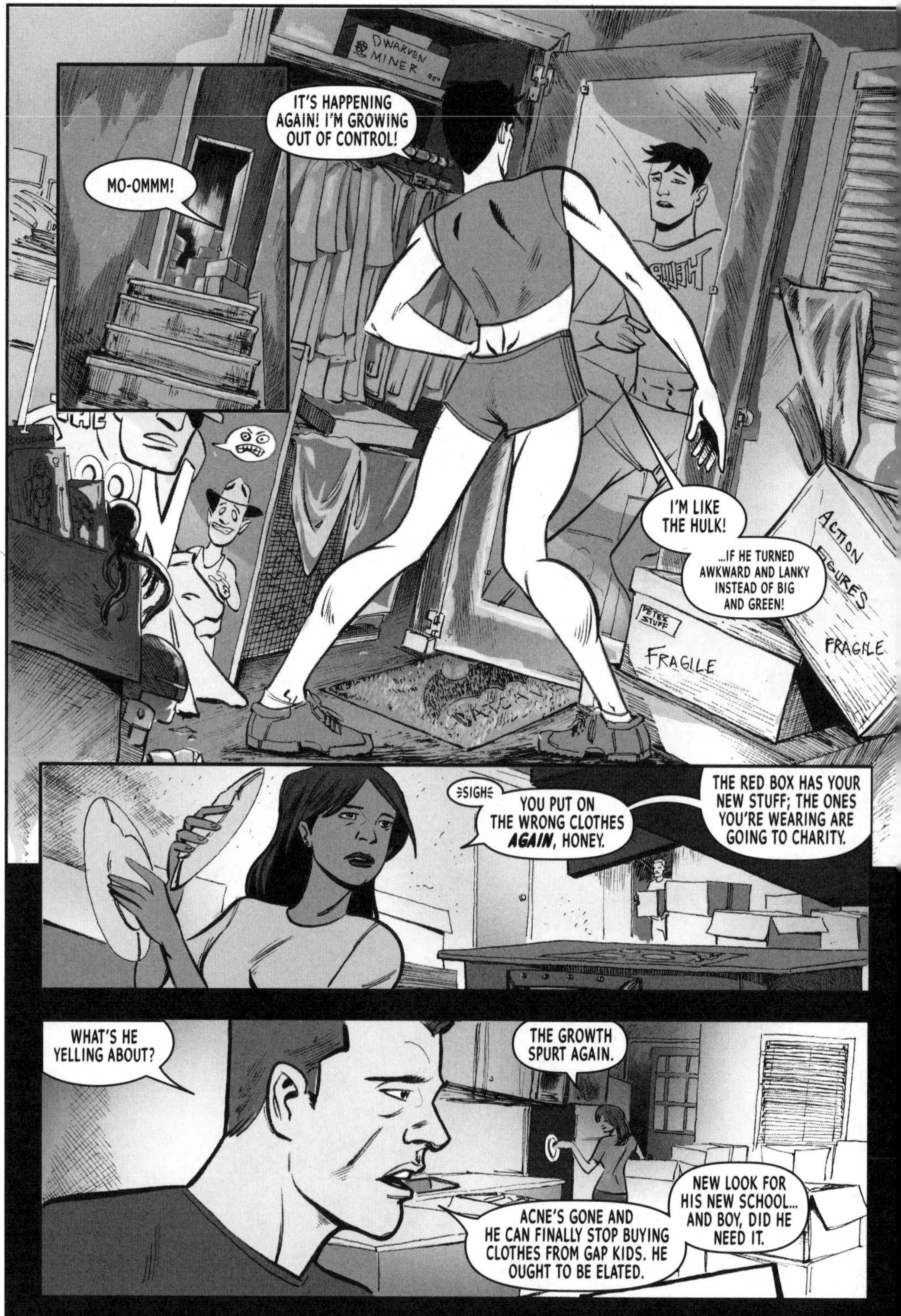
DWARVEN MINER
MO-OMMM!
IT'S HAPPENING AGAIN! I'M GROWING OUT OF CONTROL!
I'M LIKE THE HULK!
...IF HE TURNED AWKWARD AND LANKY INSTEAD OF BIG AND GREEN!
ACTION FIGURES
PETE'S STUFF
FRAGILE
FRAGILE
SIGH
YOU PUT ON THE WRONG CLOTHES ***AGAIN***, HONEY.
THE RED BOX HAS YOUR NEW STUFF; THE ONES YOU'RE WEARING ARE GOING TO CHARITY.
WHAT'S HE YELLING ABOUT?
THE GROWTH SPURT AGAIN.
ACNE'S GONE AND HE CAN FINALLY STOP BUYING CLOTHES FROM GAP KIDS. HE OUGHT TO BE ELATED.
NEW LOOK FOR HIS NEW SCHOOL... AND BOY, DID HE NEED IT.

LARP!™

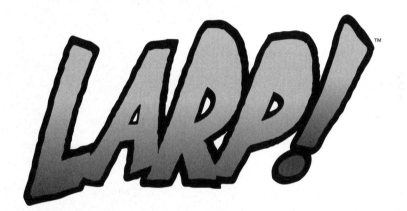

LARP! ™

TO GEEK OR NOT TO GEEK

CREATED AND WRITTEN BY
DAN JOLLEY AND SHAWN DeLOACHE

ILLUSTRATED BY
MARLIN SHOOP

LETTERING BY
GRAY GUNTER

DARK HORSE BOOKS

PRESIDENT AND PUBLISHER
MIKE RICHARDSON

EDITOR
BRENDAN WRIGHT

ASSISTANT EDITOR
IAN TUCKER

DESIGNER
JIMMY PRESLER

DIGITAL ART TECHNICIAN
CHRISTINA McKENZIE

PUBLISHED BY DARK HORSE BOOKS
A DIVISION OF DARK HORSE COMICS, INC.
10956 SE MAIN STREET
MILWAUKIE, OREGON 97222

DARKHORSE.COM

TO FIND A COMIC SHOP IN YOUR AREA CALL THE COMIC SHOP LOCATOR
SERVICE TOLL-FREE AT (888) 266-4226
INTERNATIONAL LICENSING: (503) 905-2377

FIRST EDITION: AUGUST 2015
ISBN 978-1-61655-686-0

LARP! BOOK 1: TO GEEK OR NOT TO GEEK

1 3 5 7 9 10 8 6 4 2
PRINTED IN THE UNITED STATES OF AMERICA

NEIL HANKERSON EXECUTIVE VICE PRESIDENT · TOM WEDDLE CHIEF FINANCIAL OFFICER ·
RANDY STRADLEY VICE PRESIDENT OF PUBLISHING · MICHAEL MARTENS VICE PRESIDENT
OF BOOK TRADE SALES · SCOTT ALLIE EDITOR IN CHIEF · MATT PARKINSON VICE PRESIDENT
OF MARKETING · DAVID SCROGGY VICE PRESIDENT OF PRODUCT DEVELOPMENT · DALE
LaFOUNTAIN VICE PRESIDENT OF INFORMATION TECHNOLOGY · DARLENE VOGEL SENIOR
DIRECTOR OF PRINT, DESIGN, AND PRODUCTION · KEN LIZZI GENERAL COUNSEL · DAVEY ESTRADA
EDITORIAL DIRECTOR · CHRIS WARNER SENIOR BOOKS EDITOR · CARY GRAZZINI DIRECTOR OF
PRINT AND DEVELOPMENT · LIA RIBACCHI ART DIRECTOR · CARA NIECE DIRECTOR OF
SCHEDULING · MARK BERNARDI DIRECTOR OF DIGITAL PUBLISHING

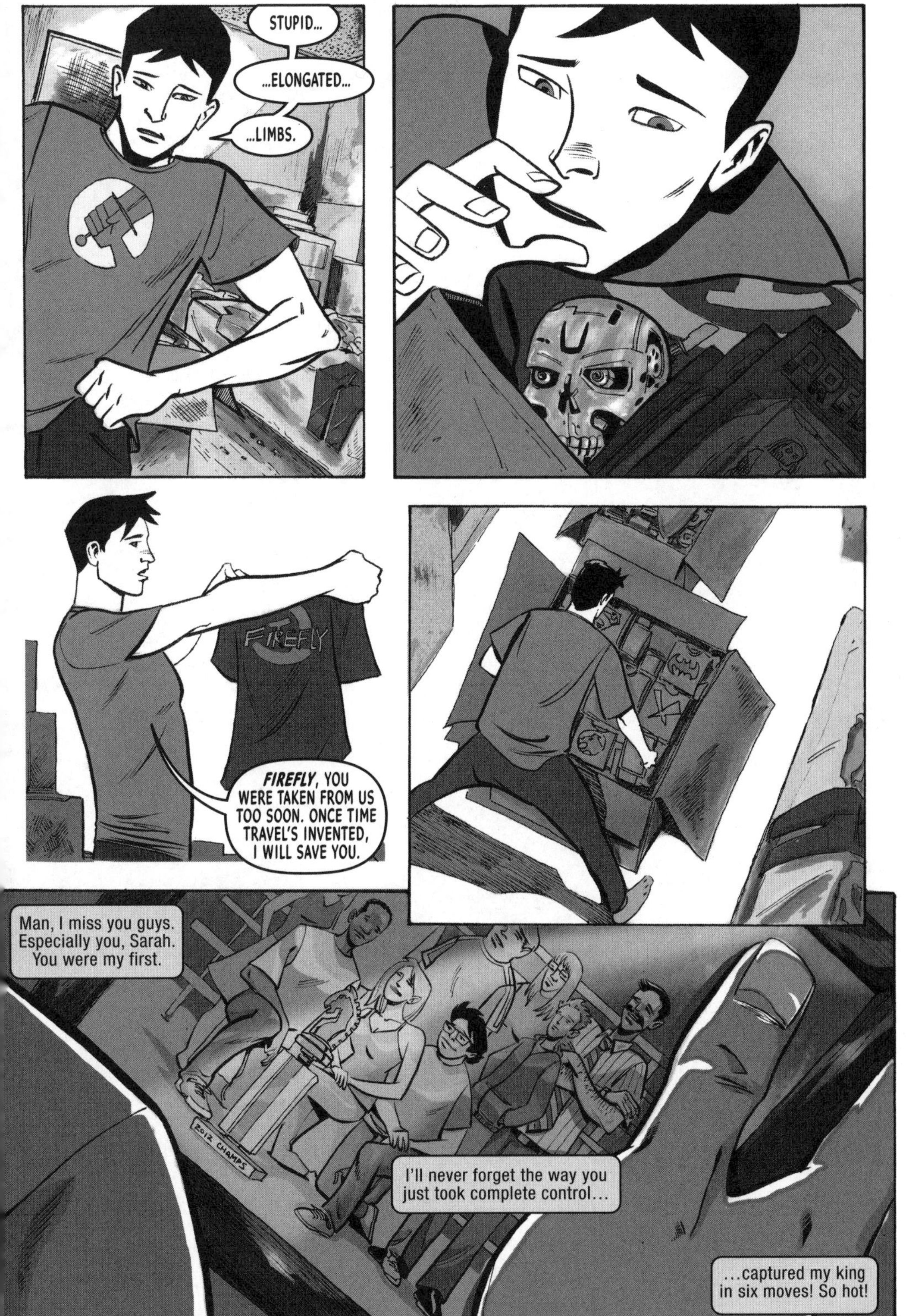
STUPID...
...ELONGATED...
...LIMBS.
FIREFLY
FIREFLY, YOU WERE TAKEN FROM US TOO SOON. ONCE TIME TRAVEL'S INVENTED, I WILL SAVE YOU.
Man, I miss you guys. Especially you, Sarah. You were my first.
2012 CHAMPS
I'll never forget the way you just took complete control...
...captured my king in six moves! So hot!

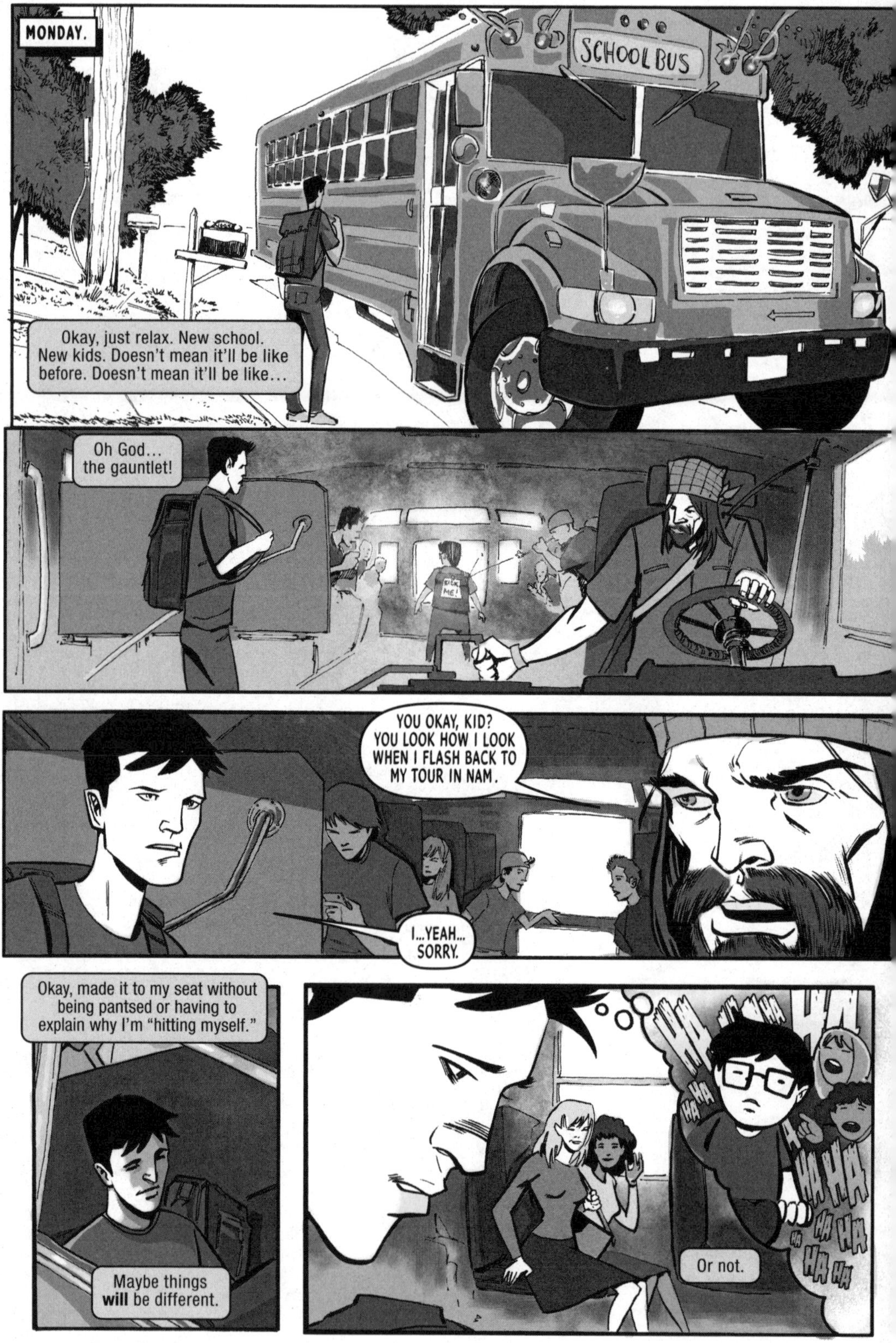

MONDAY.
SCHOOL BUS
Okay, just relax. New school. New kids. Doesn't mean it'll be like before. Doesn't mean it'll be like...
Oh God... the gauntlet!
YOU OKAY, KID? YOU LOOK HOW I LOOK WHEN I FLASH BACK TO MY TOUR IN NAM.
I...YEAH... SORRY.
Okay, made it to my seat without being pantsed or having to explain why I'm "hitting myself."
Maybe things **will** be different.
Or not.

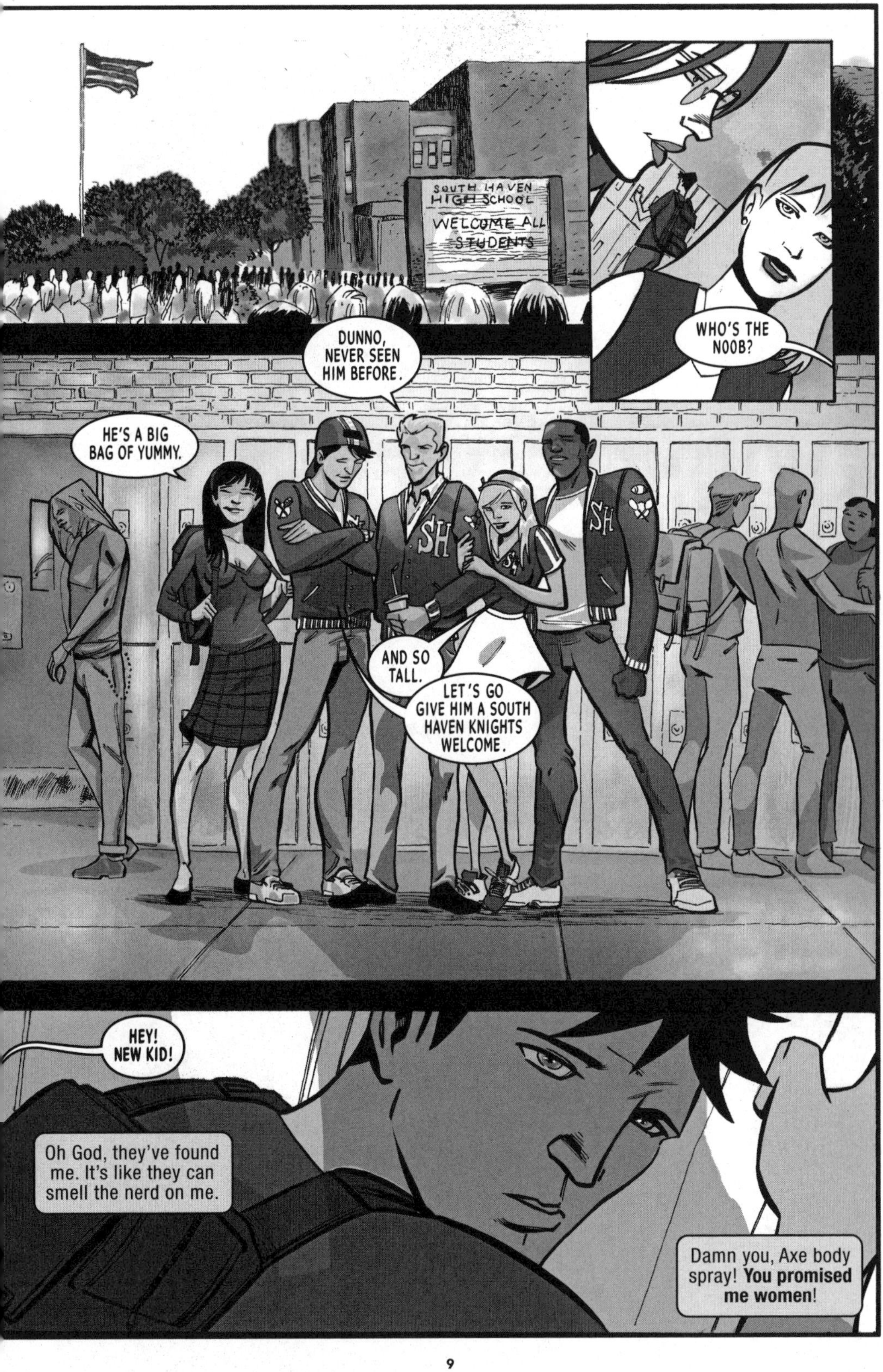
SOUTH HAVEN HIGH SCHOOL
WELCOME ALL STUDENTS
WHO'S THE NOOB?
DUNNO, NEVER SEEN HIM BEFORE.
HE'S A BIG BAG OF YUMMY.
AND SO TALL.
LET'S GO GIVE HIM A SOUTH HAVEN KNIGHTS WELCOME.
HEY! NEW KID!
Oh God, they've found me. It's like they can smell the nerd on me.
Damn you, Axe body spray! **You promised me women**!

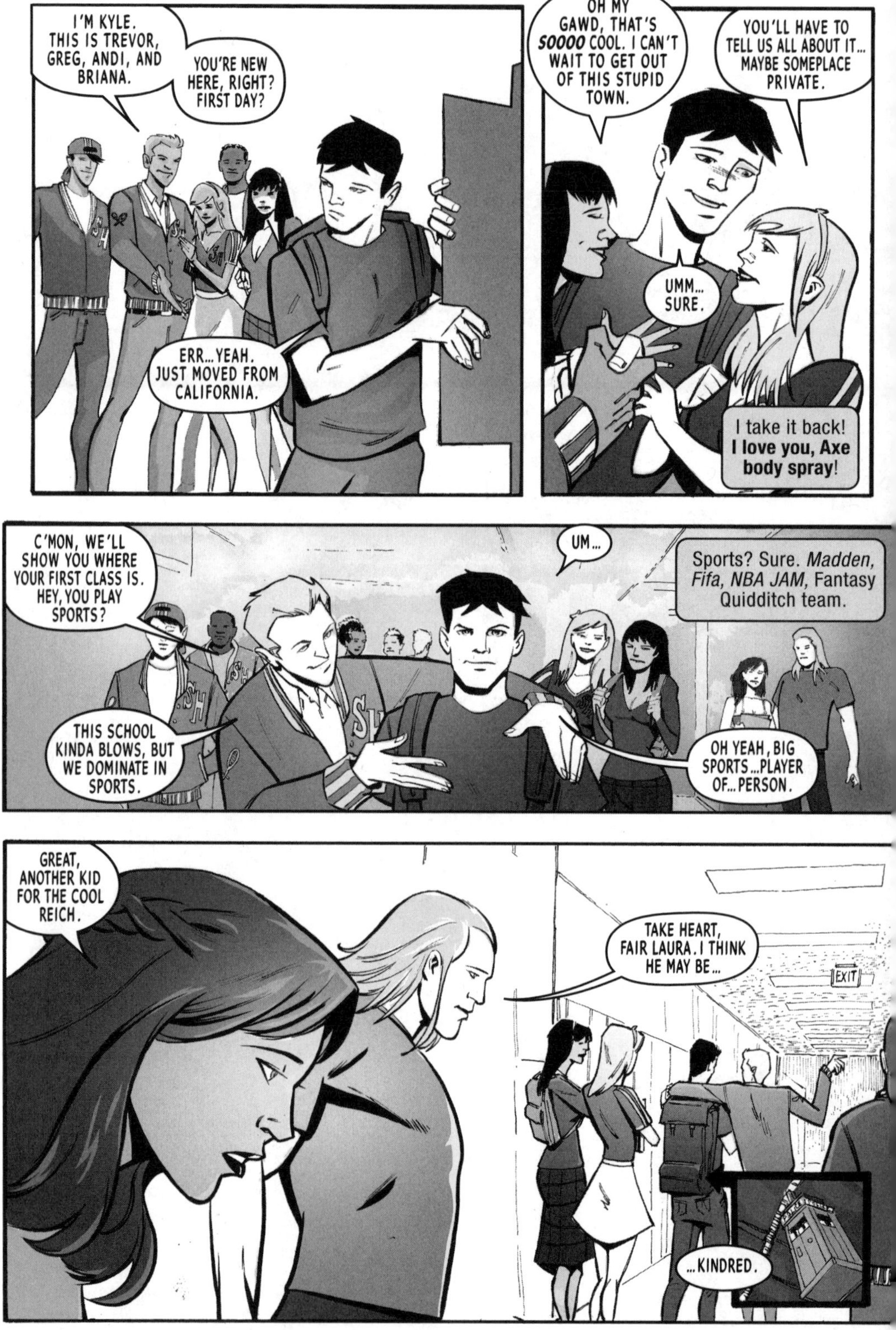
I'M KYLE. THIS IS TREVOR, GREG, ANDI, AND BRIANA.
YOU'RE NEW HERE, RIGHT? FIRST DAY?
ERR...YEAH. JUST MOVED FROM CALIFORNIA.
OH MY GAWD, THAT'S *SOOOO* COOL. I CAN'T WAIT TO GET OUT OF THIS STUPID TOWN.
YOU'LL HAVE TO TELL US ALL ABOUT IT... MAYBE SOMEPLACE PRIVATE.
UMM... SURE.
I take it back! **I love you, Axe body spray**!
C'MON, WE'LL SHOW YOU WHERE YOUR FIRST CLASS IS. HEY, YOU PLAY SPORTS?
UM...
Sports? Sure. *Madden, Fifa, NBA JAM,* Fantasy Quidditch team.
THIS SCHOOL KINDA BLOWS, BUT WE DOMINATE IN SPORTS.
OH YEAH, BIG SPORTS...PLAYER OF...PERSON.
GREAT, ANOTHER KID FOR THE COOL REICH.
TAKE HEART, FAIR LAURA. I THINK HE MAY BE...
EXIT
...KINDRED.

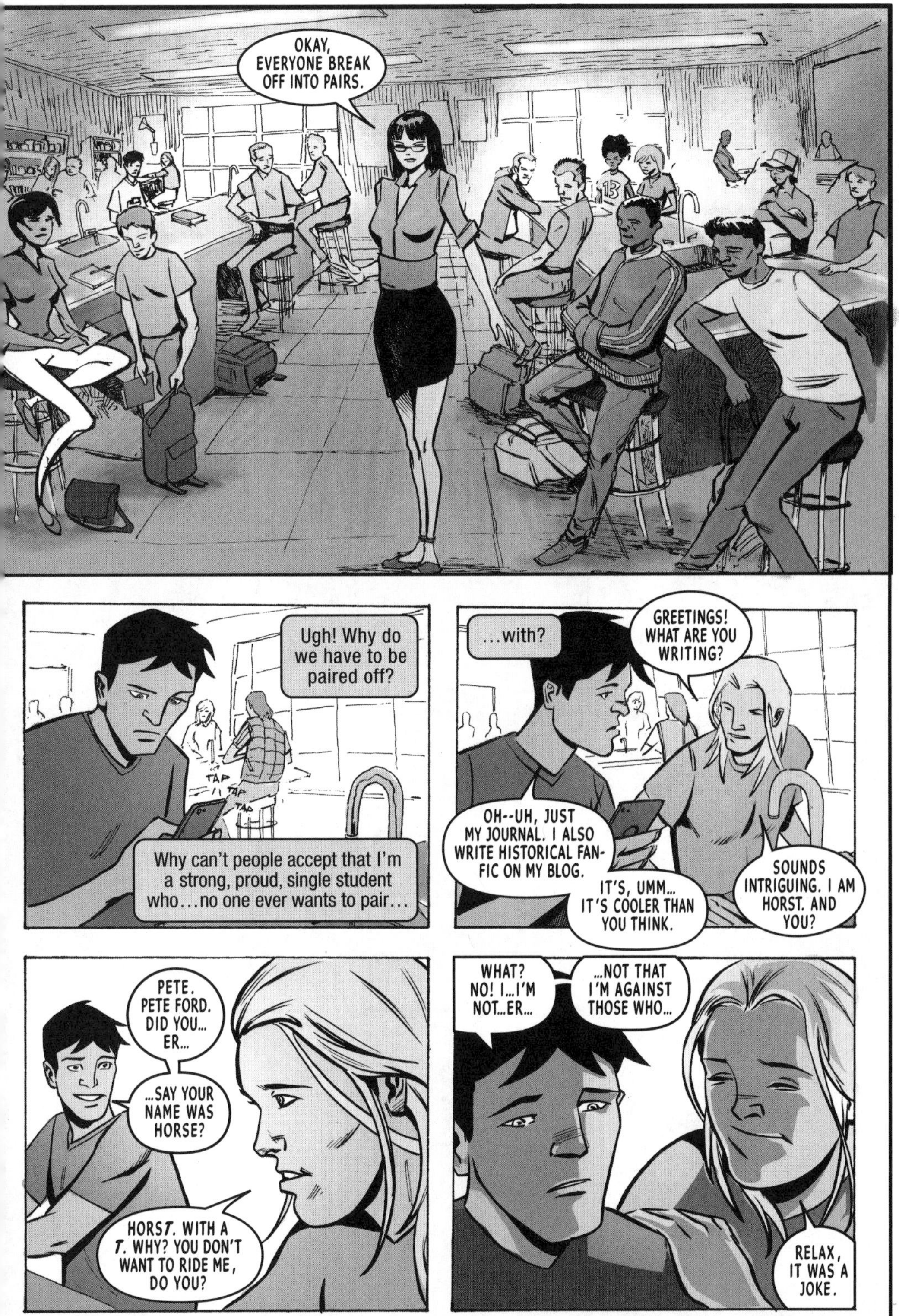
OKAY, EVERYONE BREAK OFF INTO PAIRS.
Ugh! Why do we have to be paired off?
TAP TAP TAP
Why can't people accept that I'm a strong, proud, single student who…no one ever wants to pair…
…with?
GREETINGS! WHAT ARE YOU WRITING?
OH--UH, JUST MY JOURNAL. I ALSO WRITE HISTORICAL FAN-FIC ON MY BLOG.
IT'S, UMM… IT'S COOLER THAN YOU THINK.
SOUNDS INTRIGUING. I AM HORST. AND YOU?
PETE. PETE FORD. DID YOU… ER…
…SAY YOUR NAME WAS HORSE?
HORST. WITH A T. WHY? YOU DON'T WANT TO RIDE ME, DO YOU?
WHAT? NO! I…I'M NOT…ER…
…NOT THAT I'M AGAINST THOSE WHO…
RELAX, IT WAS A JOKE.

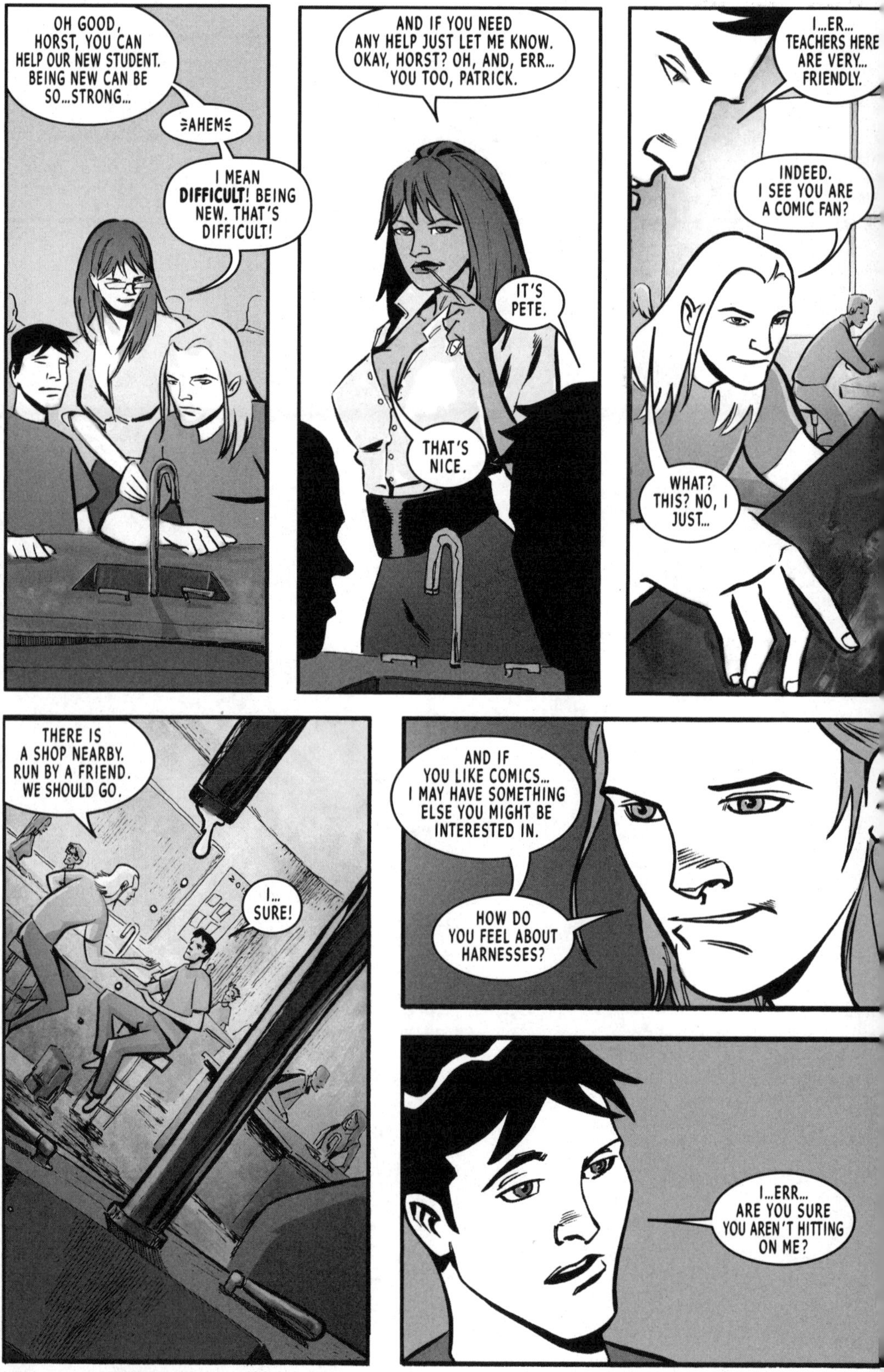
OH GOOD, HORST, YOU CAN HELP OUR NEW STUDENT. BEING NEW CAN BE SO...STRONG...
AHEM
I MEAN DIFFICULT! BEING NEW. THAT'S DIFFICULT!
AND IF YOU NEED ANY HELP JUST LET ME KNOW. OKAY, HORST? OH, AND, ERR... YOU TOO, PATRICK.
IT'S PETE.
THAT'S NICE.
I...ER... TEACHERS HERE ARE VERY... FRIENDLY.
INDEED. I SEE YOU ARE A COMIC FAN?
WHAT? THIS? NO, I JUST...
THERE IS A SHOP NEARBY. RUN BY A FRIEND. WE SHOULD GO.
I... SURE!
AND IF YOU LIKE COMICS... I MAY HAVE SOMETHING ELSE YOU MIGHT BE INTERESTED IN.
HOW DO YOU FEEL ABOUT HARNESSES?
I...ERR... ARE YOU SURE YOU AREN'T HITTING ON ME?

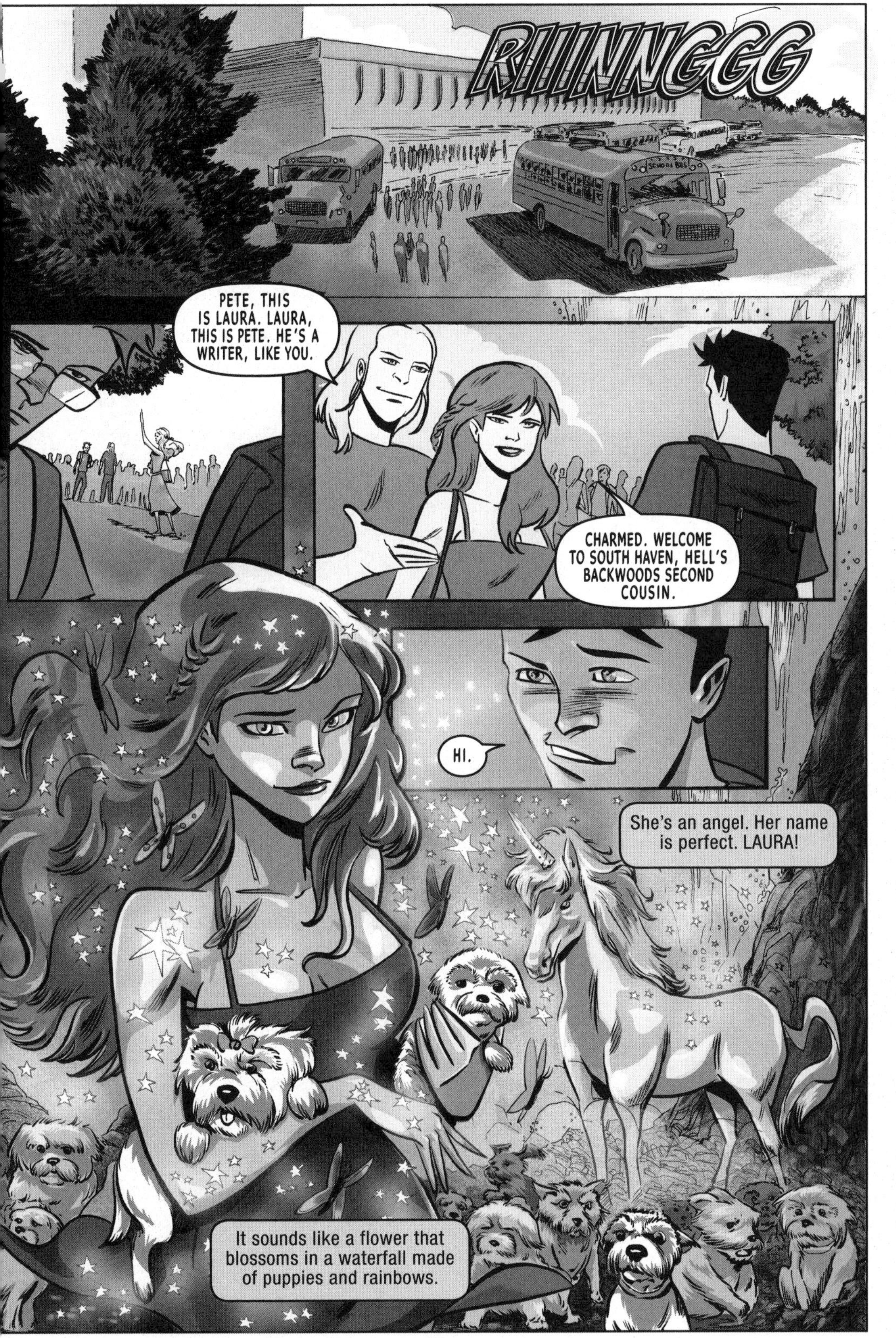
RIIINNGGG
PETE, THIS IS LAURA. LAURA, THIS IS PETE. HE'S A WRITER, LIKE YOU.
CHARMED. WELCOME TO SOUTH HAVEN, HELL'S BACKWOODS SECOND COUSIN.
HI.
She's an angel. Her name is perfect. LAURA!
It sounds like a flower that blossoms in a waterfall made of puppies and rainbows.

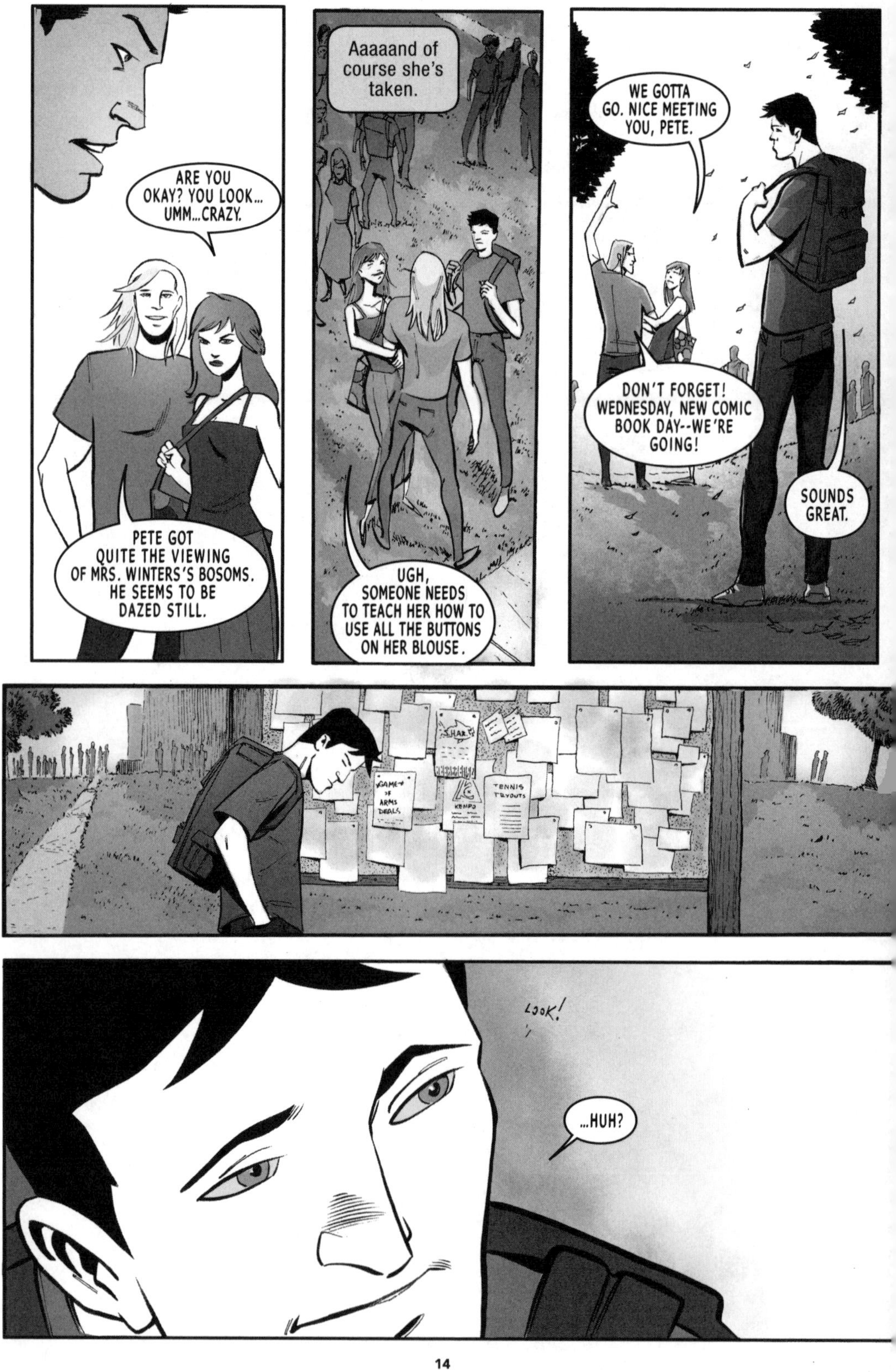
ARE YOU OKAY? YOU LOOK... UMM...CRAZY.
PETE GOT QUITE THE VIEWING OF MRS. WINTERS'S BOSOMS. HE SEEMS TO BE DAZED STILL.
Aaaaand of course she's taken.
UGH, SOMEONE NEEDS TO TEACH HER HOW TO USE ALL THE BUTTONS ON HER BLOUSE.
WE GOTTA GO. NICE MEETING YOU, PETE.
DON'T FORGET! WEDNESDAY, NEW COMIC BOOK DAY--WE'RE GOING!
SOUNDS GREAT.
GAME OF ARMS DEALS
TENNIS TRYOUTS
LOOK!
...HUH?

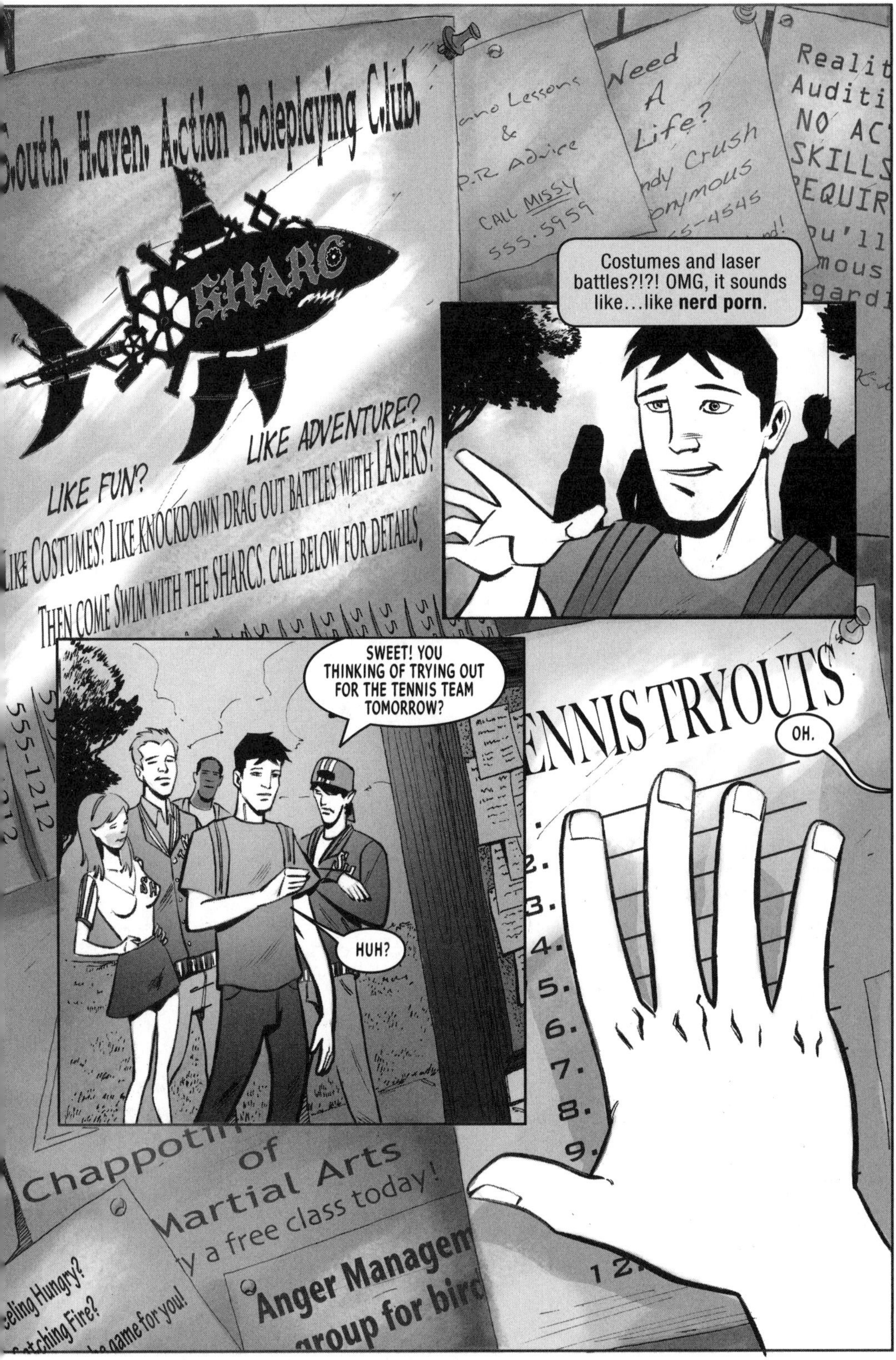
South Haven Action Roleplaying Club
SHARC
LIKE FUN?
LIKE ADVENTURE?
LIKE COSTUMES? LIKE KNOCKDOWN DRAG OUT BATTLES WITH LASERS?
THEN COME SWIM WITH THE SHARCS. CALL BELOW FOR DETAILS.
Costumes and laser battles?!?! OMG, it sounds like…like **nerd porn**.
SWEET! YOU THINKING OF TRYING OUT FOR THE TENNIS TEAM TOMORROW?
HUH?
TENNIS TRYOUTS
OH.
Martial Arts
a free class today!
Anger Managem
group for bir

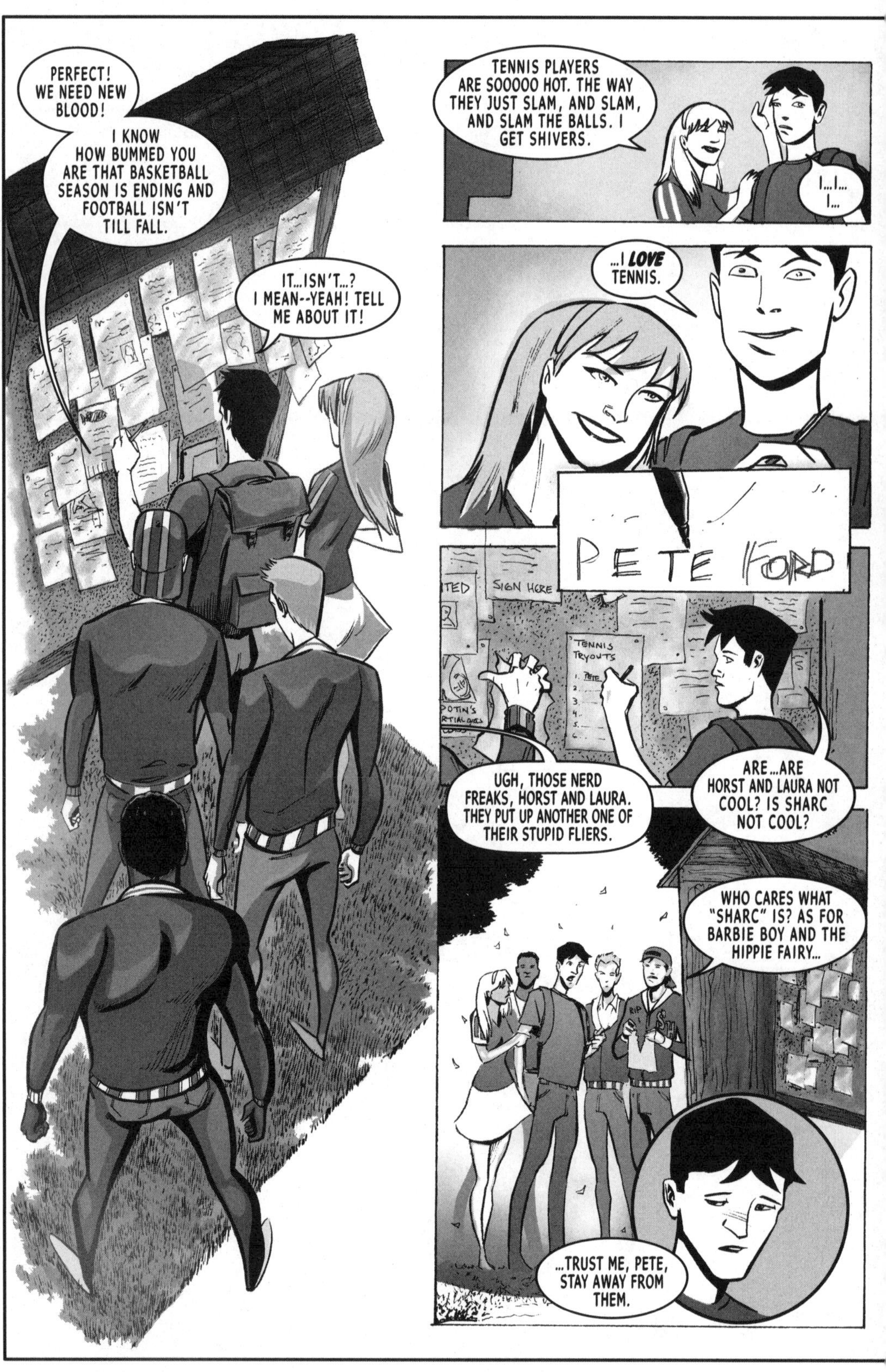
PERFECT! WE NEED NEW BLOOD!
I KNOW HOW BUMMED YOU ARE THAT BASKETBALL SEASON IS ENDING AND FOOTBALL ISN'T TILL FALL.
IT...ISN'T...? I MEAN--YEAH! TELL ME ABOUT IT!
TENNIS PLAYERS ARE SOOOOO HOT. THE WAY THEY JUST SLAM, AND SLAM, AND SLAM THE BALLS. I GET SHIVERS.
I...I... I...
...I LOVE TENNIS.
PETE FORD
SIGN HERE
TENNIS TRYOUTS
UGH, THOSE NERD FREAKS, HORST AND LAURA. THEY PUT UP ANOTHER ONE OF THEIR STUPID FLIERS.
ARE...ARE HORST AND LAURA NOT COOL? IS SHARC NOT COOL?
WHO CARES WHAT "SHARC" IS? AS FOR BARBIE BOY AND THE HIPPIE FAIRY...
...TRUST ME, PETE, STAY AWAY FROM THEM.

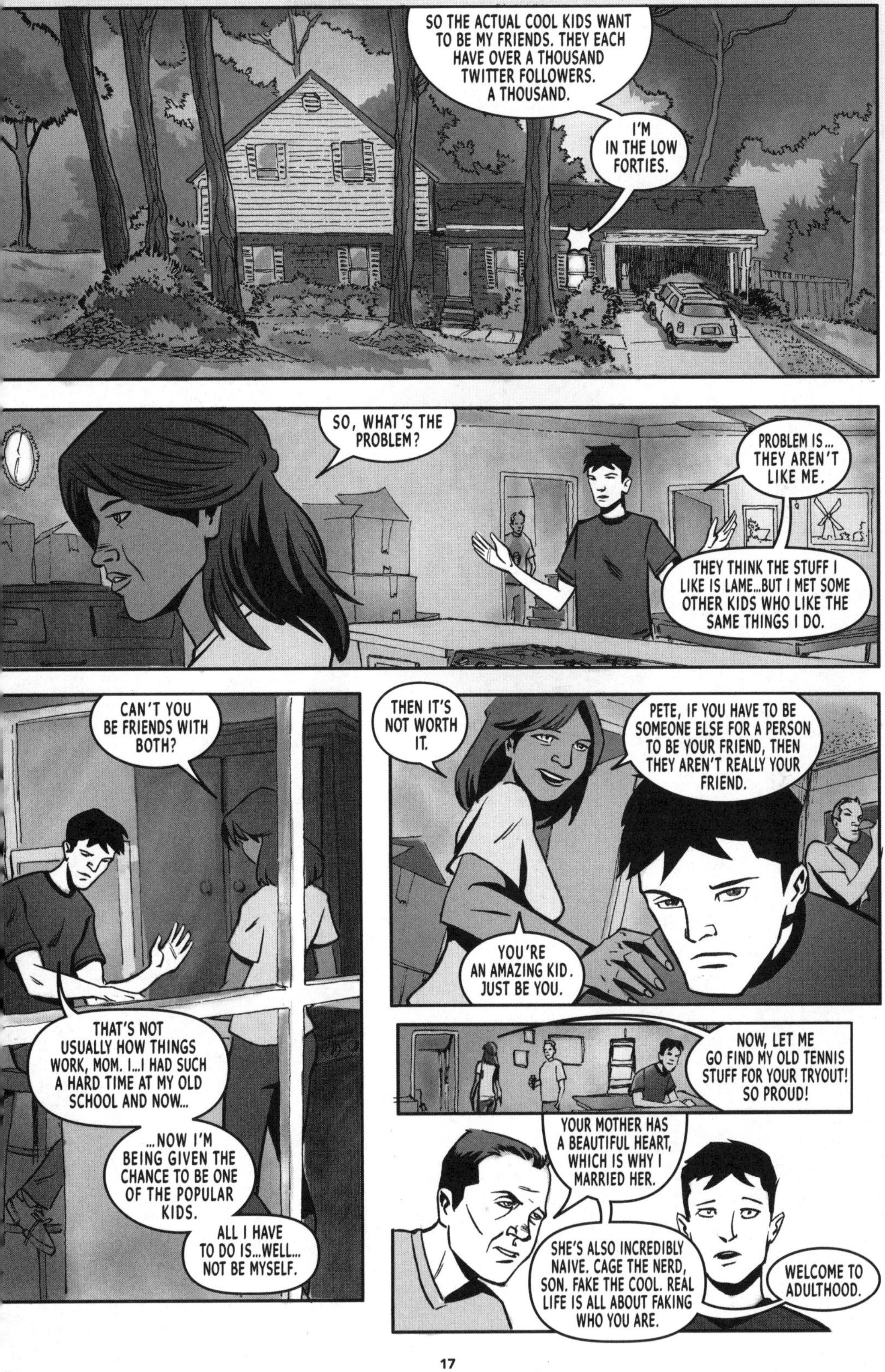
SO THE ACTUAL COOL KIDS WANT TO BE MY FRIENDS. THEY EACH HAVE OVER A THOUSAND TWITTER FOLLOWERS. A THOUSAND.
I'M IN THE LOW FORTIES.
SO, WHAT'S THE PROBLEM?
PROBLEM IS... THEY AREN'T LIKE ME.
THEY THINK THE STUFF I LIKE IS LAME...BUT I MET SOME OTHER KIDS WHO LIKE THE SAME THINGS I DO.
CAN'T YOU BE FRIENDS WITH BOTH?
THAT'S NOT USUALLY HOW THINGS WORK, MOM. I...I HAD SUCH A HARD TIME AT MY OLD SCHOOL AND NOW...
...NOW I'M BEING GIVEN THE CHANCE TO BE ONE OF THE POPULAR KIDS.
ALL I HAVE TO DO IS...WELL... NOT BE MYSELF.
THEN IT'S NOT WORTH IT.
PETE, IF YOU HAVE TO BE SOMEONE ELSE FOR A PERSON TO BE YOUR FRIEND, THEN THEY AREN'T REALLY YOUR FRIEND.
YOU'RE AN AMAZING KID. JUST BE YOU.
NOW, LET ME GO FIND MY OLD TENNIS STUFF FOR YOUR TRYOUT! SO PROUD!
YOUR MOTHER HAS A BEAUTIFUL HEART, WHICH IS WHY I MARRIED HER.
SHE'S ALSO INCREDIBLY NAIVE. CAGE THE NERD, SON. FAKE THE COOL. REAL LIFE IS ALL ABOUT FAKING WHO YOU ARE.
WELCOME TO ADULTHOOD.

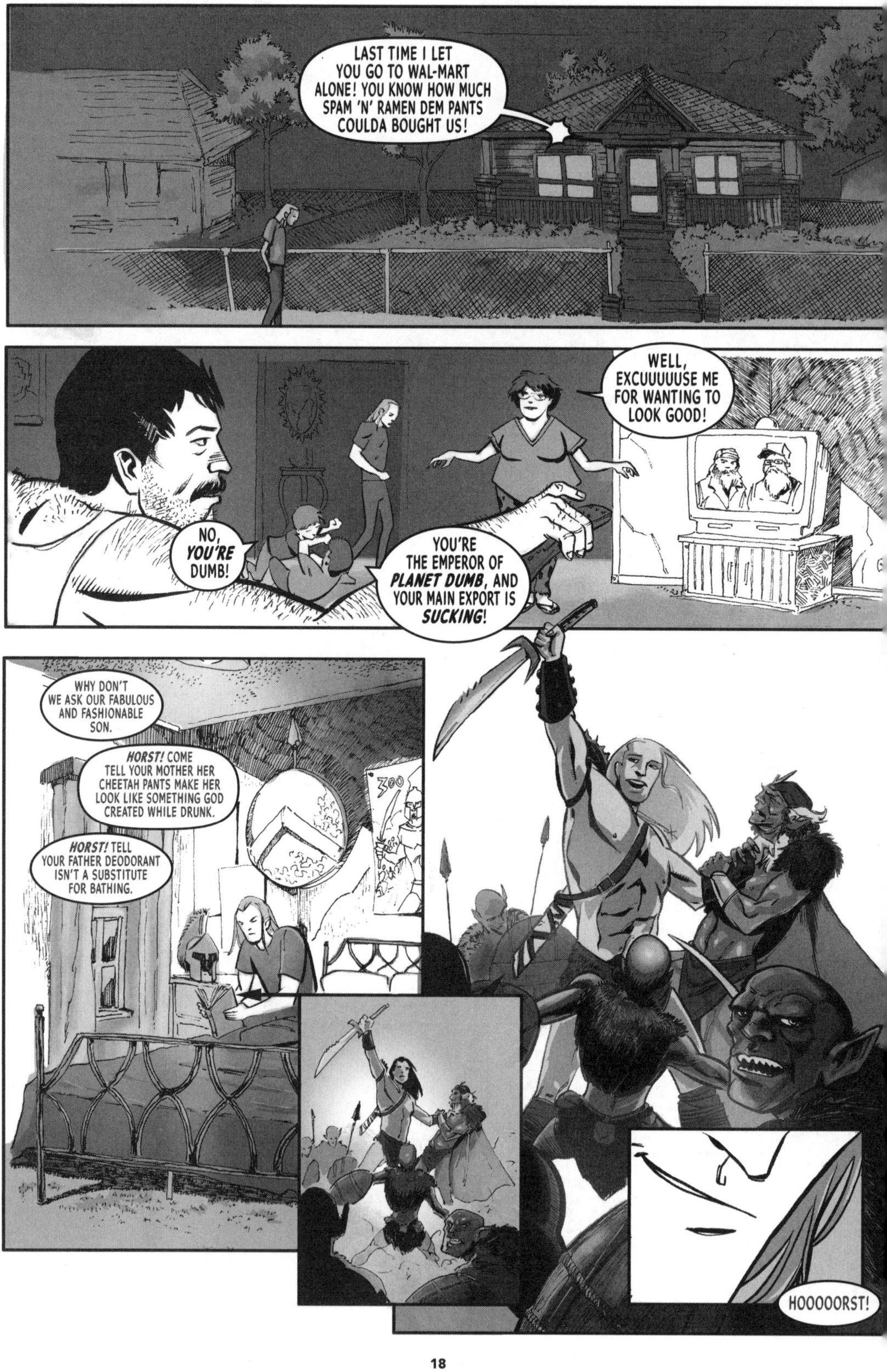
LAST TIME I LET YOU GO TO WAL-MART ALONE! YOU KNOW HOW MUCH SPAM 'N' RAMEN DEM PANTS COULDA BOUGHT US!
WELL, EXCUUUUUSE ME FOR WANTING TO LOOK GOOD!
NO, YOU'RE DUMB!
YOU'RE THE EMPEROR OF PLANET DUMB, AND YOUR MAIN EXPORT IS SUCKING!
WHY DON'T WE ASK OUR FABULOUS AND FASHIONABLE SON.
HORST! COME TELL YOUR MOTHER HER CHEETAH PANTS MAKE HER LOOK LIKE SOMETHING GOD CREATED WHILE DRUNK.
HORST! TELL YOUR FATHER DEODORANT ISN'T A SUBSTITUTE FOR BATHING.
300
HOOOOORST!

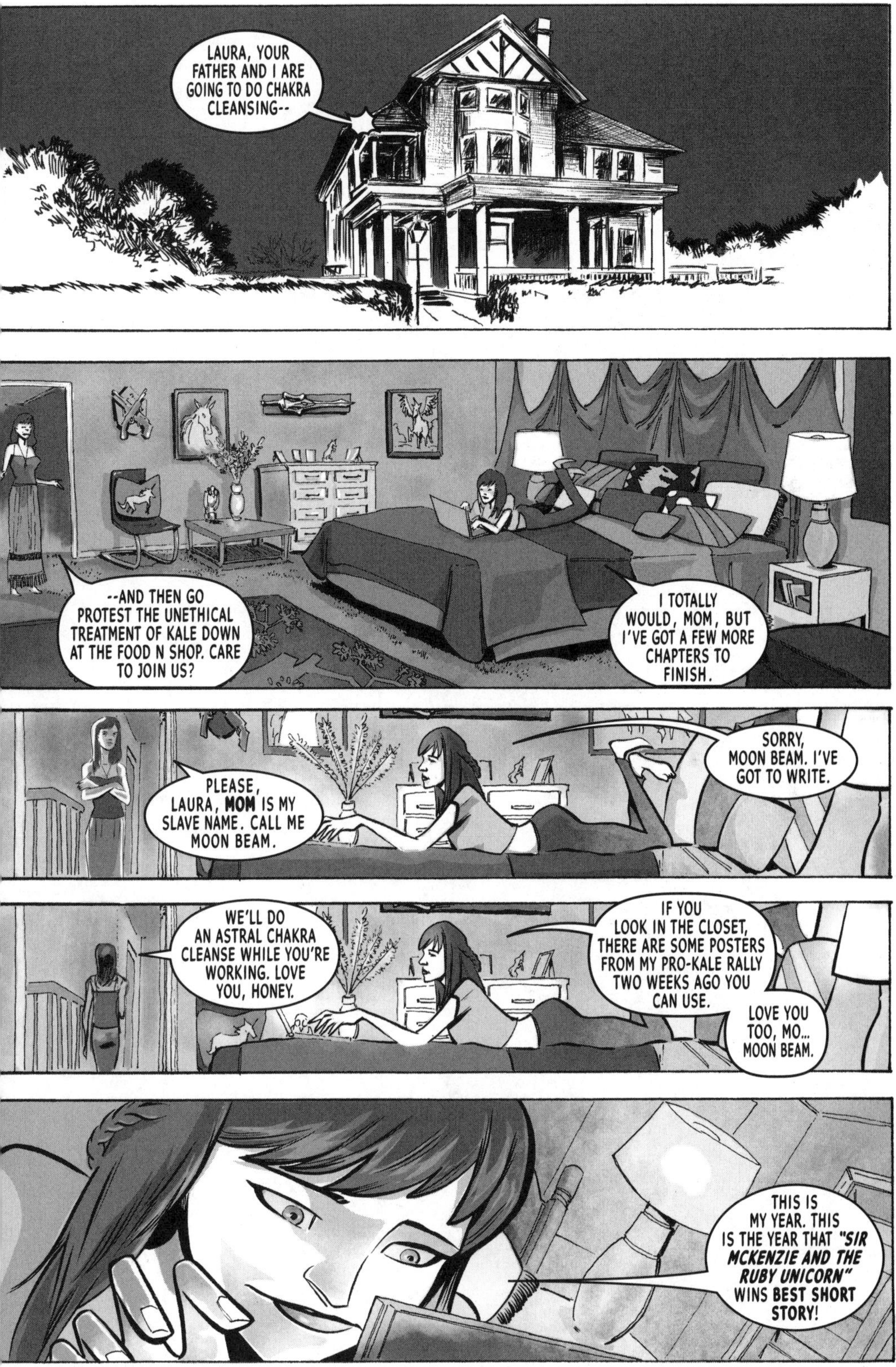

LAURA, YOUR FATHER AND I ARE GOING TO DO CHAKRA CLEANSING--
--AND THEN GO PROTEST THE UNETHICAL TREATMENT OF KALE DOWN AT THE FOOD N SHOP. CARE TO JOIN US?
I TOTALLY WOULD, MOM, BUT I'VE GOT A FEW MORE CHAPTERS TO FINISH.
PLEASE, LAURA, **MOM** IS MY SLAVE NAME. CALL ME MOON BEAM.
SORRY, MOON BEAM. I'VE GOT TO WRITE.
WE'LL DO AN ASTRAL CHAKRA CLEANSE WHILE YOU'RE WORKING. LOVE YOU, HONEY.
IF YOU LOOK IN THE CLOSET, THERE ARE SOME POSTERS FROM MY PRO-KALE RALLY TWO WEEKS AGO YOU CAN USE.
LOVE YOU TOO, MO... MOON BEAM.
THIS IS MY YEAR. THIS IS THE YEAR THAT ***"SIR MCKENZIE AND THE RUBY UNICORN"*** WINS **BEST SHORT STORY!**

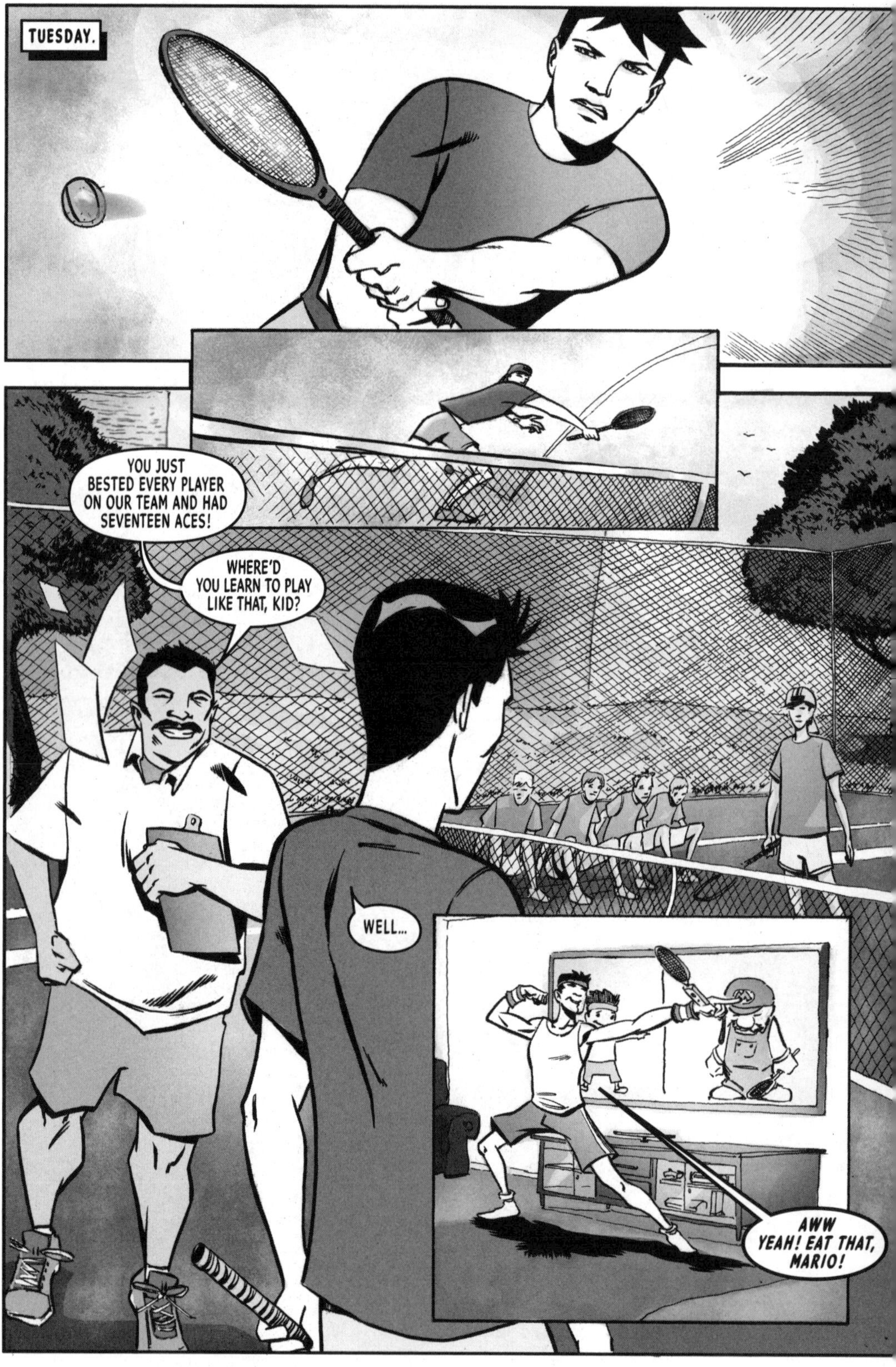
TUESDAY.
YOU JUST BESTED EVERY PLAYER ON OUR TEAM AND HAD SEVENTEEN ACES!
WHERE'D YOU LEARN TO PLAY LIKE THAT, KID?
WELL...
AWW YEAH! EAT THAT, MARIO!

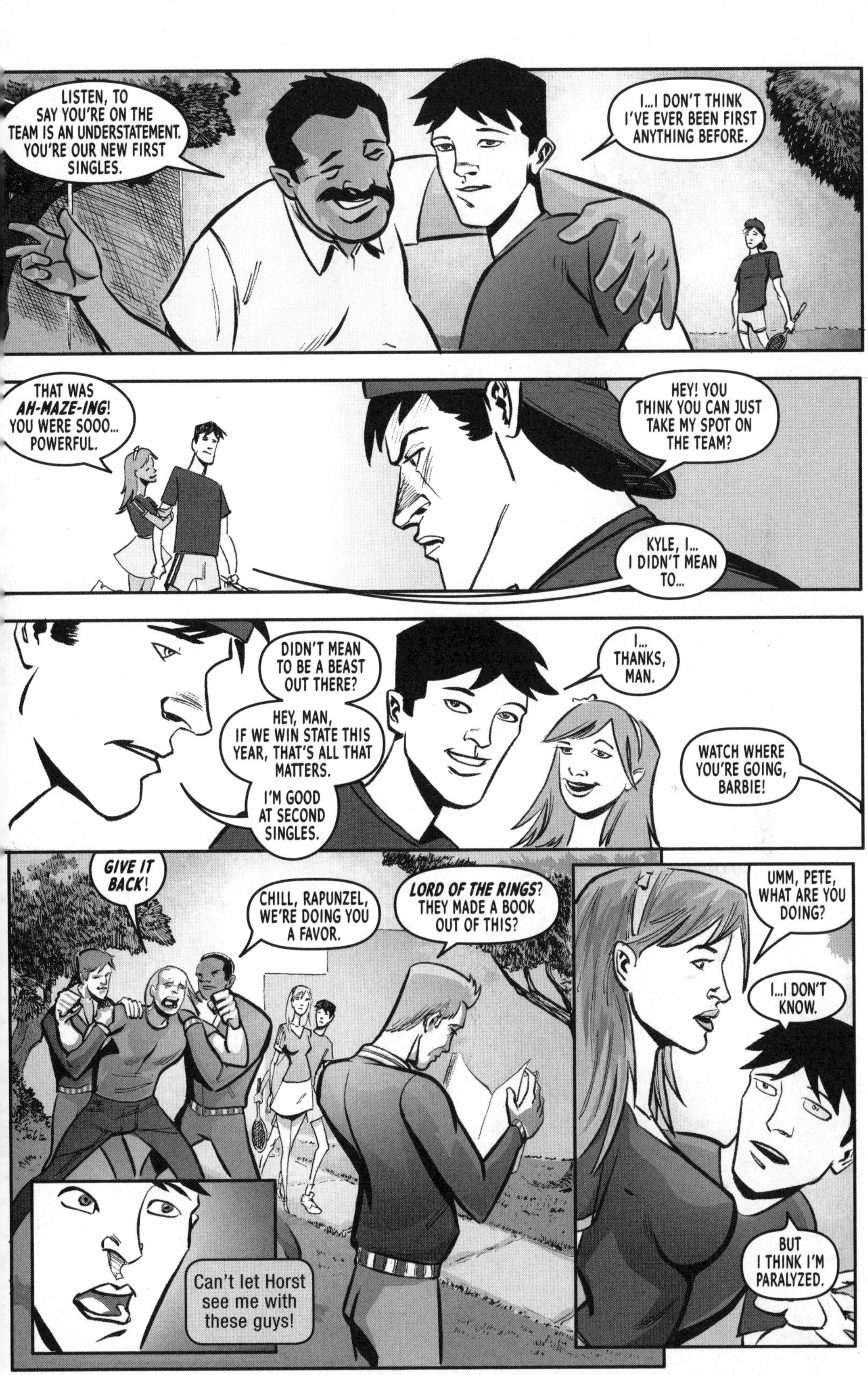
LISTEN, TO SAY YOU'RE ON THE TEAM IS AN UNDERSTATEMENT. YOU'RE OUR NEW FIRST SINGLES.
I...I DON'T THINK I'VE EVER BEEN FIRST ANYTHING BEFORE.
THAT WAS *AH-MAZE-ING*! YOU WERE SOOO... POWERFUL.
HEY! YOU THINK YOU CAN JUST TAKE MY SPOT ON THE TEAM?
KYLE, I... I DIDN'T MEAN TO...
DIDN'T MEAN TO BE A BEAST OUT THERE?
HEY, MAN, IF WE WIN STATE THIS YEAR, THAT'S ALL THAT MATTERS.
I'M GOOD AT SECOND SINGLES.
I... THANKS, MAN.
WATCH WHERE YOU'RE GOING, BARBIE!
GIVE IT BACK!
CHILL, RAPUNZEL, WE'RE DOING YOU A FAVOR.
LORD OF THE RINGS? THEY MADE A BOOK OUT OF THIS?
Can't let Horst see me with these guys!
UMM, PETE, WHAT ARE YOU DOING?
I...I DON'T KNOW.
BUT I THINK I'M PARALYZED.

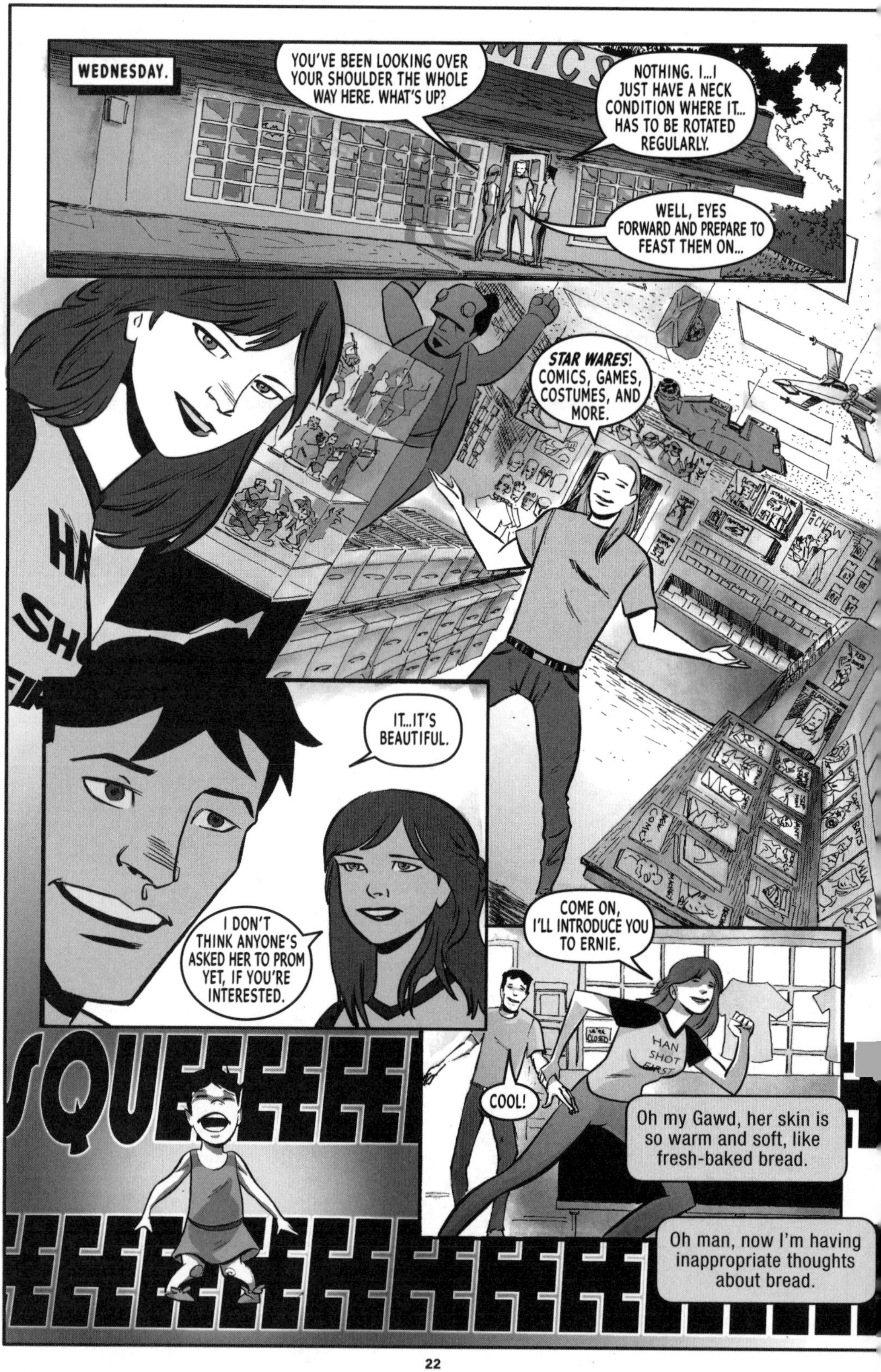

WEDNESDAY.
YOU'VE BEEN LOOKING OVER YOUR SHOULDER THE WHOLE WAY HERE. WHAT'S UP?
NOTHING. I...I JUST HAVE A NECK CONDITION WHERE IT... HAS TO BE ROTATED REGULARLY.
WELL, EYES FORWARD AND PREPARE TO FEAST THEM ON...
STAR WARES! COMICS, GAMES, COSTUMES, AND MORE.
IT...IT'S BEAUTIFUL.
I DON'T THINK ANYONE'S ASKED HER TO PROM YET, IF YOU'RE INTERESTED.
COME ON, I'LL INTRODUCE YOU TO ERNIE.
COOL!
HAN SHOT FIRST
SQUEEEEEEEEEEEEEEEEEEEEE
Oh my Gawd, her skin is so warm and soft, like fresh-baked bread.
Oh man, now I'm having inappropriate thoughts about bread.

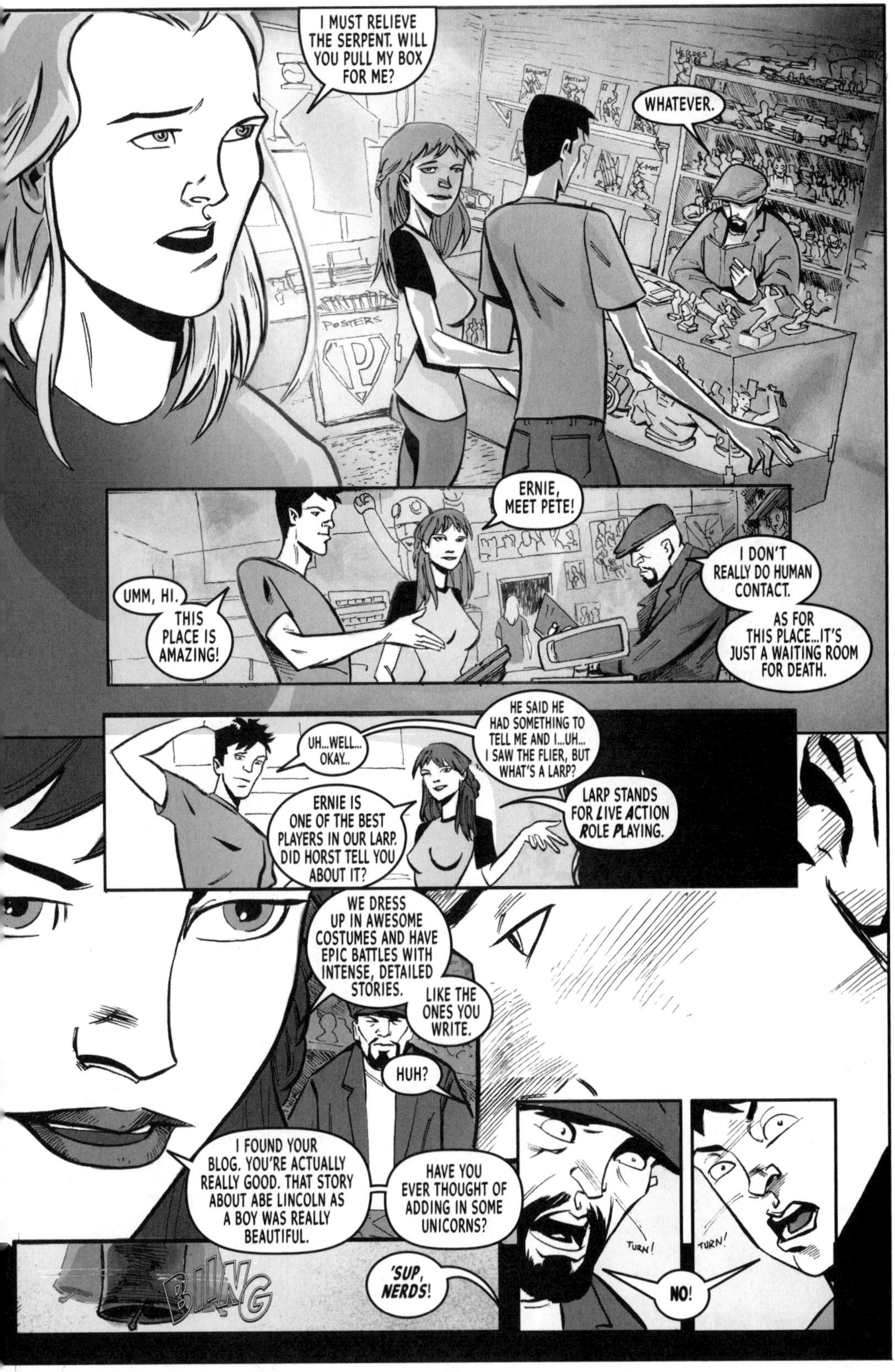
I MUST RELIEVE THE SERPENT. WILL YOU PULL MY BOX FOR ME?
WHATEVER.
HEROES
POSTERS
X-MEN
ERNIE, MEET PETE!
UMM, HI.
THIS PLACE IS AMAZING!
I DON'T REALLY DO HUMAN CONTACT.
AS FOR THIS PLACE...IT'S JUST A WAITING ROOM FOR DEATH.
UH...WELL... OKAY...
HE SAID HE HAD SOMETHING TO TELL ME AND I...UH... I SAW THE FLIER, BUT WHAT'S A LARP?
ERNIE IS ONE OF THE BEST PLAYERS IN OUR LARP. DID HORST TELL YOU ABOUT IT?
LARP STANDS FOR LIVE ACTION ROLE PLAYING.
WE DRESS UP IN AWESOME COSTUMES AND HAVE EPIC BATTLES WITH INTENSE, DETAILED STORIES.
LIKE THE ONES YOU WRITE.
HUH?
I FOUND YOUR BLOG. YOU'RE ACTUALLY REALLY GOOD. THAT STORY ABOUT ABE LINCOLN AS A BOY WAS REALLY BEAUTIFUL.
HAVE YOU EVER THOUGHT OF ADDING IN SOME UNICORNS?
BLING
'SUP, NERDS!
TURN!
TURN!
NO!

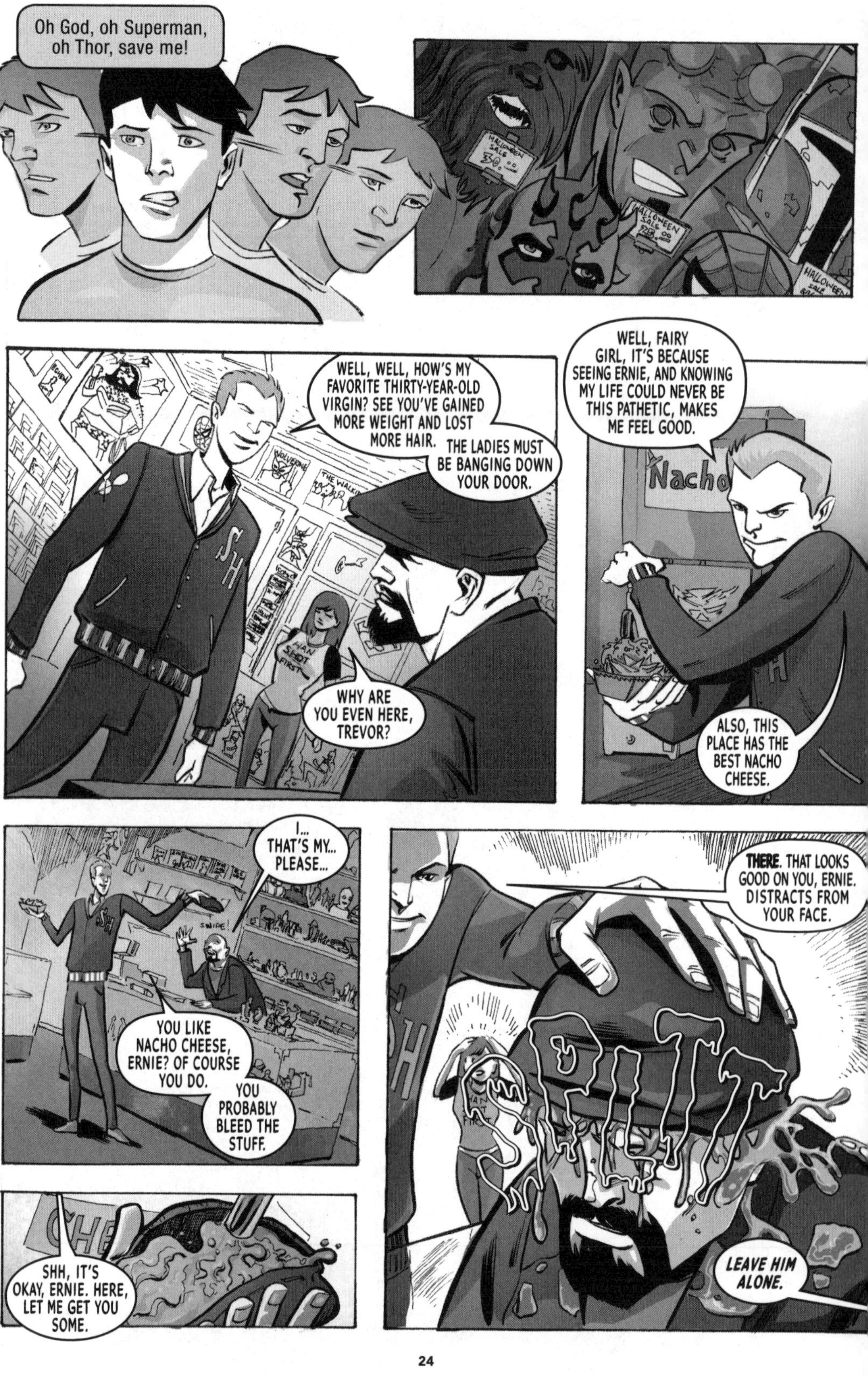
Oh God, oh Superman, oh Thor, save me!
WELL, WELL, HOW'S MY FAVORITE THIRTY-YEAR-OLD VIRGIN? SEE YOU'VE GAINED MORE WEIGHT AND LOST MORE HAIR.
THE LADIES MUST BE BANGING DOWN YOUR DOOR.
WOLVERINE
HAN SHOT FIRST
WHY ARE YOU EVEN HERE, TREVOR?
WELL, FAIRY GIRL, IT'S BECAUSE SEEING ERNIE, AND KNOWING MY LIFE COULD NEVER BE THIS PATHETIC, MAKES ME FEEL GOOD.
Nacho
ALSO, THIS PLACE HAS THE BEST NACHO CHEESE.
I... THAT'S MY... PLEASE...
SWIPE!
YOU LIKE NACHO CHEESE, ERNIE? OF COURSE YOU DO.
YOU PROBABLY BLEED THE STUFF.
SHH, IT'S OKAY, ERNIE. HERE, LET ME GET YOU SOME.
THERE. THAT LOOKS GOOD ON YOU, ERNIE. DISTRACTS FROM YOUR FACE.
SPLUT
LEAVE HIM ALONE.

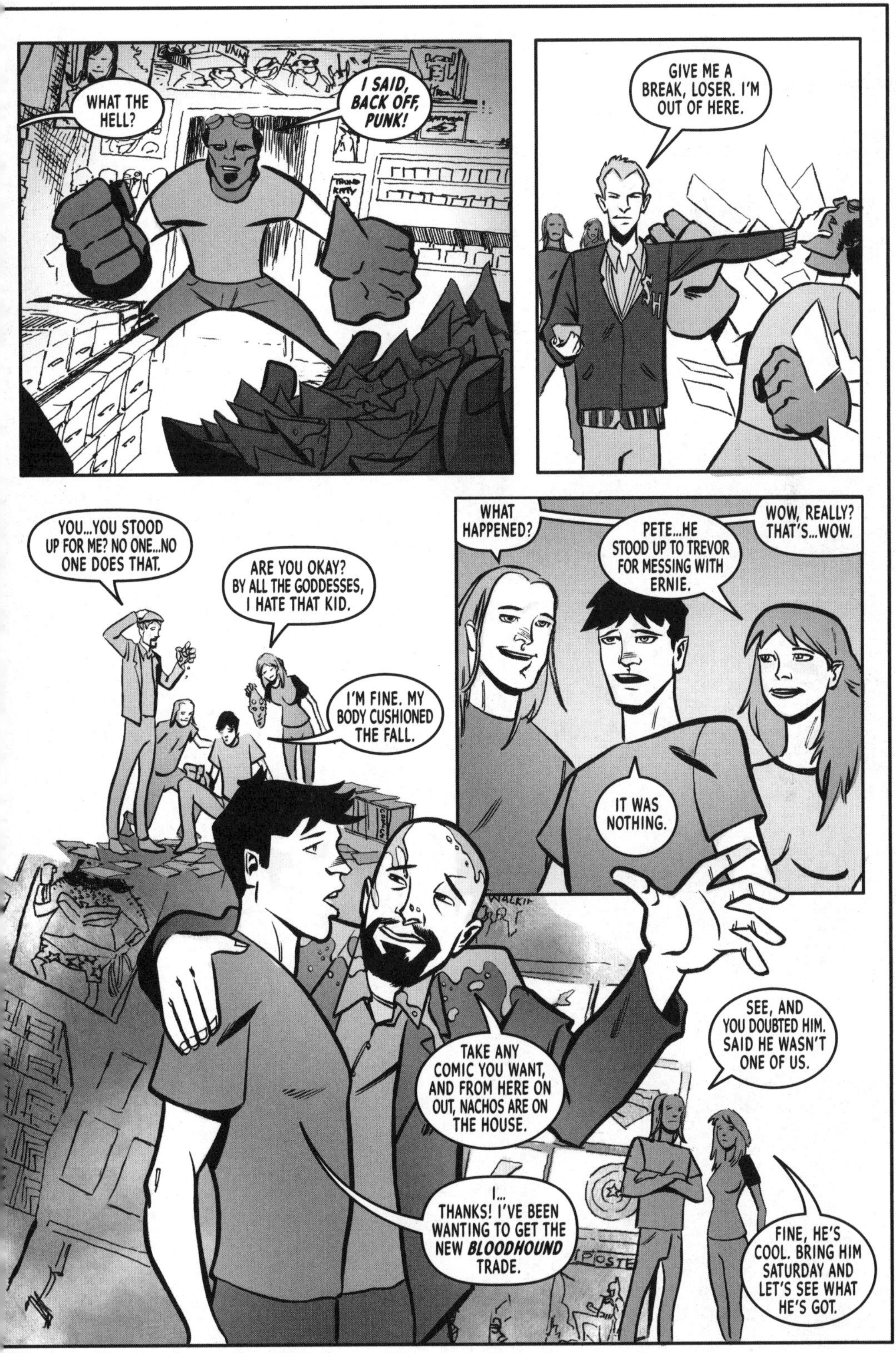
WHAT THE HELL?
I SAID, BACK OFF, PUNK!
GIVE ME A BREAK, LOSER. I'M OUT OF HERE.
YOU...YOU STOOD UP FOR ME? NO ONE...NO ONE DOES THAT.
ARE YOU OKAY? BY ALL THE GODDESSES, I HATE THAT KID.
I'M FINE. MY BODY CUSHIONED THE FALL.
WHAT HAPPENED?
PETE...HE STOOD UP TO TREVOR FOR MESSING WITH ERNIE.
WOW, REALLY? THAT'S...WOW.
IT WAS NOTHING.
TAKE ANY COMIC YOU WANT, AND FROM HERE ON OUT, NACHOS ARE ON THE HOUSE.
I... THANKS! I'VE BEEN WANTING TO GET THE NEW BLOODHOUND TRADE.
SEE, AND YOU DOUBTED HIM. SAID HE WASN'T ONE OF US.
FINE, HE'S COOL. BRING HIM SATURDAY AND LET'S SEE WHAT HE'S GOT.

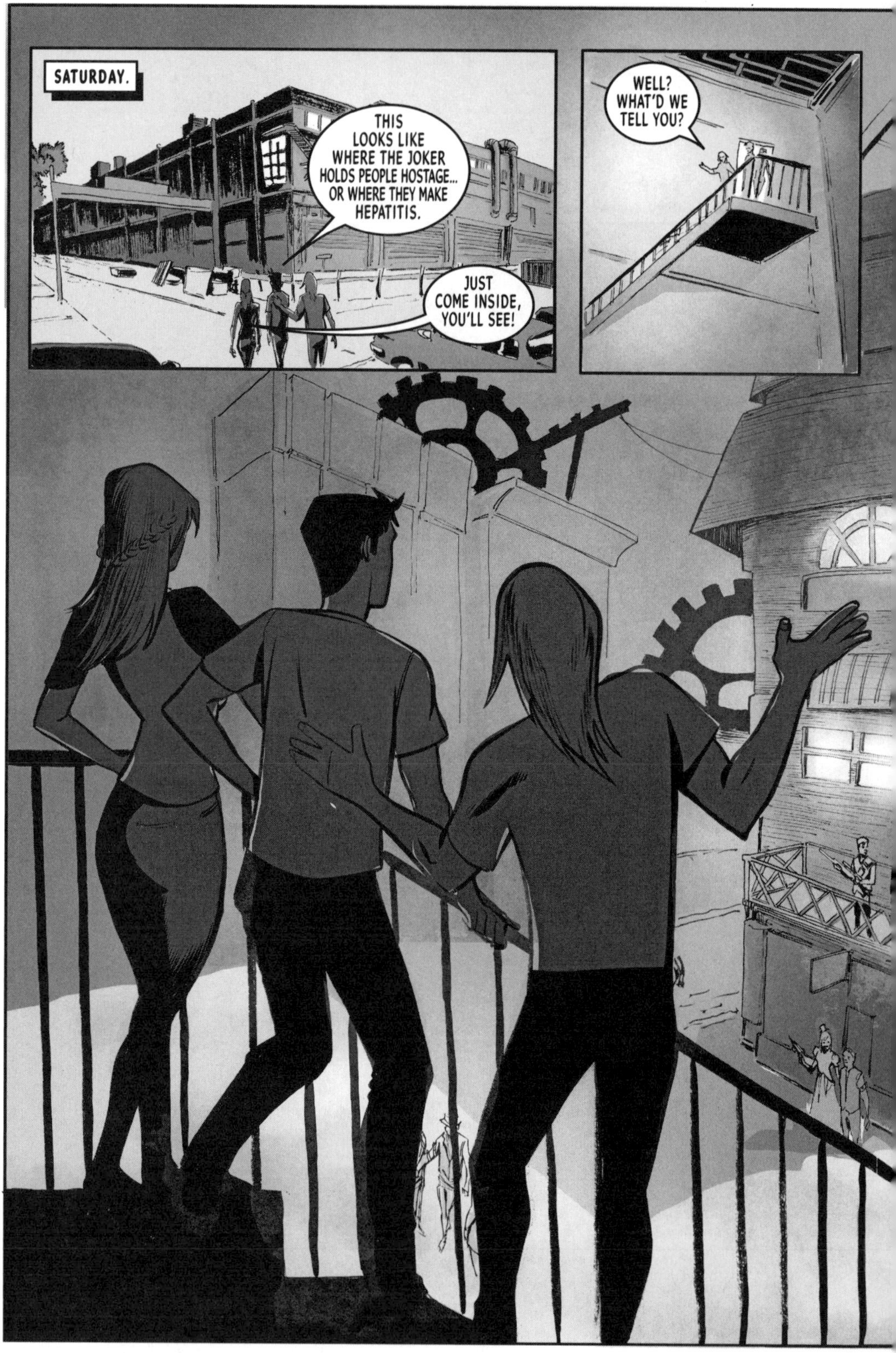
SATURDAY.
THIS LOOKS LIKE WHERE THE JOKER HOLDS PEOPLE HOSTAGE... OR WHERE THEY MAKE HEPATITIS.
JUST COME INSIDE, YOU'LL SEE!
WELL? WHAT'D WE TELL YOU?

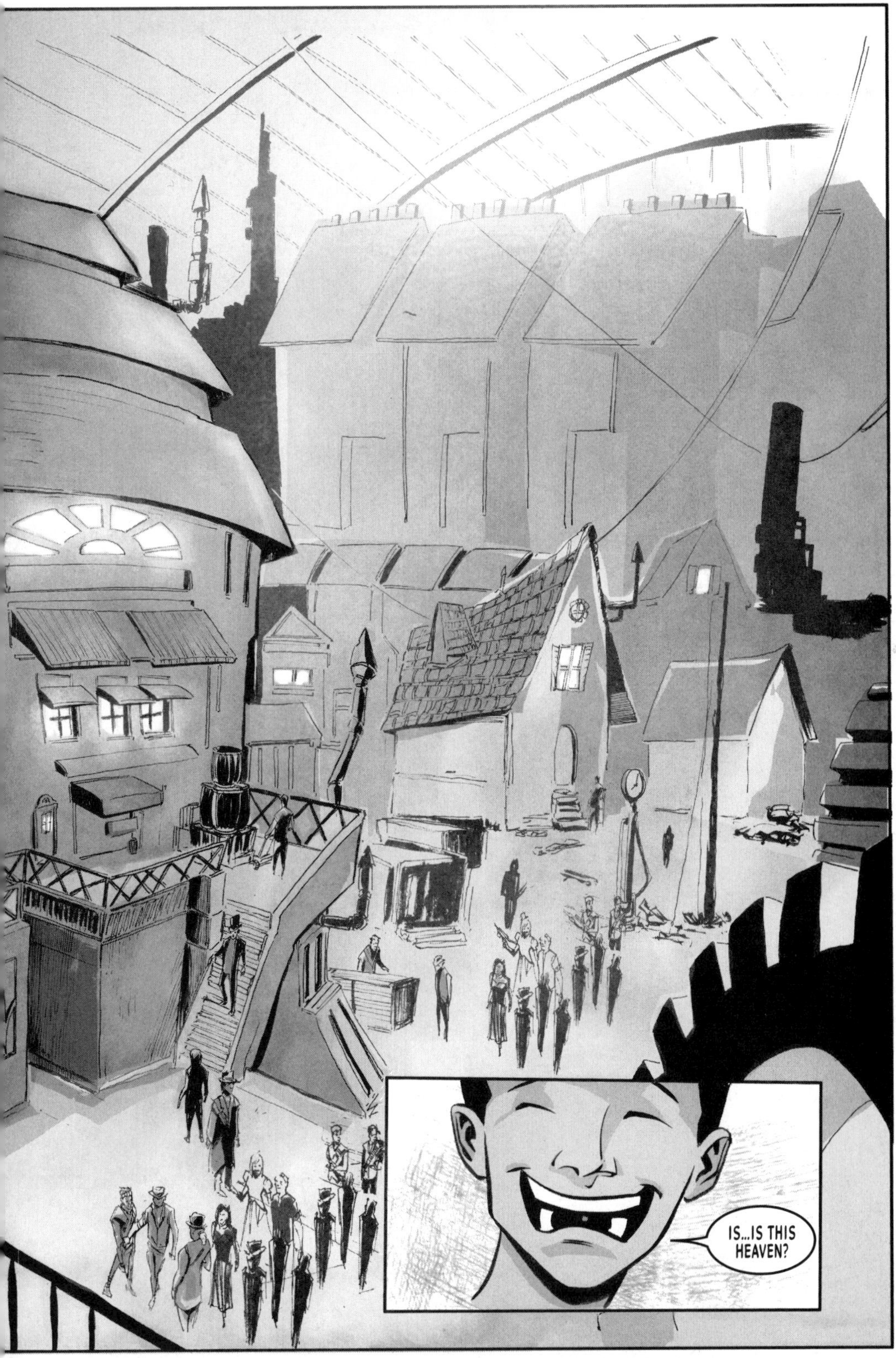
IS...IS THIS HEAVEN?

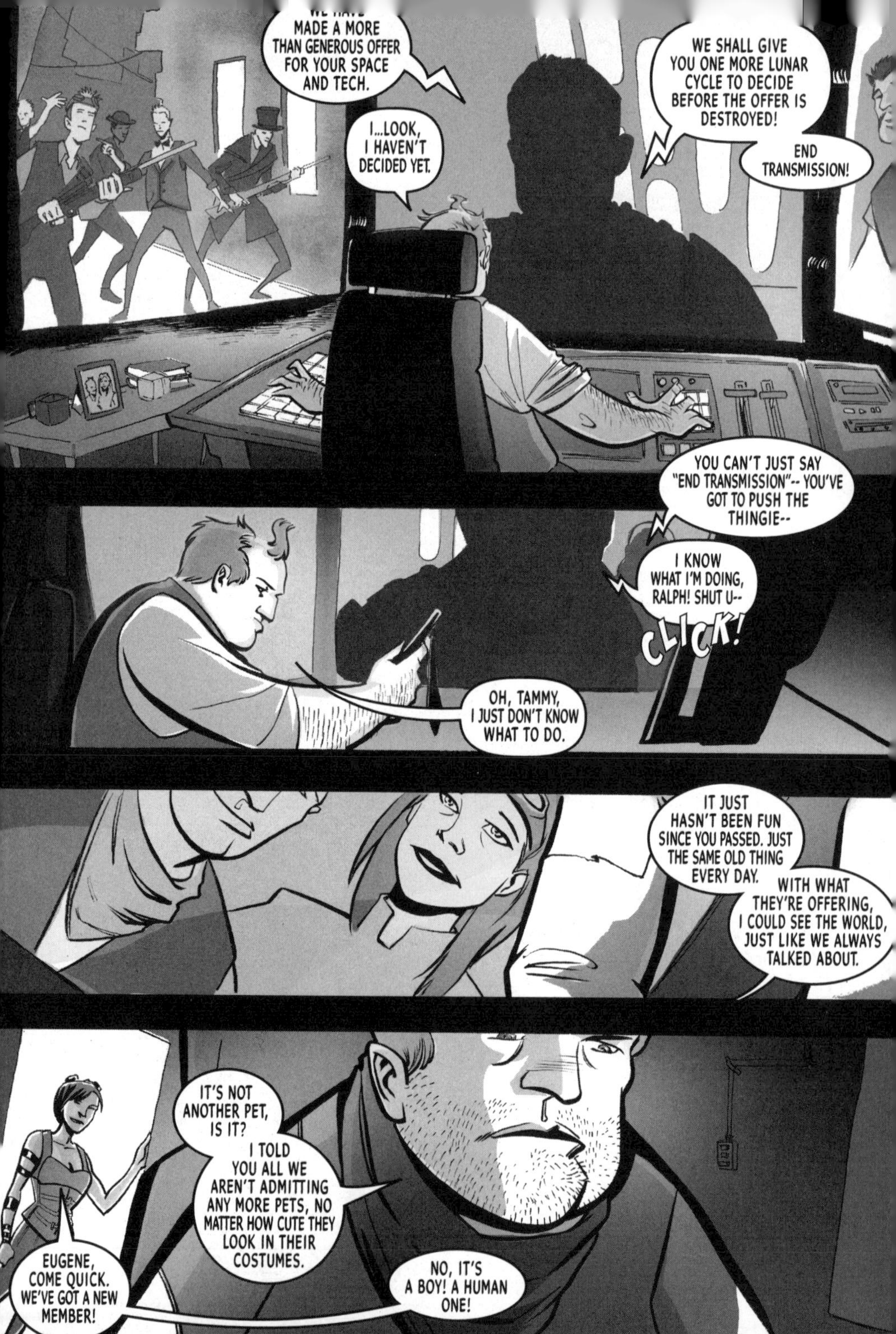

MADE A MORE THAN GENEROUS OFFER FOR YOUR SPACE AND TECH.
I...LOOK, I HAVEN'T DECIDED YET.
WE SHALL GIVE YOU ONE MORE LUNAR CYCLE TO DECIDE BEFORE THE OFFER IS DESTROYED!
END TRANSMISSION!
YOU CAN'T JUST SAY "END TRANSMISSION"-- YOU'VE GOT TO PUSH THE THINGIE--
I KNOW WHAT I'M DOING, RALPH! SHUT U--
CLICK!
OH, TAMMY, I JUST DON'T KNOW WHAT TO DO.
IT JUST HASN'T BEEN FUN SINCE YOU PASSED. JUST THE SAME OLD THING EVERY DAY.
WITH WHAT THEY'RE OFFERING, I COULD SEE THE WORLD, JUST LIKE WE ALWAYS TALKED ABOUT.
EUGENE, COME QUICK. WE'VE GOT A NEW MEMBER!
IT'S NOT ANOTHER PET, IS IT?
I TOLD YOU ALL WE AREN'T ADMITTING ANY MORE PETS, NO MATTER HOW CUTE THEY LOOK IN THEIR COSTUMES.
NO, IT'S A BOY! A HUMAN ONE!

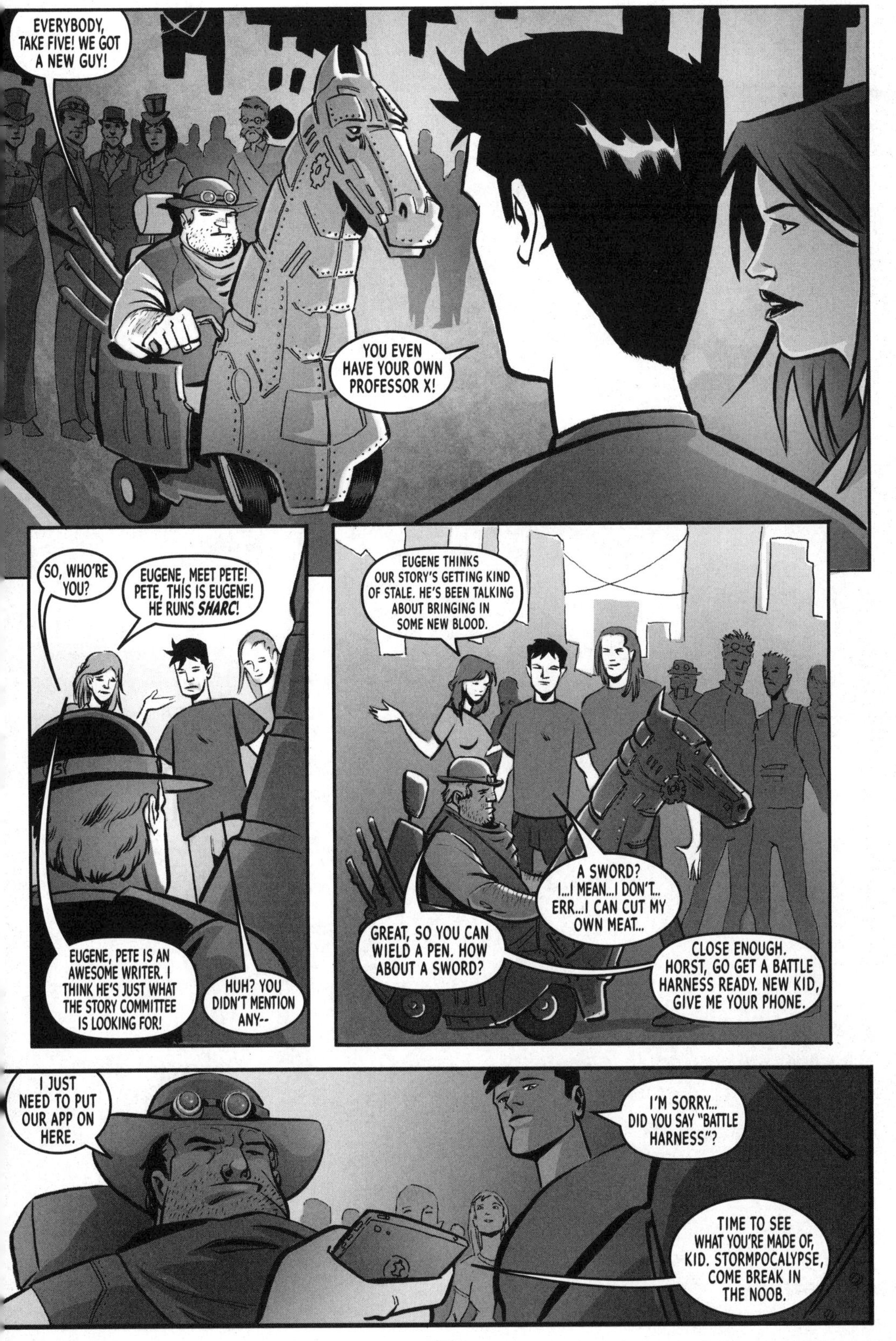
EVERYBODY, TAKE FIVE! WE GOT A NEW GUY!
YOU EVEN HAVE YOUR OWN PROFESSOR X!
SO, WHO'RE YOU?
EUGENE, MEET PETE! PETE, THIS IS EUGENE! HE RUNS *SHARC*!
EUGENE, PETE IS AN AWESOME WRITER. I THINK HE'S JUST WHAT THE STORY COMMITTEE IS LOOKING FOR!
HUH? YOU DIDN'T MENTION ANY--
EUGENE THINKS OUR STORY'S GETTING KIND OF STALE. HE'S BEEN TALKING ABOUT BRINGING IN SOME NEW BLOOD.
GREAT, SO YOU CAN WIELD A PEN. HOW ABOUT A SWORD?
A SWORD? I...I MEAN...I DON'T... ERR...I CAN CUT MY OWN MEAT...
CLOSE ENOUGH. HORST, GO GET A BATTLE HARNESS READY. NEW KID, GIVE ME YOUR PHONE.
I JUST NEED TO PUT OUR APP ON HERE.
I'M SORRY... DID YOU SAY "BATTLE HARNESS"?
TIME TO SEE WHAT YOU'RE MADE OF, KID. STORMPOCALYPSE, COME BREAK IN THE NOOB.

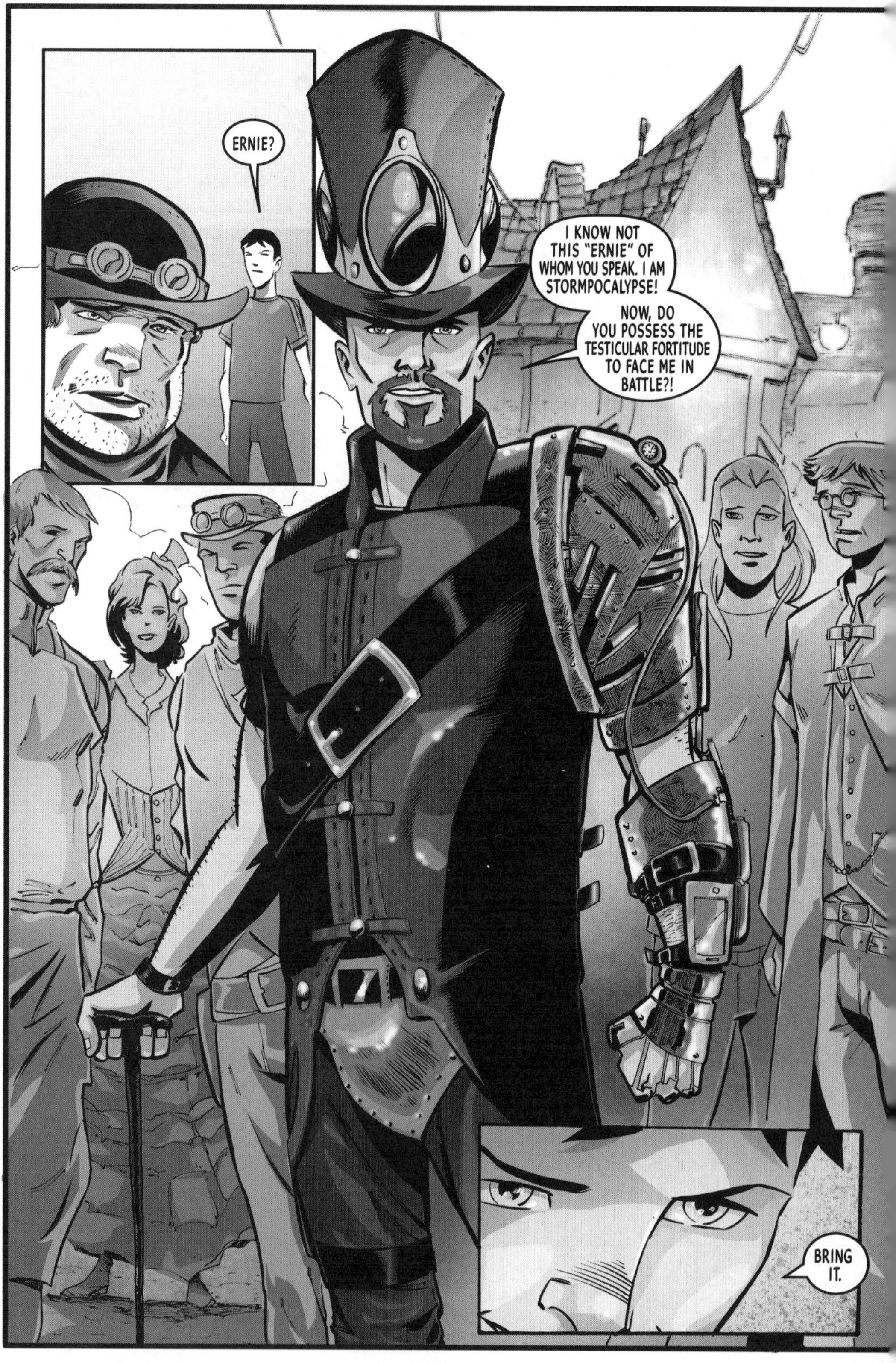
ERNIE?
I KNOW NOT THIS "ERNIE" OF WHOM YOU SPEAK. I AM STORMPOCALYPSE!
NOW, DO YOU POSSESS THE TESTICULAR FORTITUDE TO FACE ME IN BATTLE?!
BRING IT.

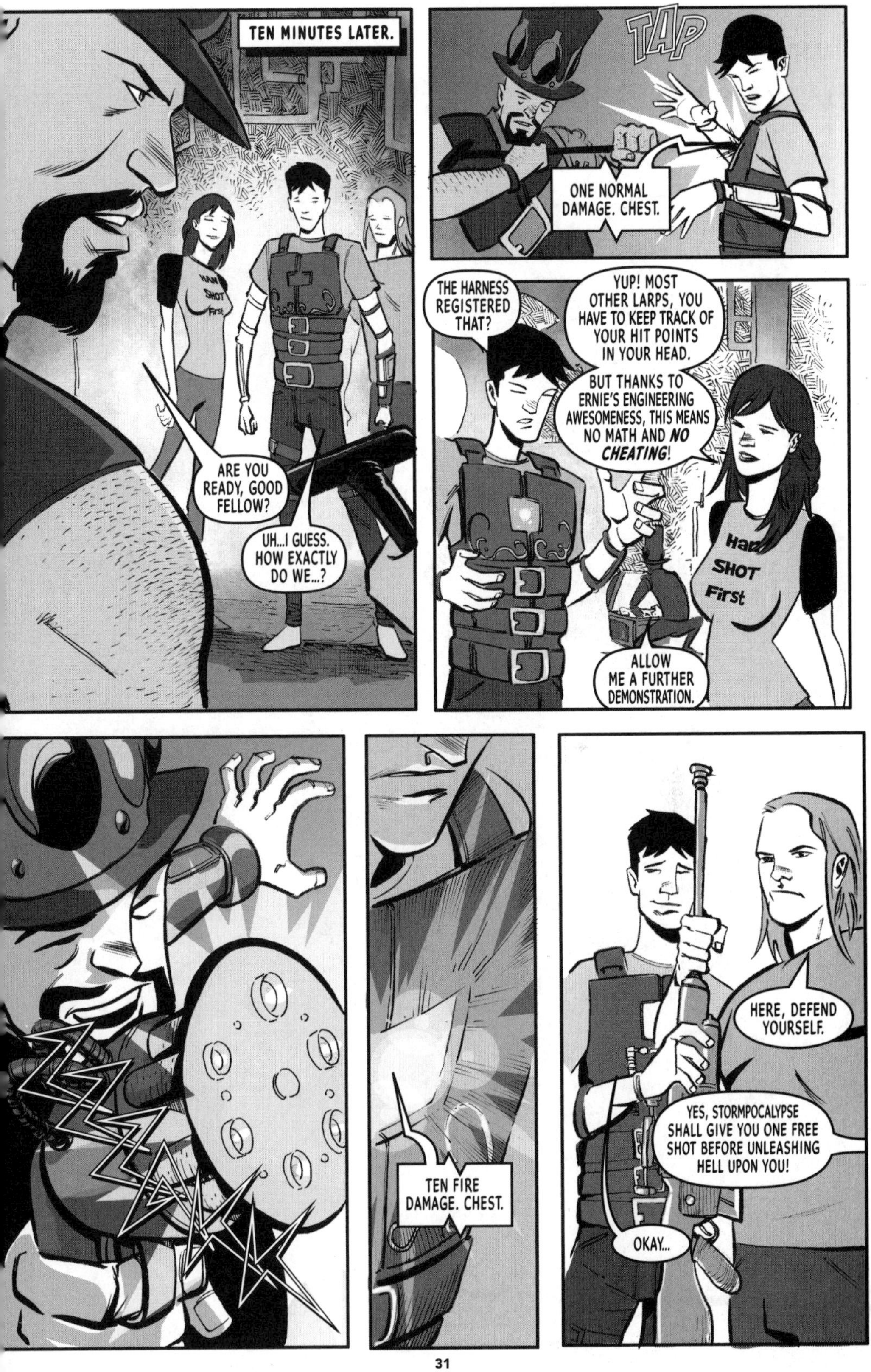
TEN MINUTES LATER.
ARE YOU READY, GOOD FELLOW?
UH...I GUESS. HOW EXACTLY DO WE...?
TAP
ONE NORMAL DAMAGE. CHEST.
THE HARNESS REGISTERED THAT?
YUP! MOST OTHER LARPS, YOU HAVE TO KEEP TRACK OF YOUR HIT POINTS IN YOUR HEAD.
BUT THANKS TO ERNIE'S ENGINEERING AWESOMENESS, THIS MEANS NO MATH AND NO CHEATING!
HAN SHOT FIRST
ALLOW ME A FURTHER DEMONSTRATION.
TEN FIRE DAMAGE. CHEST.
HERE, DEFEND YOURSELF.
YES, STORMPOCALYPSE SHALL GIVE YOU ONE FREE SHOT BEFORE UNLEASHING HELL UPON YOU!
OKAY...

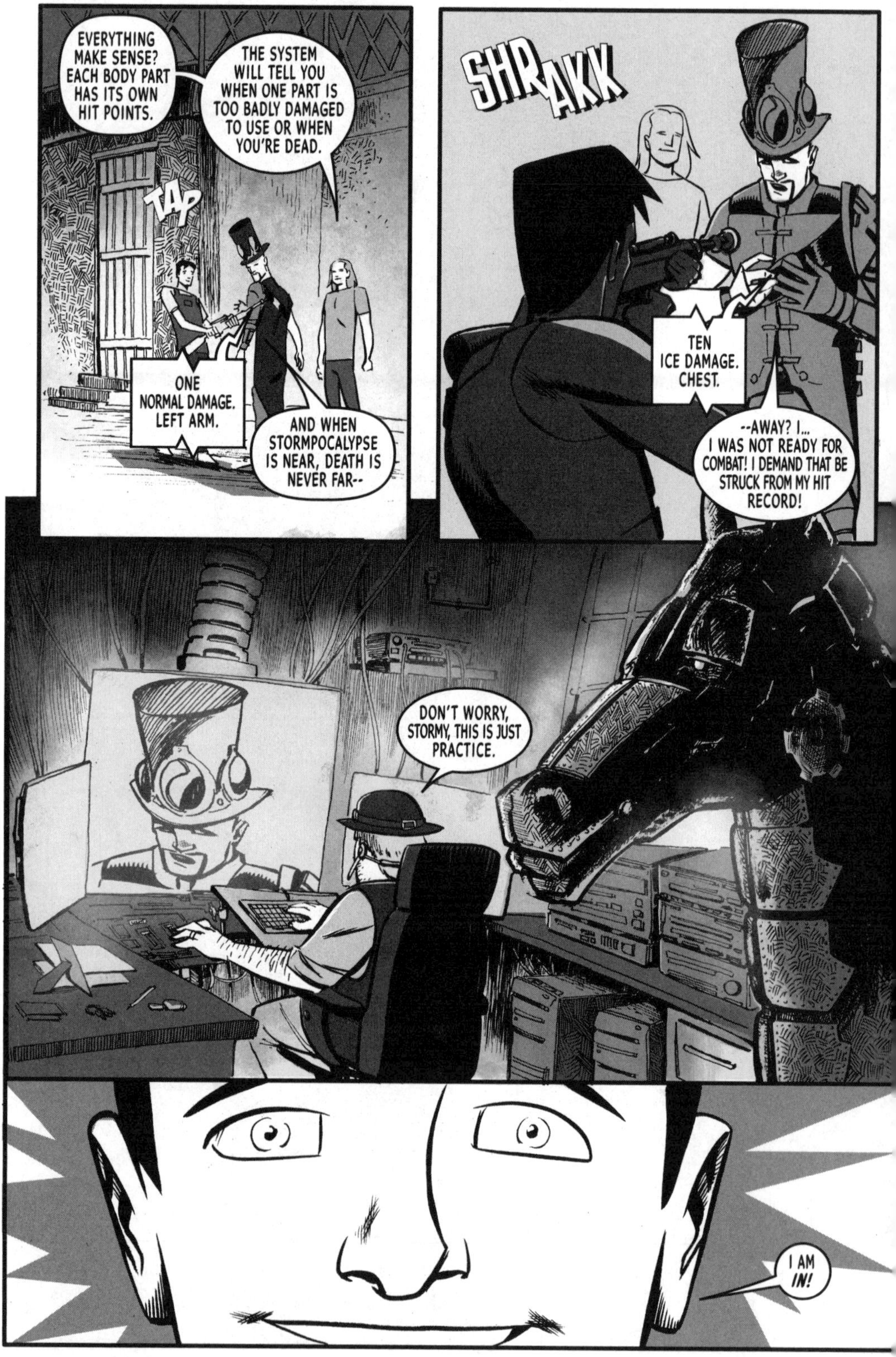
EVERYTHING MAKE SENSE? EACH BODY PART HAS ITS OWN HIT POINTS.
THE SYSTEM WILL TELL YOU WHEN ONE PART IS TOO BADLY DAMAGED TO USE OR WHEN YOU'RE DEAD.
TAP
ONE NORMAL DAMAGE. LEFT ARM.
AND WHEN STORMPOCALYPSE IS NEAR, DEATH IS NEVER FAR--
SHRAKK
TEN ICE DAMAGE. CHEST.
--AWAY? I... I WAS NOT READY FOR COMBAT! I DEMAND THAT BE STRUCK FROM MY HIT RECORD!
DON'T WORRY, STORMY, THIS IS JUST PRACTICE.
I AM *IN!*

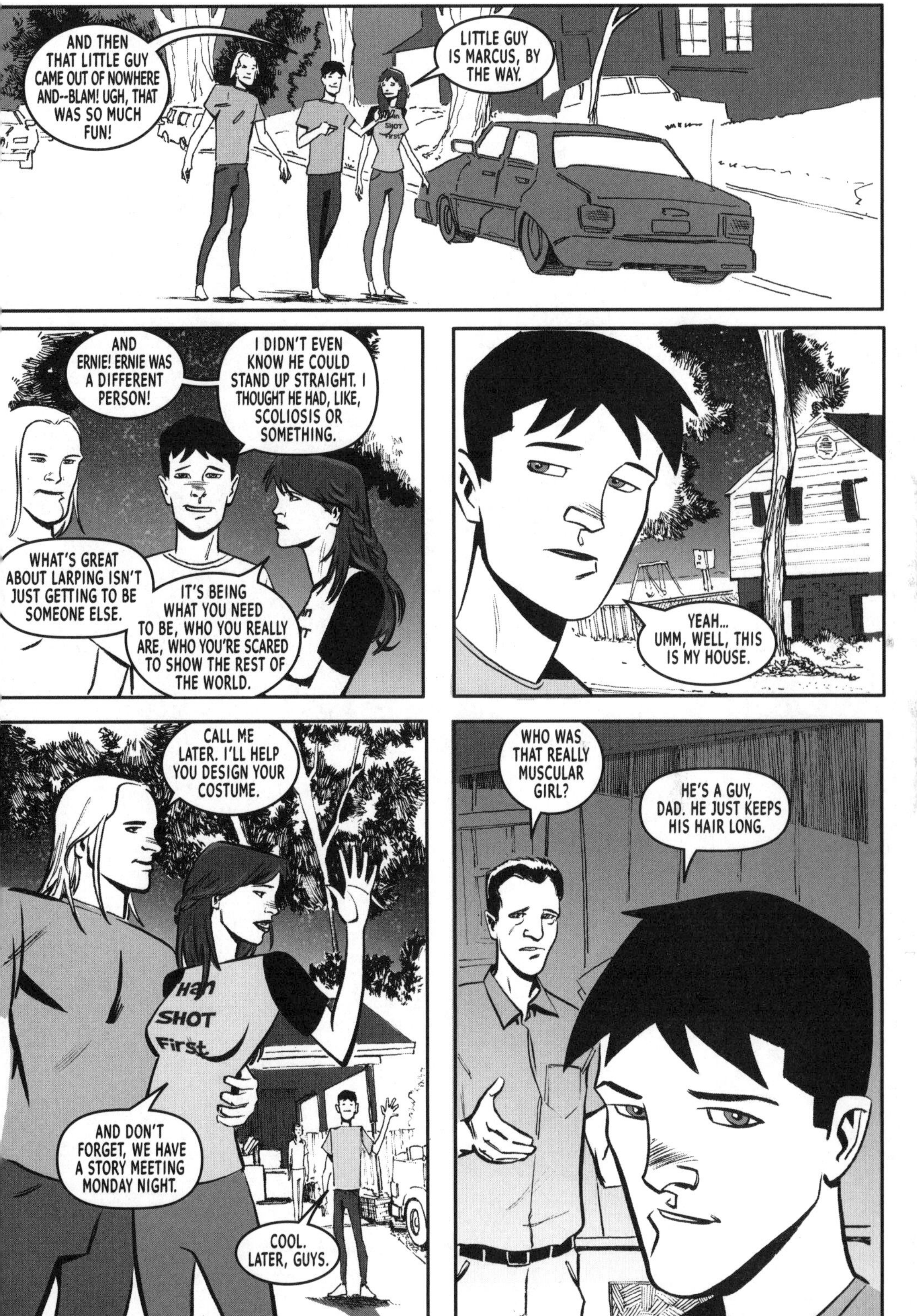
AND THEN THAT LITTLE GUY CAME OUT OF NOWHERE AND--BLAM! UGH, THAT WAS SO MUCH FUN!
LITTLE GUY IS MARCUS, BY THE WAY.
AND ERNIE! ERNIE WAS A DIFFERENT PERSON!
I DIDN'T EVEN KNOW HE COULD STAND UP STRAIGHT. I THOUGHT HE HAD, LIKE, SCOLIOSIS OR SOMETHING.
WHAT'S GREAT ABOUT LARPING ISN'T JUST GETTING TO BE SOMEONE ELSE.
IT'S BEING WHAT YOU NEED TO BE, WHO YOU REALLY ARE, WHO YOU'RE SCARED TO SHOW THE REST OF THE WORLD.
YEAH... UMM, WELL, THIS IS MY HOUSE.
CALL ME LATER. I'LL HELP YOU DESIGN YOUR COSTUME.
Han SHOT First
AND DON'T FORGET, WE HAVE A STORY MEETING MONDAY NIGHT.
COOL. LATER, GUYS.
WHO WAS THAT REALLY MUSCULAR GIRL?
HE'S A GUY, DAD. HE JUST KEEPS HIS HAIR LONG.

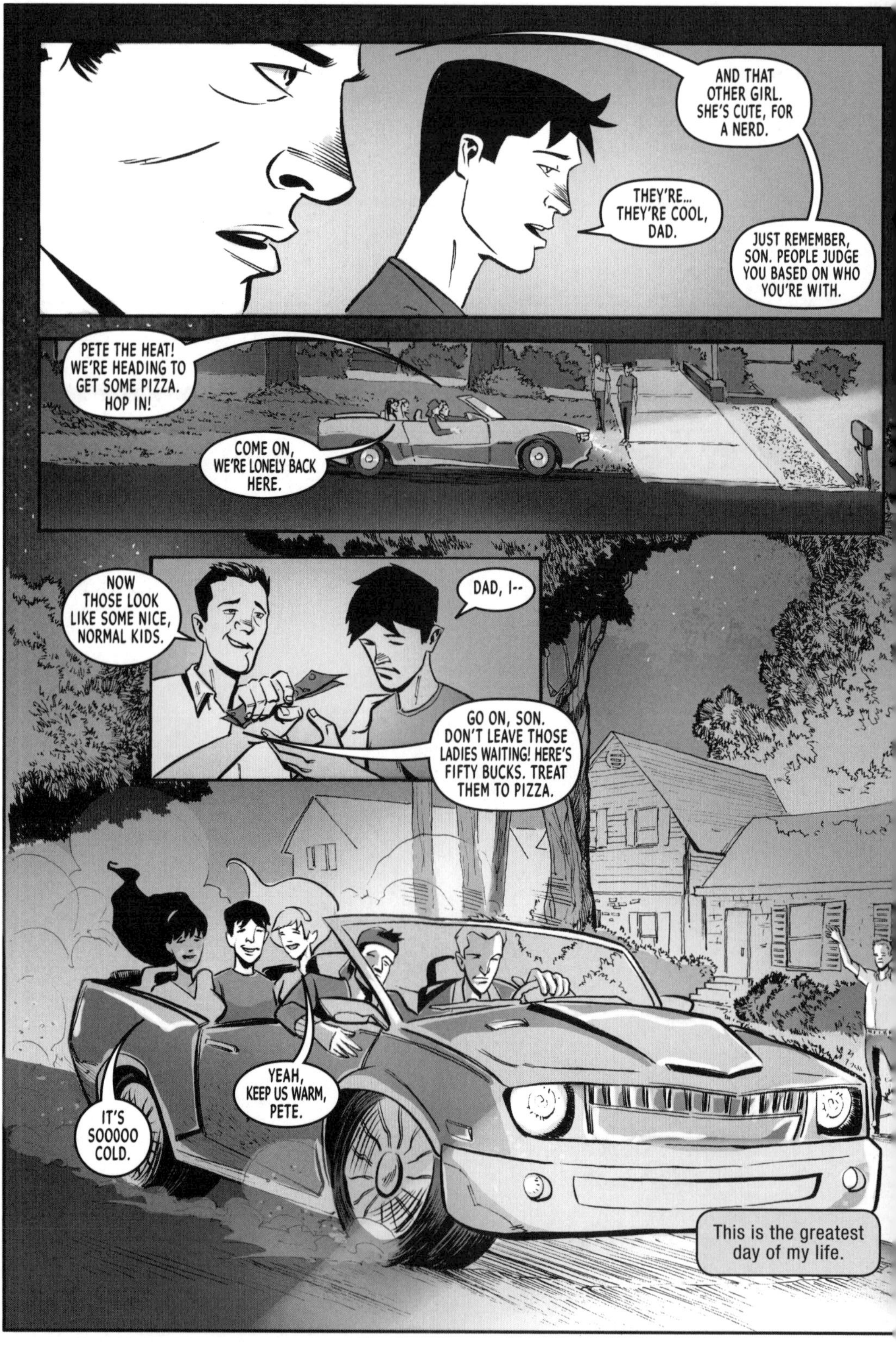
THEY'RE... THEY'RE COOL, DAD.
AND THAT OTHER GIRL. SHE'S CUTE, FOR A NERD.
JUST REMEMBER, SON. PEOPLE JUDGE YOU BASED ON WHO YOU'RE WITH.
PETE THE HEAT! WE'RE HEADING TO GET SOME PIZZA. HOP IN!
COME ON, WE'RE LONELY BACK HERE.
NOW THOSE LOOK LIKE SOME NICE, NORMAL KIDS.
DAD, I--
GO ON, SON. DON'T LEAVE THOSE LADIES WAITING! HERE'S FIFTY BUCKS. TREAT THEM TO PIZZA.
IT'S SOOOOO COLD.
YEAH, KEEP US WARM, PETE.
This is the greatest day of my life.

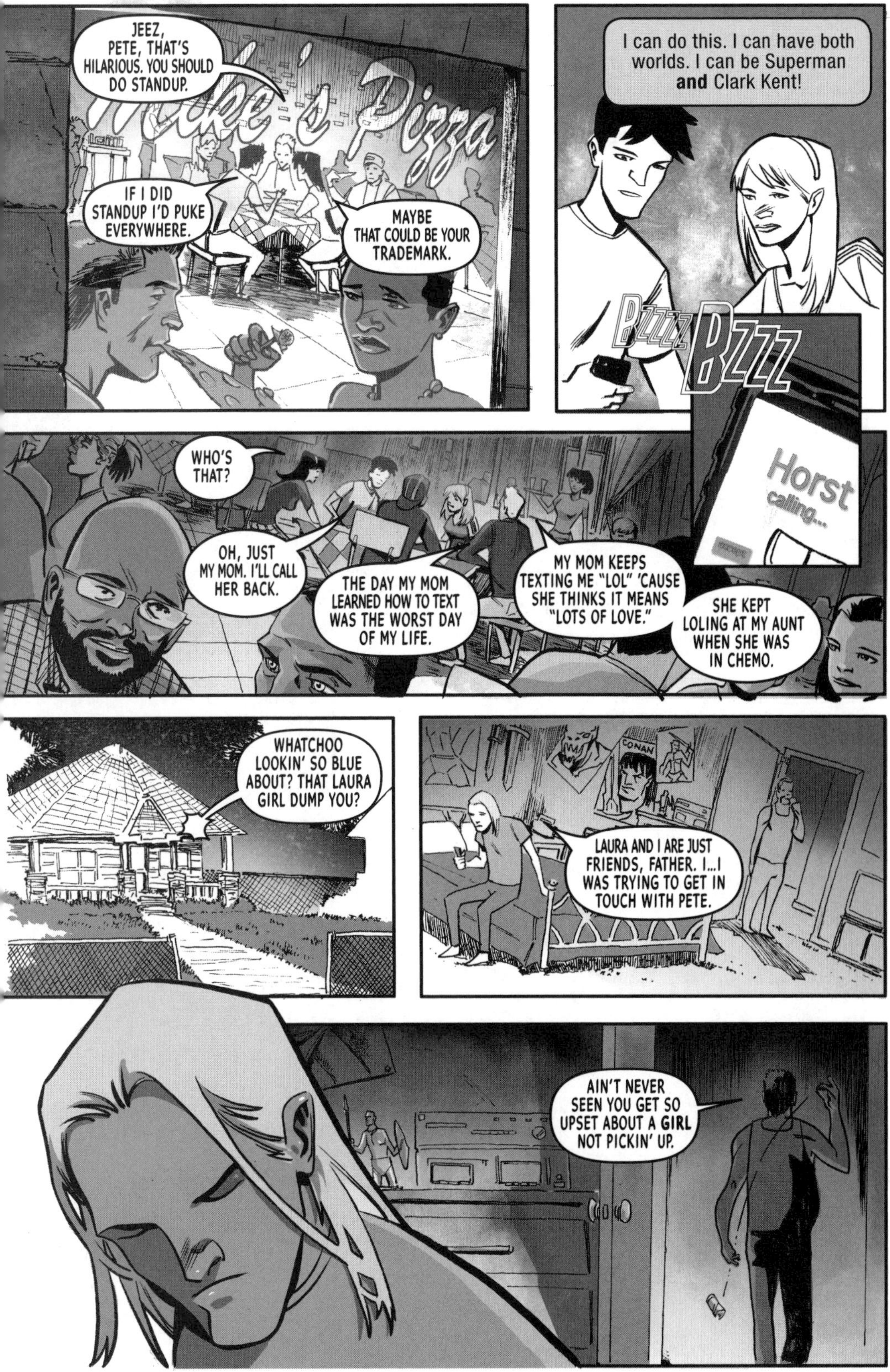

JEEZ, PETE, THAT'S HILARIOUS. YOU SHOULD DO STANDUP.
Mike's Pizza
IF I DID STANDUP I'D PUKE EVERYWHERE.
MAYBE THAT COULD BE YOUR TRADEMARK.
I can do this. I can have both worlds. I can be Superman **and** Clark Kent!
BZZZZ BZZZ
Horst calling...
WHO'S THAT?
OH, JUST MY MOM. I'LL CALL HER BACK.
THE DAY MY MOM LEARNED HOW TO TEXT WAS THE WORST DAY OF MY LIFE.
MY MOM KEEPS TEXTING ME "LOL" 'CAUSE SHE THINKS IT MEANS "LOTS OF LOVE."
SHE KEPT LOLING AT MY AUNT WHEN SHE WAS IN CHEMO.
WHATCHOO LOOKIN' SO BLUE ABOUT? THAT LAURA GIRL DUMP YOU?
CONAN
LAURA AND I ARE JUST FRIENDS, FATHER. I...I WAS TRYING TO GET IN TOUCH WITH PETE.
AIN'T NEVER SEEN YOU GET SO UPSET ABOUT A **GIRL** NOT PICKIN' UP.

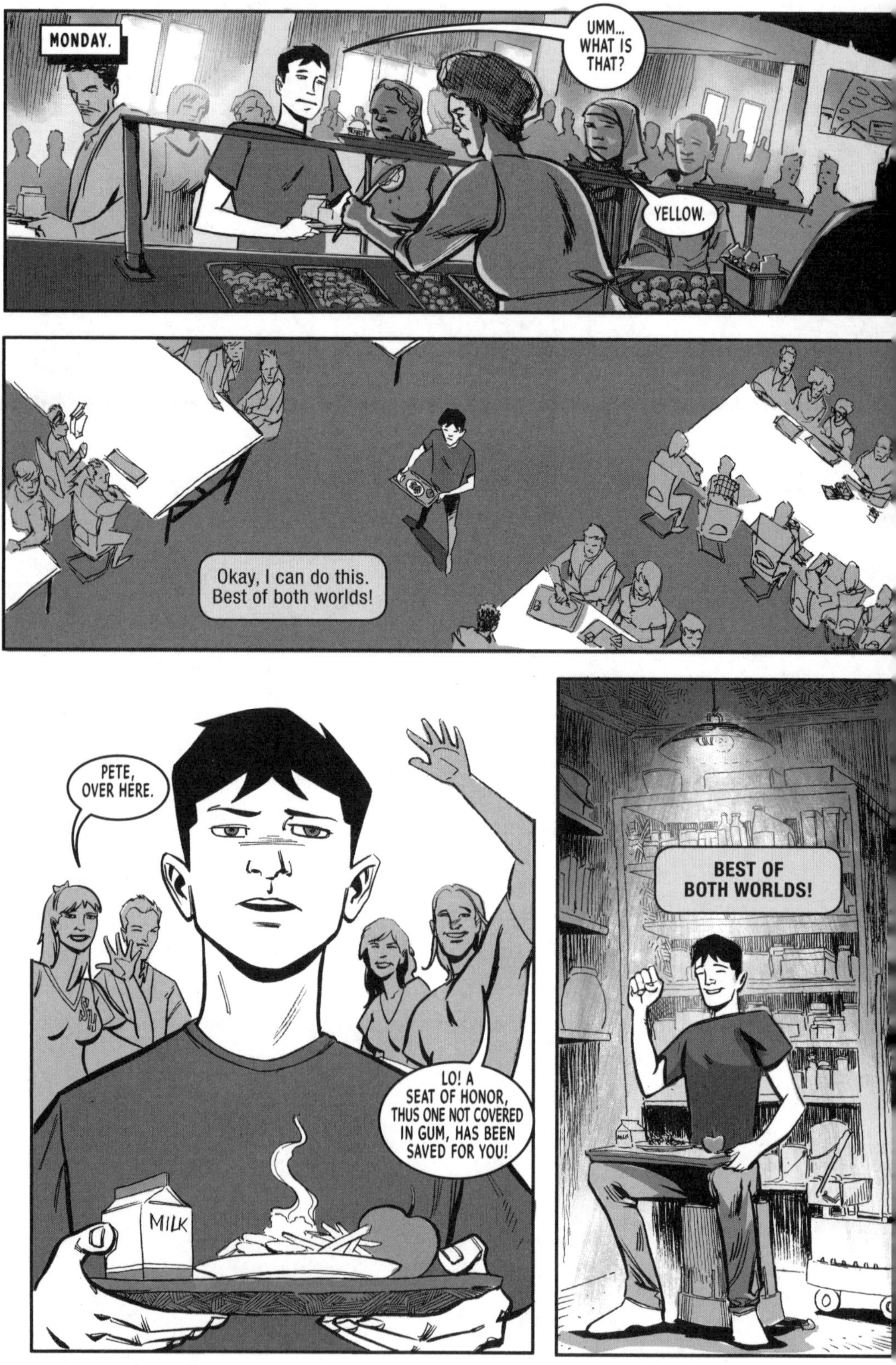
MONDAY.
UMM... WHAT IS THAT?
YELLOW.
Okay, I can do this. Best of both worlds!
PETE, OVER HERE.
LO! A SEAT OF HONOR, THUS ONE NOT COVERED IN GUM, HAS BEEN SAVED FOR YOU!
MILK
BEST OF BOTH WORLDS!

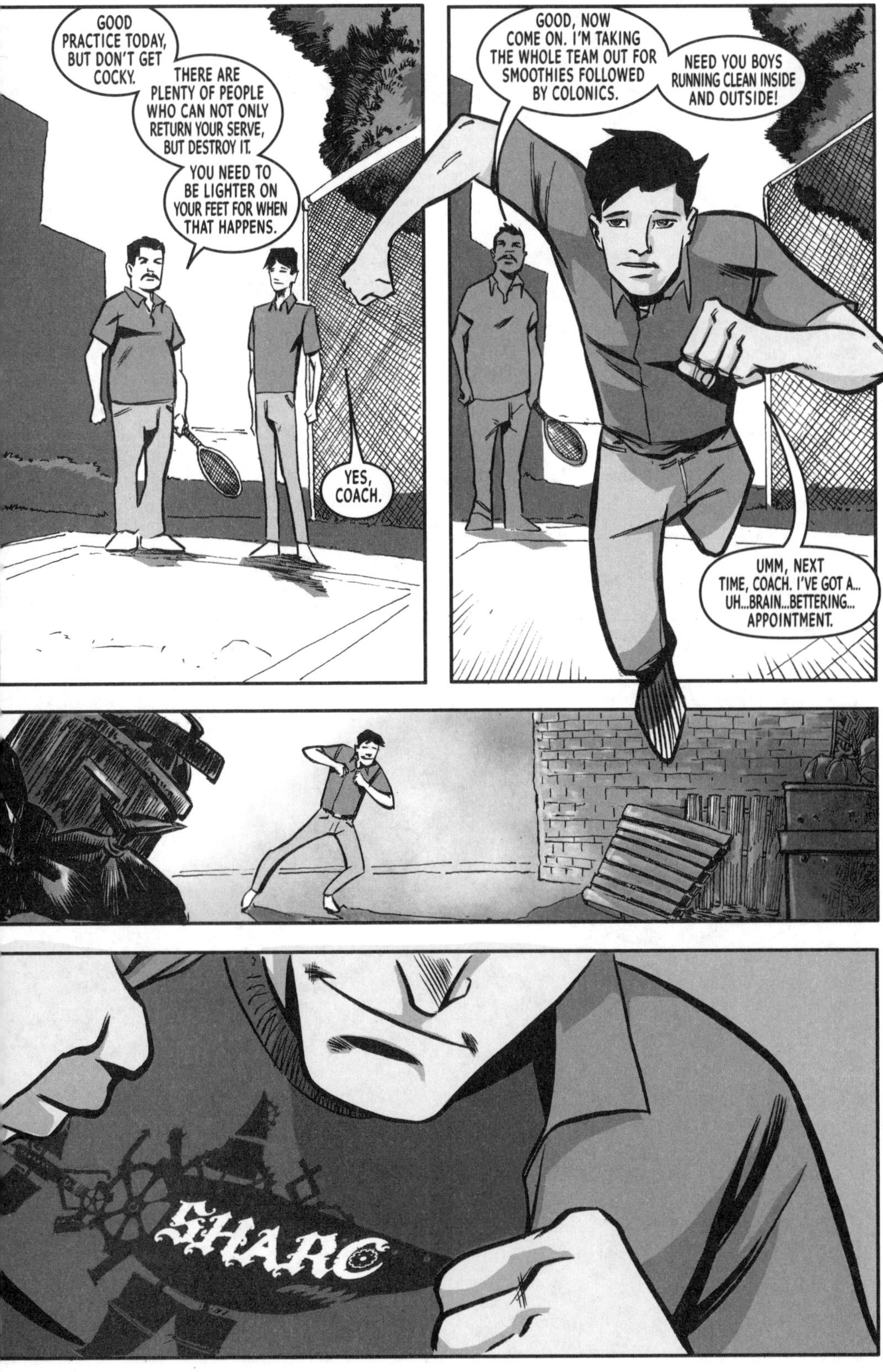
GOOD PRACTICE TODAY, BUT DON'T GET COCKY.
THERE ARE PLENTY OF PEOPLE WHO CAN NOT ONLY RETURN YOUR SERVE, BUT DESTROY IT.
YOU NEED TO BE LIGHTER ON YOUR FEET FOR WHEN THAT HAPPENS.
YES, COACH.
GOOD, NOW COME ON. I'M TAKING THE WHOLE TEAM OUT FOR SMOOTHIES FOLLOWED BY COLONICS.
NEED YOU BOYS RUNNING CLEAN INSIDE AND OUTSIDE!
UMM, NEXT TIME, COACH. I'VE GOT A... UH...BRAIN...BETTERING... APPOINTMENT.
SHARC

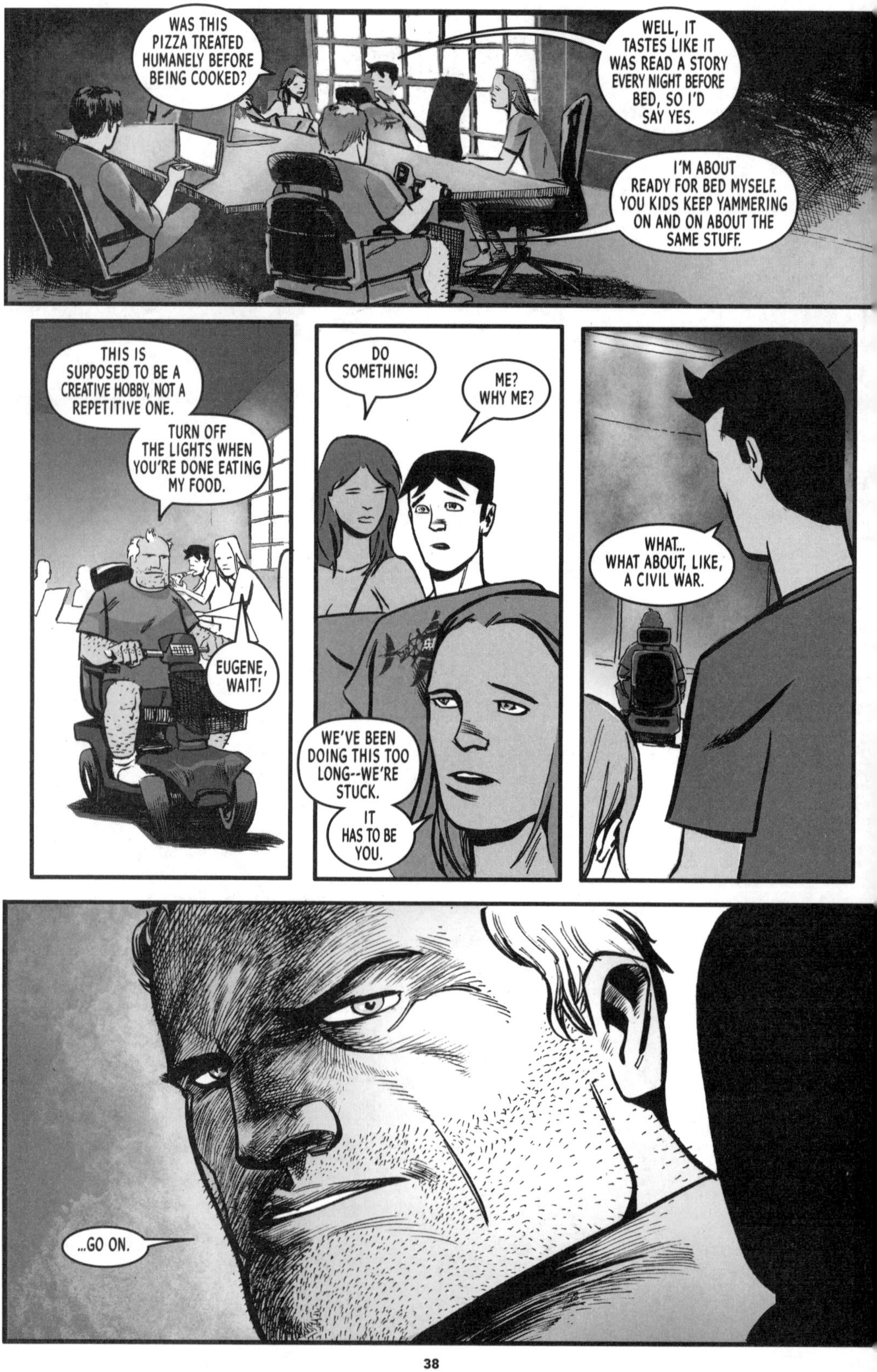
WAS THIS PIZZA TREATED HUMANELY BEFORE BEING COOKED?
WELL, IT TASTES LIKE IT WAS READ A STORY EVERY NIGHT BEFORE BED, SO I'D SAY YES.
I'M ABOUT READY FOR BED MYSELF. YOU KIDS KEEP YAMMERING ON AND ON ABOUT THE SAME STUFF.
THIS IS SUPPOSED TO BE A CREATIVE HOBBY, NOT A REPETITIVE ONE.
TURN OFF THE LIGHTS WHEN YOU'RE DONE EATING MY FOOD.
EUGENE, WAIT!
DO SOMETHING!
ME? WHY ME?
WE'VE BEEN DOING THIS TOO LONG--WE'RE STUCK.
IT HAS TO BE YOU.
WHAT... WHAT ABOUT, LIKE, A CIVIL WAR.
...GO ON.

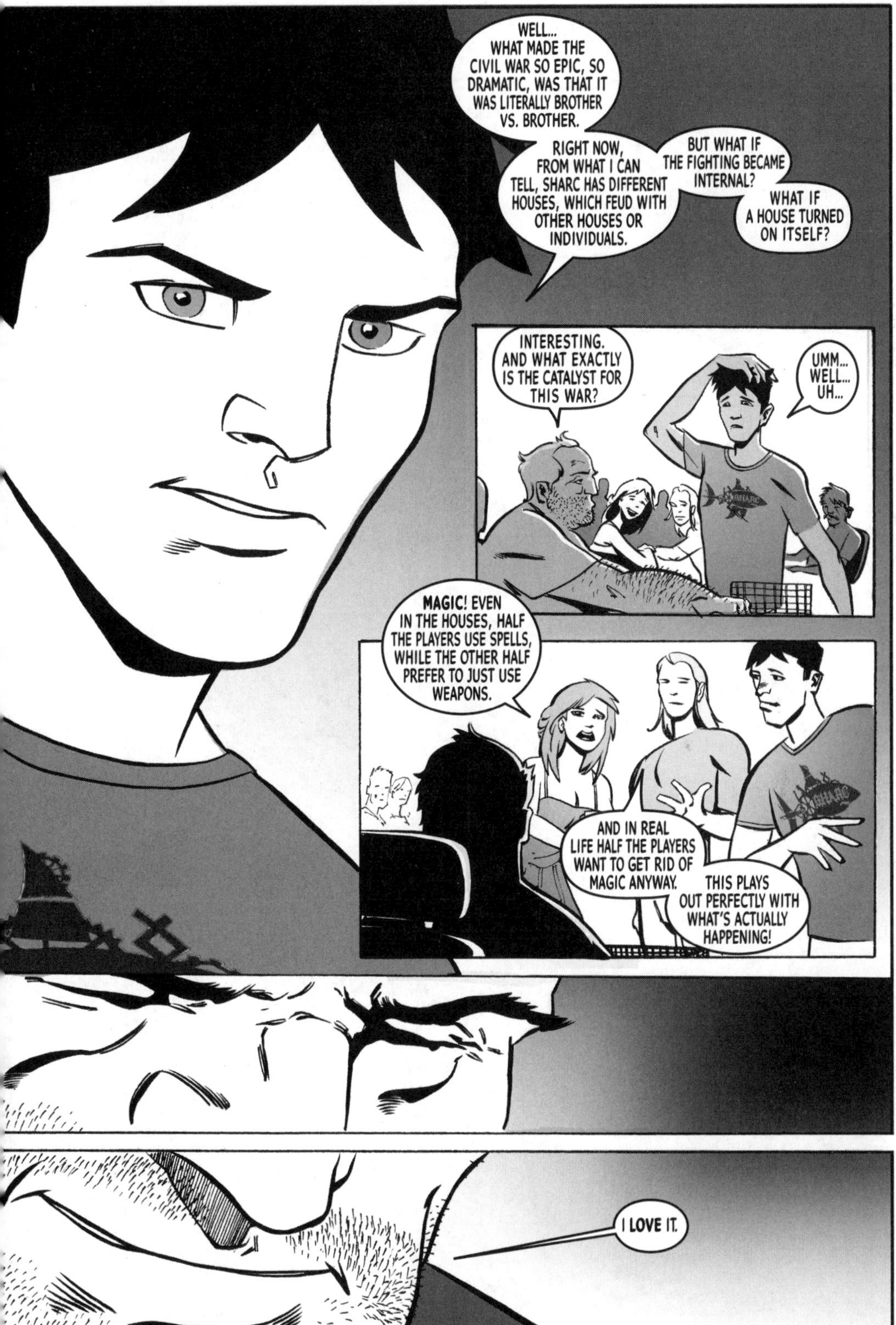
WELL... WHAT MADE THE CIVIL WAR SO EPIC, SO DRAMATIC, WAS THAT IT WAS LITERALLY BROTHER VS. BROTHER.
RIGHT NOW, FROM WHAT I CAN TELL, SHARC HAS DIFFERENT HOUSES, WHICH FEUD WITH OTHER HOUSES OR INDIVIDUALS.
BUT WHAT IF THE FIGHTING BECAME INTERNAL?
WHAT IF A HOUSE TURNED ON ITSELF?
INTERESTING. AND WHAT EXACTLY IS THE CATALYST FOR THIS WAR?
UMM... WELL... UH...
MAGIC! EVEN IN THE HOUSES, HALF THE PLAYERS USE SPELLS, WHILE THE OTHER HALF PREFER TO JUST USE WEAPONS.
AND IN REAL LIFE HALF THE PLAYERS WANT TO GET RID OF MAGIC ANYWAY.
THIS PLAYS OUT PERFECTLY WITH WHAT'S ACTUALLY HAPPENING!
I LOVE IT.

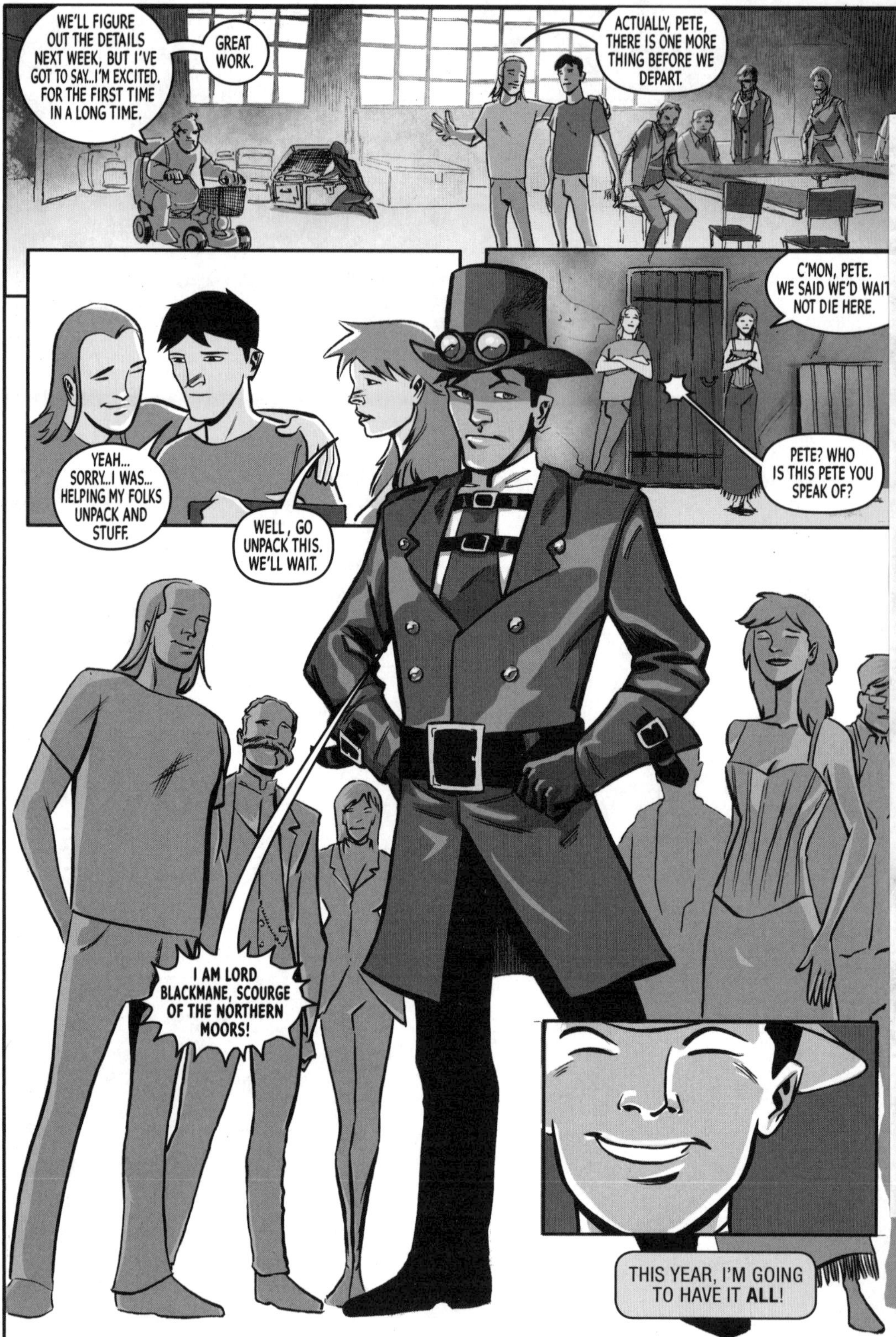
WE'LL FIGURE OUT THE DETAILS NEXT WEEK, BUT I'VE GOT TO SAY...I'M EXCITED. FOR THE FIRST TIME IN A LONG TIME.
GREAT WORK.
ACTUALLY, PETE, THERE IS ONE MORE THING BEFORE WE DEPART.
YEAH... SORRY...I WAS... HELPING MY FOLKS UNPACK AND STUFF.
WELL, GO UNPACK THIS. WE'LL WAIT.
C'MON, PETE. WE SAID WE'D WAIT NOT DIE HERE.
PETE? WHO IS THIS PETE YOU SPEAK OF?
I AM LORD BLACKMANE, SCOURGE OF THE NORTHERN MOORS!
THIS YEAR, I'M GOING TO HAVE IT ALL!

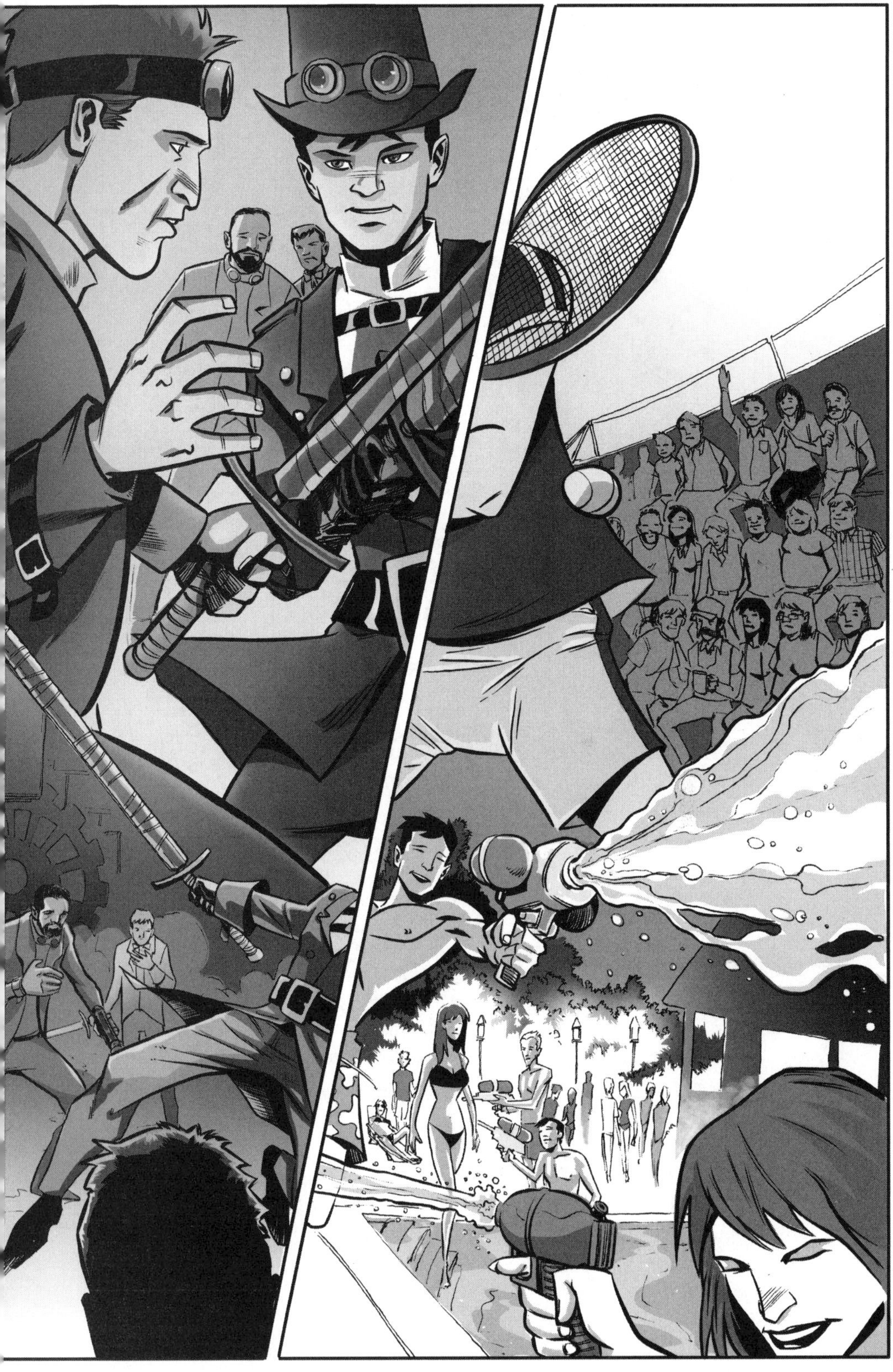

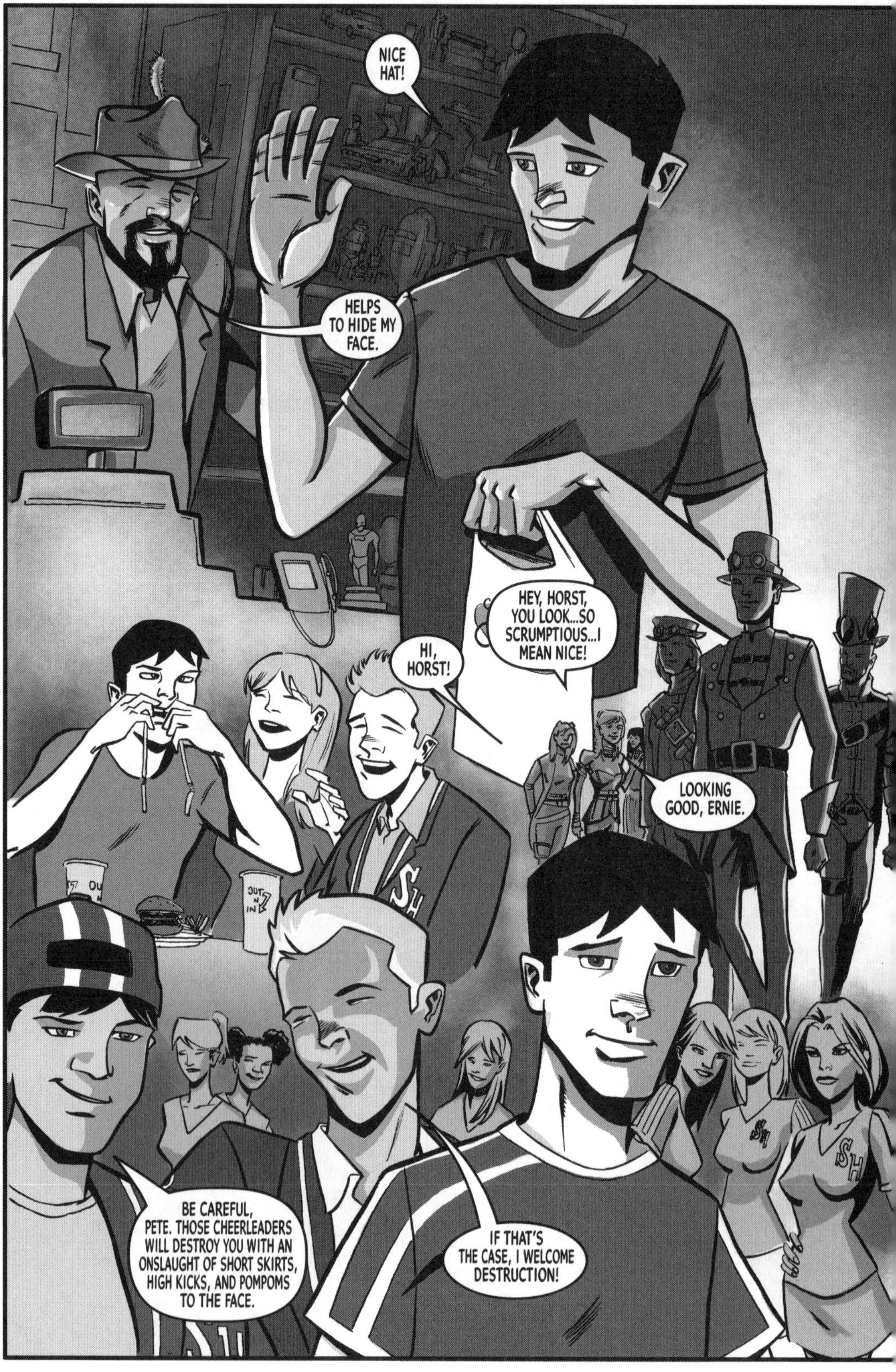
NICE HAT!
HELPS TO HIDE MY FACE.
HEY, HORST, YOU LOOK...SO SCRUMPTIOUS...I MEAN NICE!
HI, HORST!
LOOKING GOOD, ERNIE.
BE CAREFUL, PETE. THOSE CHEERLEADERS WILL DESTROY YOU WITH AN ONSLAUGHT OF SHORT SKIRTS, HIGH KICKS, AND POMPOMS TO THE FACE.
IF THAT'S THE CASE, I WELCOME DESTRUCTION!

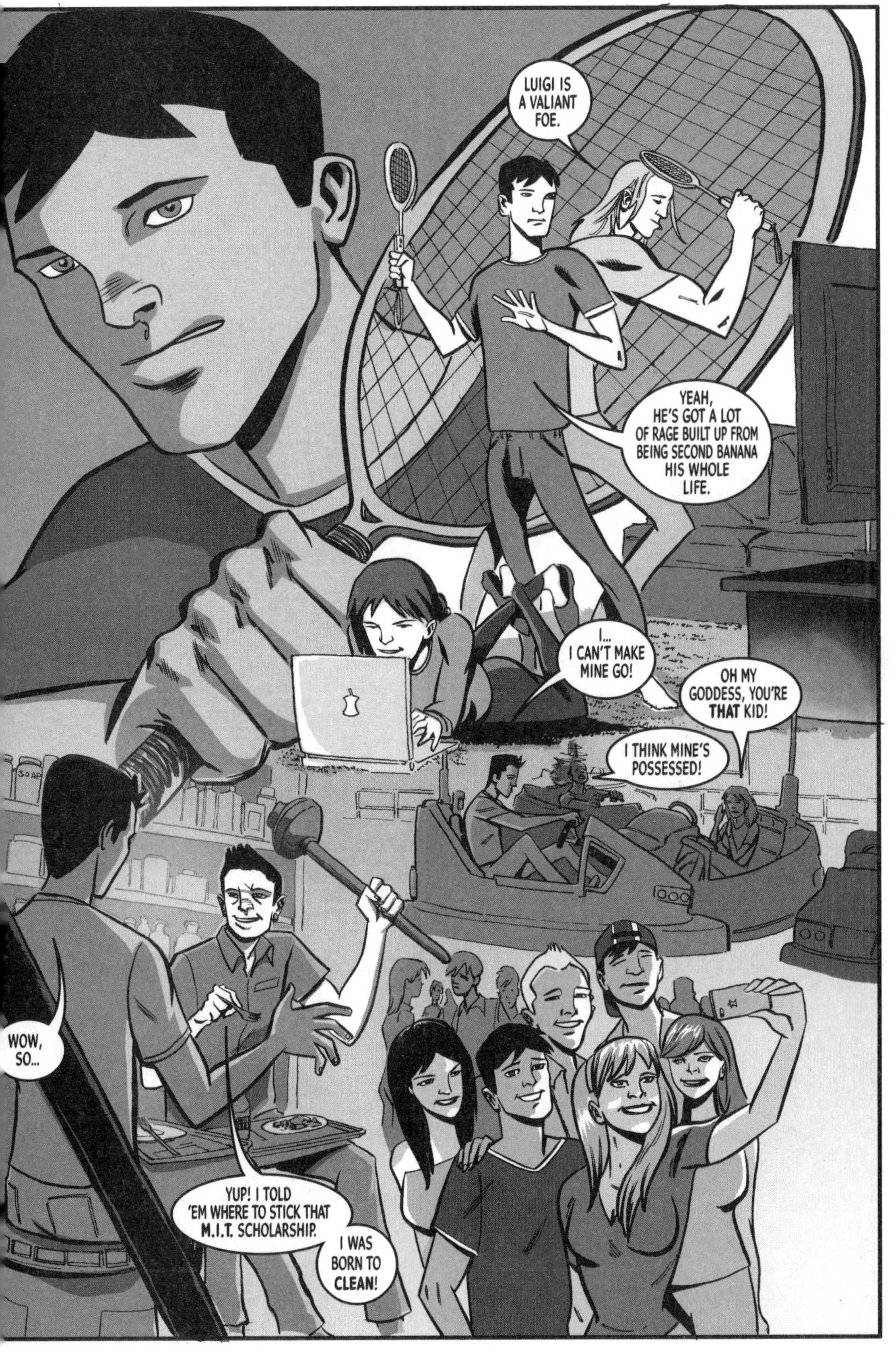
LUIGI IS A VALIANT FOE.
YEAH, HE'S GOT A LOT OF RAGE BUILT UP FROM BEING SECOND BANANA HIS WHOLE LIFE.
I... I CAN'T MAKE MINE GO!
OH MY GODDESS, YOU'RE **THAT** KID!
I THINK MINE'S POSSESSED!
WOW, SO...
YUP! I TOLD 'EM WHERE TO STICK THAT **M.I.T.** SCHOLARSHIP.
I WAS BORN TO **CLEAN**!

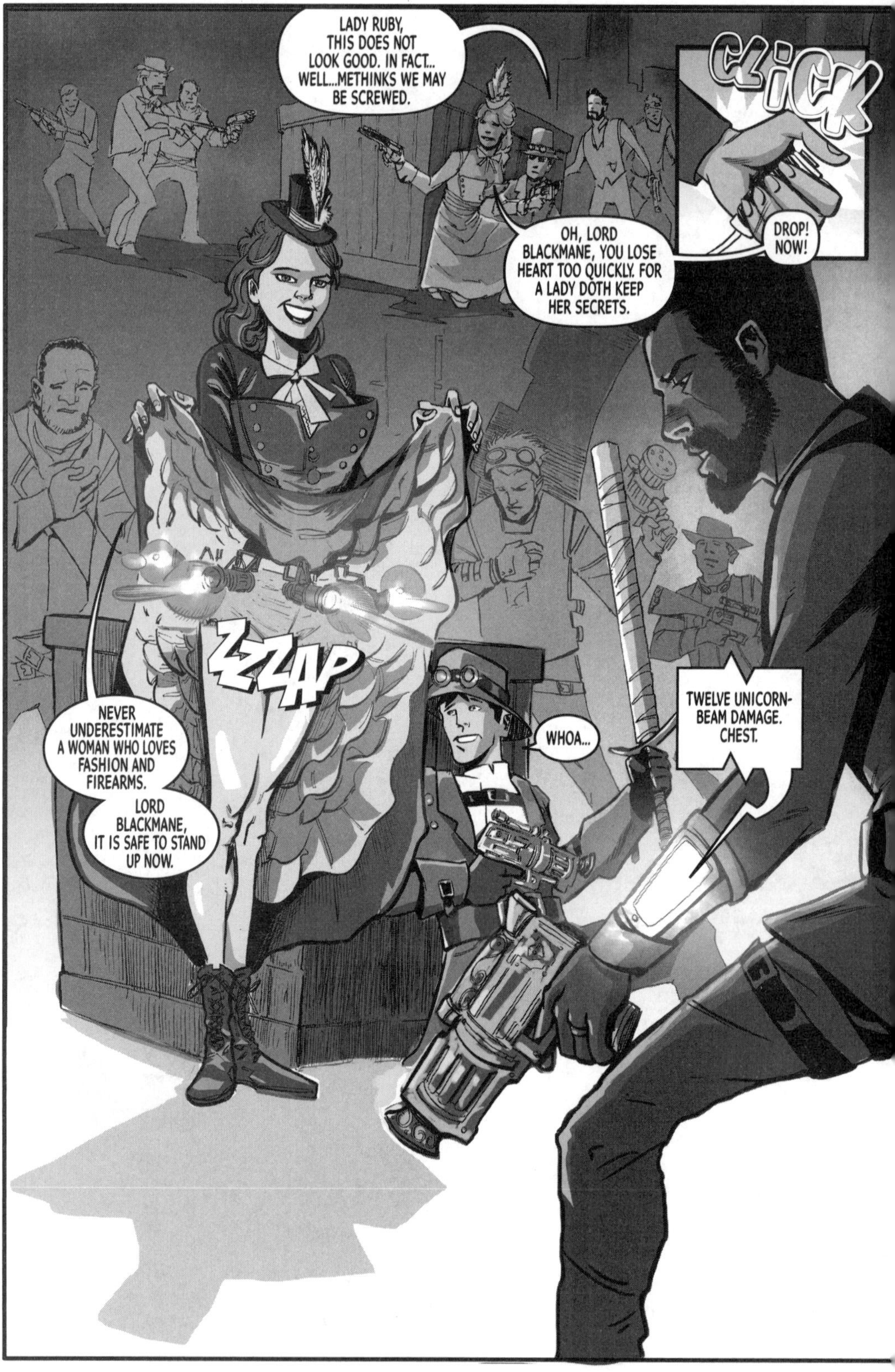
LADY RUBY, THIS DOES NOT LOOK GOOD. IN FACT... WELL...METHINKS WE MAY BE SCREWED.
OH, LORD BLACKMANE, YOU LOSE HEART TOO QUICKLY. FOR A LADY DOTH KEEP HER SECRETS.
CLICK
DROP! NOW!
ZZZAP
NEVER UNDERESTIMATE A WOMAN WHO LOVES FASHION AND FIREARMS.
LORD BLACKMANE, IT IS SAFE TO STAND UP NOW.
WHOA...
TWELVE UNICORN-BEAM DAMAGE. CHEST.

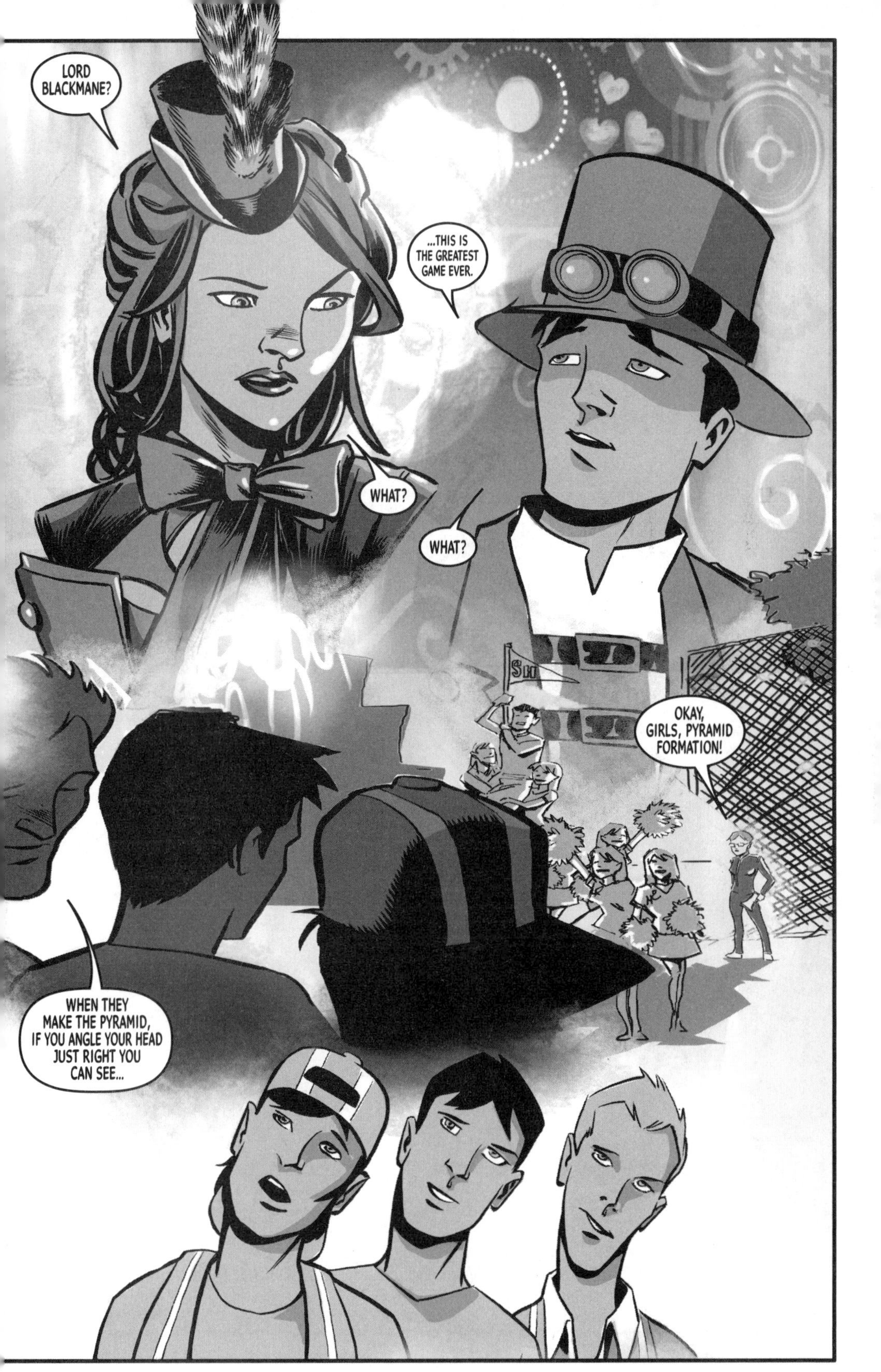
LORD BLACKMANE?
...THIS IS THE GREATEST GAME EVER.
WHAT?
WHAT?
OKAY, GIRLS, PYRAMID FORMATION!
WHEN THEY MAKE THE PYRAMID, IF YOU ANGLE YOUR HEAD JUST RIGHT YOU CAN SEE...

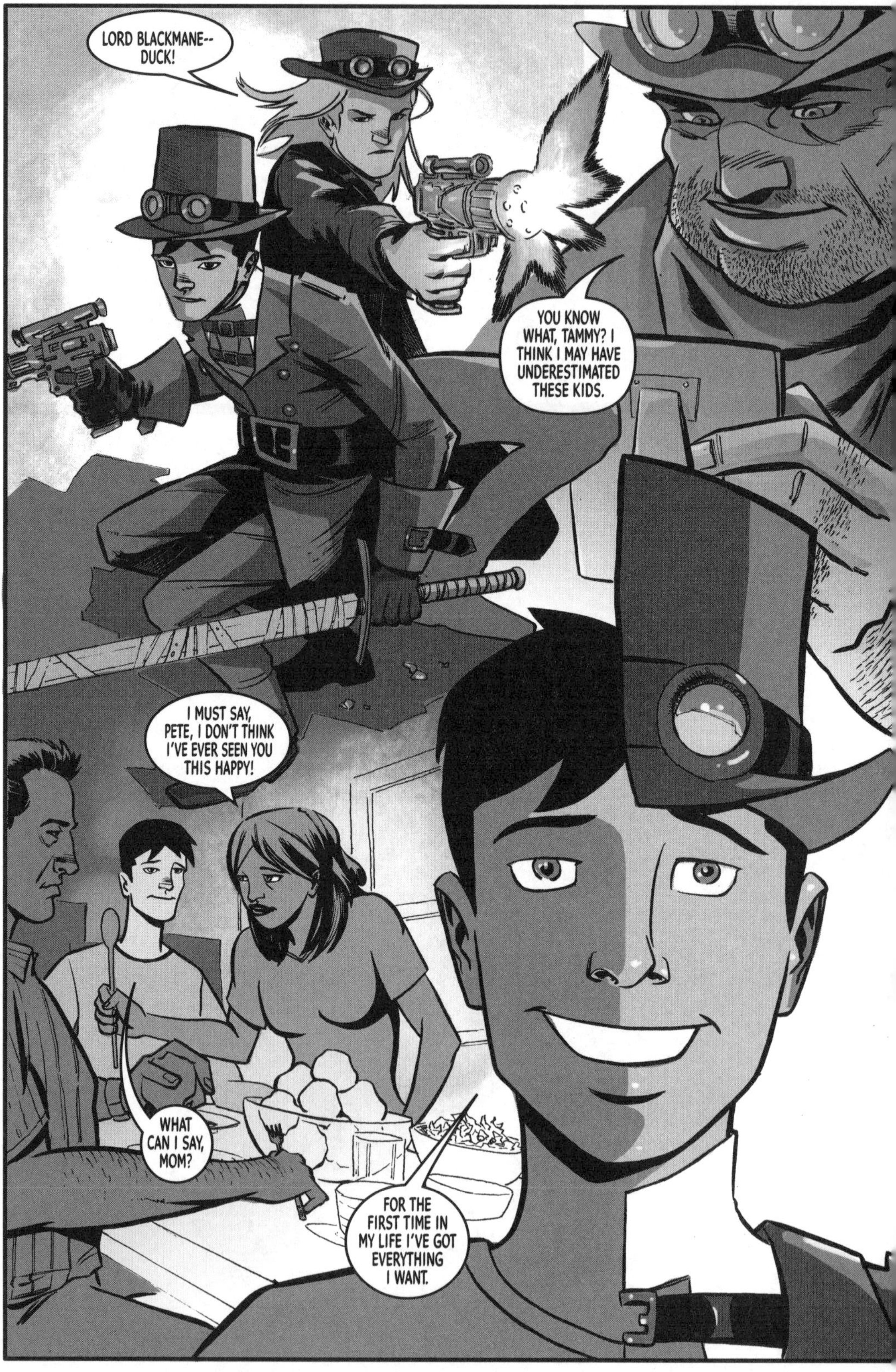
LORD BLACKMANE-- DUCK!
YOU KNOW WHAT, TAMMY? I THINK I MAY HAVE UNDERESTIMATED THESE KIDS.
I MUST SAY, PETE, I DON'T THINK I'VE EVER SEEN YOU THIS HAPPY!
WHAT CAN I SAY, MOM?
FOR THE FIRST TIME IN MY LIFE I'VE GOT EVERYTHING I WANT.

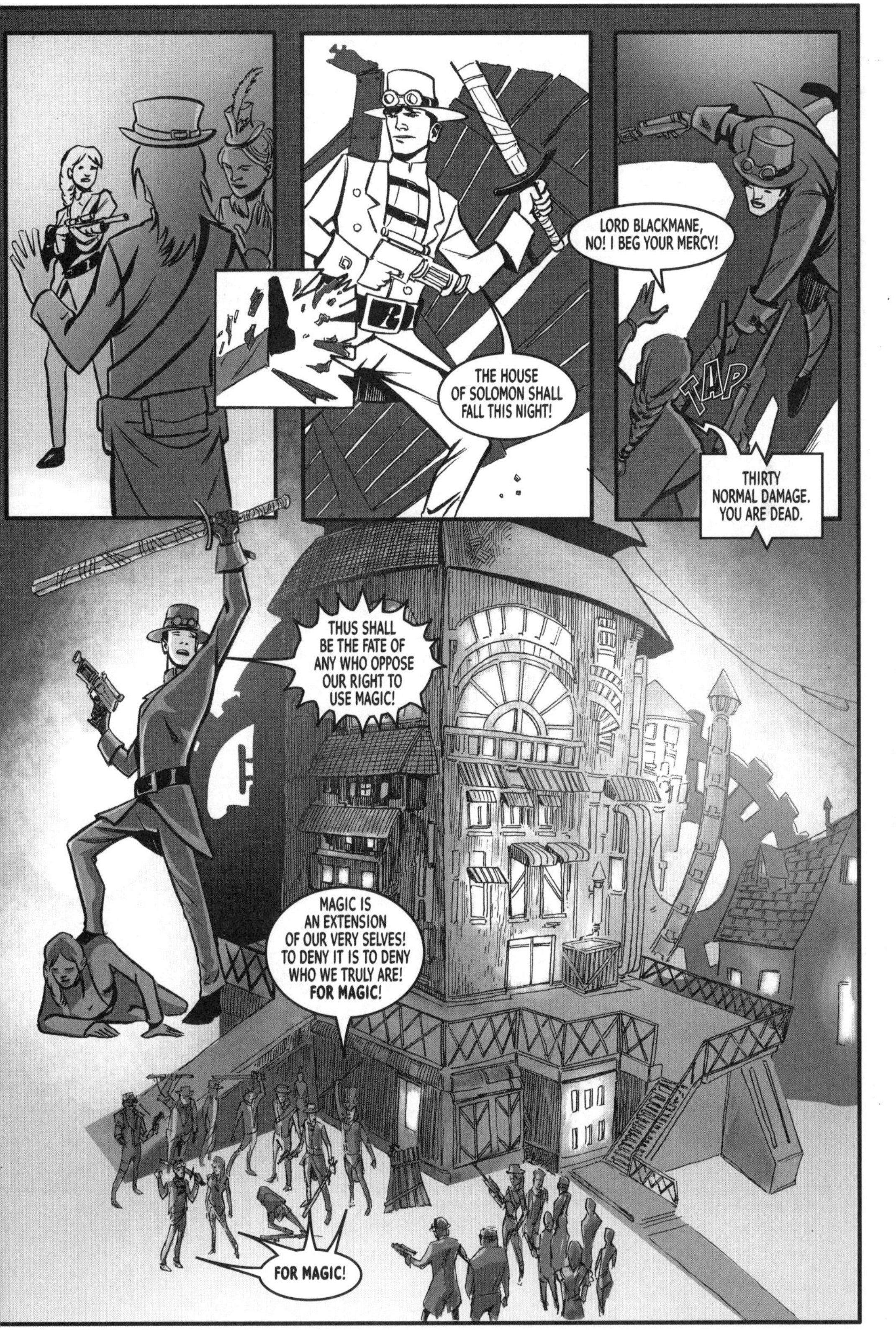
THE HOUSE OF SOLOMON SHALL FALL THIS NIGHT!
LORD BLACKMANE, NO! I BEG YOUR MERCY!
TAP
THIRTY NORMAL DAMAGE. YOU ARE DEAD.
THUS SHALL BE THE FATE OF ANY WHO OPPOSE OUR RIGHT TO USE MAGIC!
MAGIC IS AN EXTENSION OF OUR VERY SELVES! TO DENY IT IS TO DENY WHO WE TRULY ARE! **FOR MAGIC!**
FOR MAGIC!

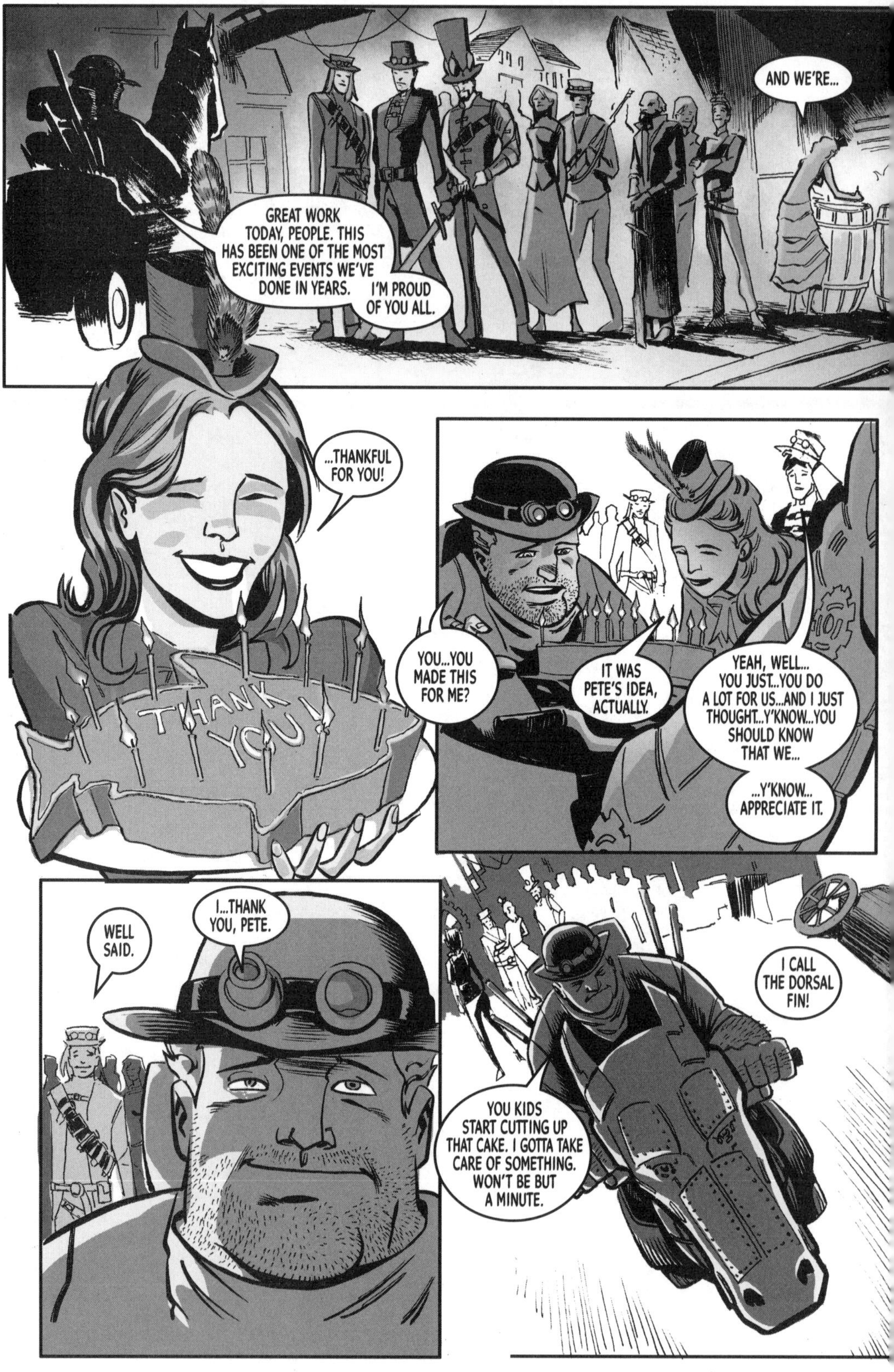
GREAT WORK TODAY, PEOPLE. THIS HAS BEEN ONE OF THE MOST EXCITING EVENTS WE'VE DONE IN YEARS.
I'M PROUD OF YOU ALL.
AND WE'RE...
...THANKFUL FOR YOU!
THANK YOU
YOU...YOU MADE THIS FOR ME?
IT WAS PETE'S IDEA, ACTUALLY.
YEAH, WELL... YOU JUST...YOU DO A LOT FOR US...AND I JUST THOUGHT...Y'KNOW...YOU SHOULD KNOW THAT WE...
...Y'KNOW... APPRECIATE IT.
WELL SAID.
I...THANK YOU, PETE.
I CALL THE DORSAL FIN!
YOU KIDS START CUTTING UP THAT CAKE. I GOTTA TAKE CARE OF SOMETHING. WON'T BE BUT A MINUTE.

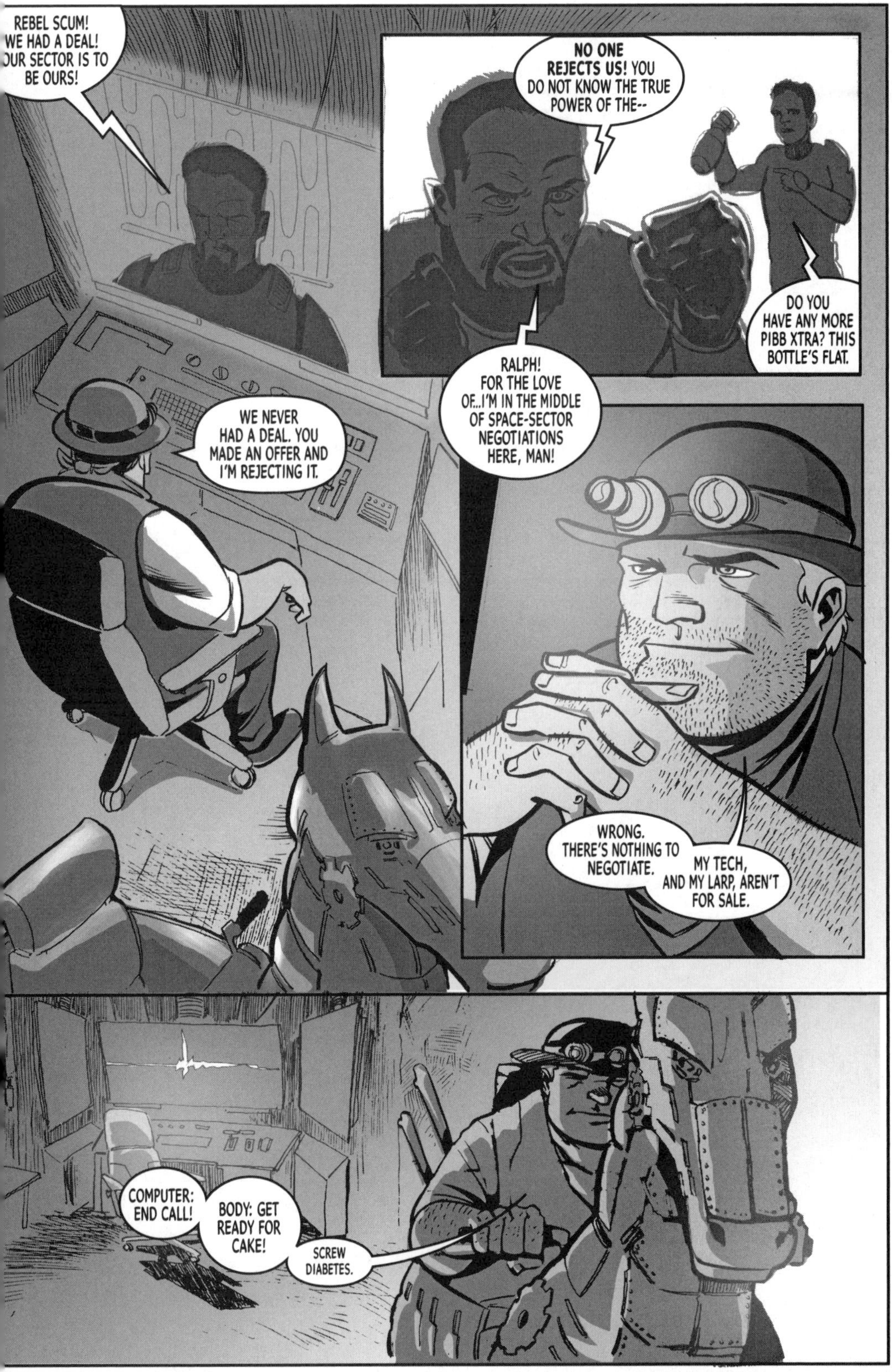
REBEL SCUM! WE HAD A DEAL! OUR SECTOR IS TO BE OURS!
NO ONE REJECTS US! YOU DO NOT KNOW THE TRUE POWER OF THE--
DO YOU HAVE ANY MORE PIBB XTRA? THIS BOTTLE'S FLAT.
RALPH! FOR THE LOVE OF...I'M IN THE MIDDLE OF SPACE-SECTOR NEGOTIATIONS HERE, MAN!
WE NEVER HAD A DEAL. YOU MADE AN OFFER AND I'M REJECTING IT.
WRONG. THERE'S NOTHING TO NEGOTIATE.
MY TECH, AND MY LARP, AREN'T FOR SALE.
COMPUTER: END CALL!
BODY: GET READY FOR CAKE!
SCREW DIABETES.

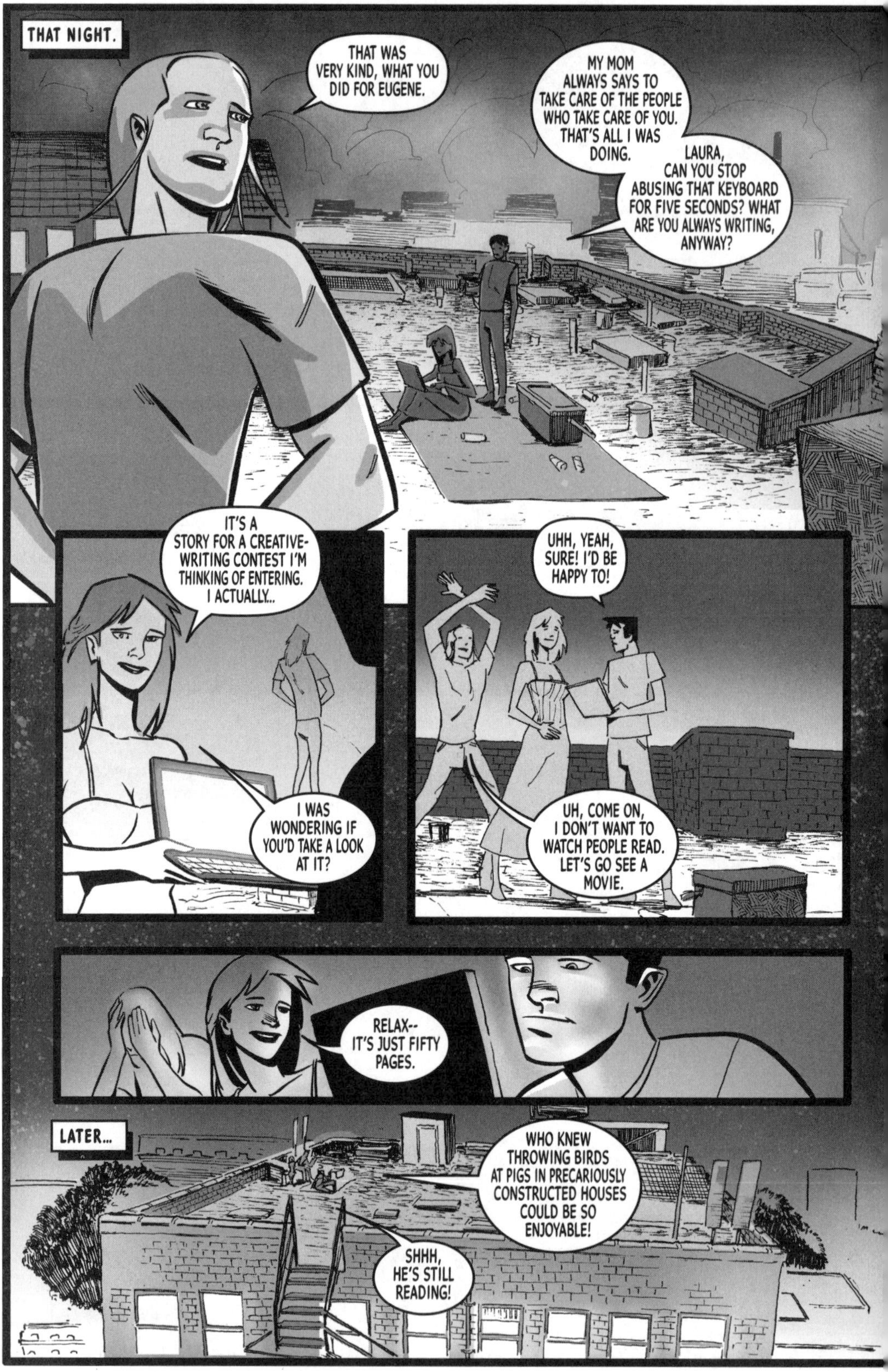
THAT NIGHT.
THAT WAS VERY KIND, WHAT YOU DID FOR EUGENE.
MY MOM ALWAYS SAYS TO TAKE CARE OF THE PEOPLE WHO TAKE CARE OF YOU. THAT'S ALL I WAS DOING.
LAURA, CAN YOU STOP ABUSING THAT KEYBOARD FOR FIVE SECONDS? WHAT ARE YOU ALWAYS WRITING, ANYWAY?
IT'S A STORY FOR A CREATIVE-WRITING CONTEST I'M THINKING OF ENTERING. I ACTUALLY...
I WAS WONDERING IF YOU'D TAKE A LOOK AT IT?
UHH, YEAH, SURE! I'D BE HAPPY TO!
UH, COME ON, I DON'T WANT TO WATCH PEOPLE READ. LET'S GO SEE A MOVIE.
RELAX-- IT'S JUST FIFTY PAGES.
LATER...
WHO KNEW THROWING BIRDS AT PIGS IN PRECARIOUSLY CONSTRUCTED HOUSES COULD BE SO ENJOYABLE!
SHHH, HE'S STILL READING!

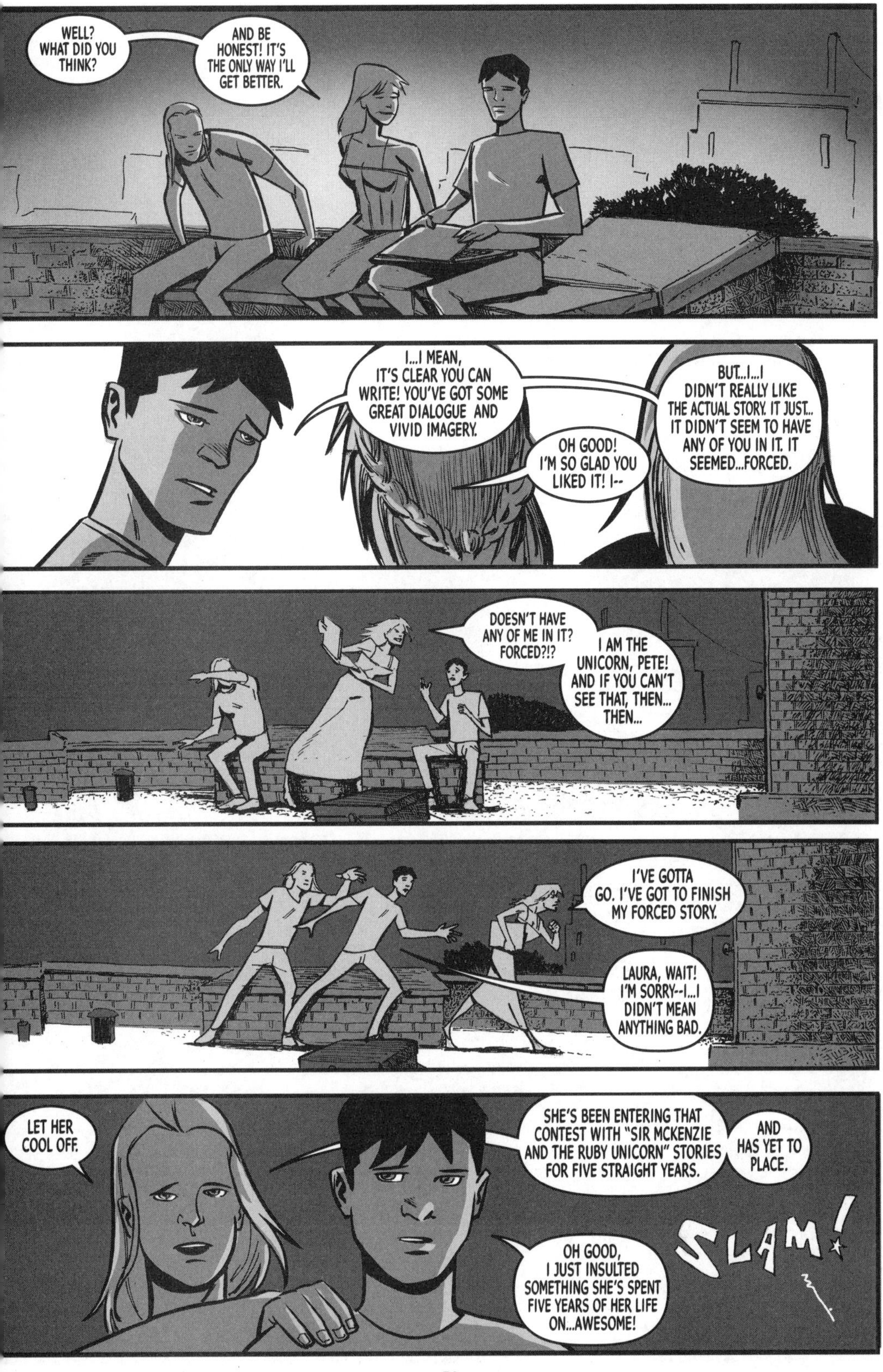
WELL? WHAT DID YOU THINK?
AND BE HONEST! IT'S THE ONLY WAY I'LL GET BETTER.
I...I MEAN, IT'S CLEAR YOU CAN WRITE! YOU'VE GOT SOME GREAT DIALOGUE AND VIVID IMAGERY.
OH GOOD! I'M SO GLAD YOU LIKED IT! I--
BUT...I...I DIDN'T REALLY LIKE THE ACTUAL STORY. IT JUST... IT DIDN'T SEEM TO HAVE ANY OF YOU IN IT. IT SEEMED...FORCED.
DOESN'T HAVE ANY OF ME IN IT? FORCED?!?
I AM THE UNICORN, PETE! AND IF YOU CAN'T SEE THAT, THEN... THEN...
I'VE GOTTA GO. I'VE GOT TO FINISH MY FORCED STORY.
LAURA, WAIT! I'M SORRY--I...I DIDN'T MEAN ANYTHING BAD.
LET HER COOL OFF.
SHE'S BEEN ENTERING THAT CONTEST WITH "SIR MCKENZIE AND THE RUBY UNICORN" STORIES FOR FIVE STRAIGHT YEARS.
AND HAS YET TO PLACE.
SLAM!
OH GOOD, I JUST INSULTED SOMETHING SHE'S SPENT FIVE YEARS OF HER LIFE ON...AWESOME!

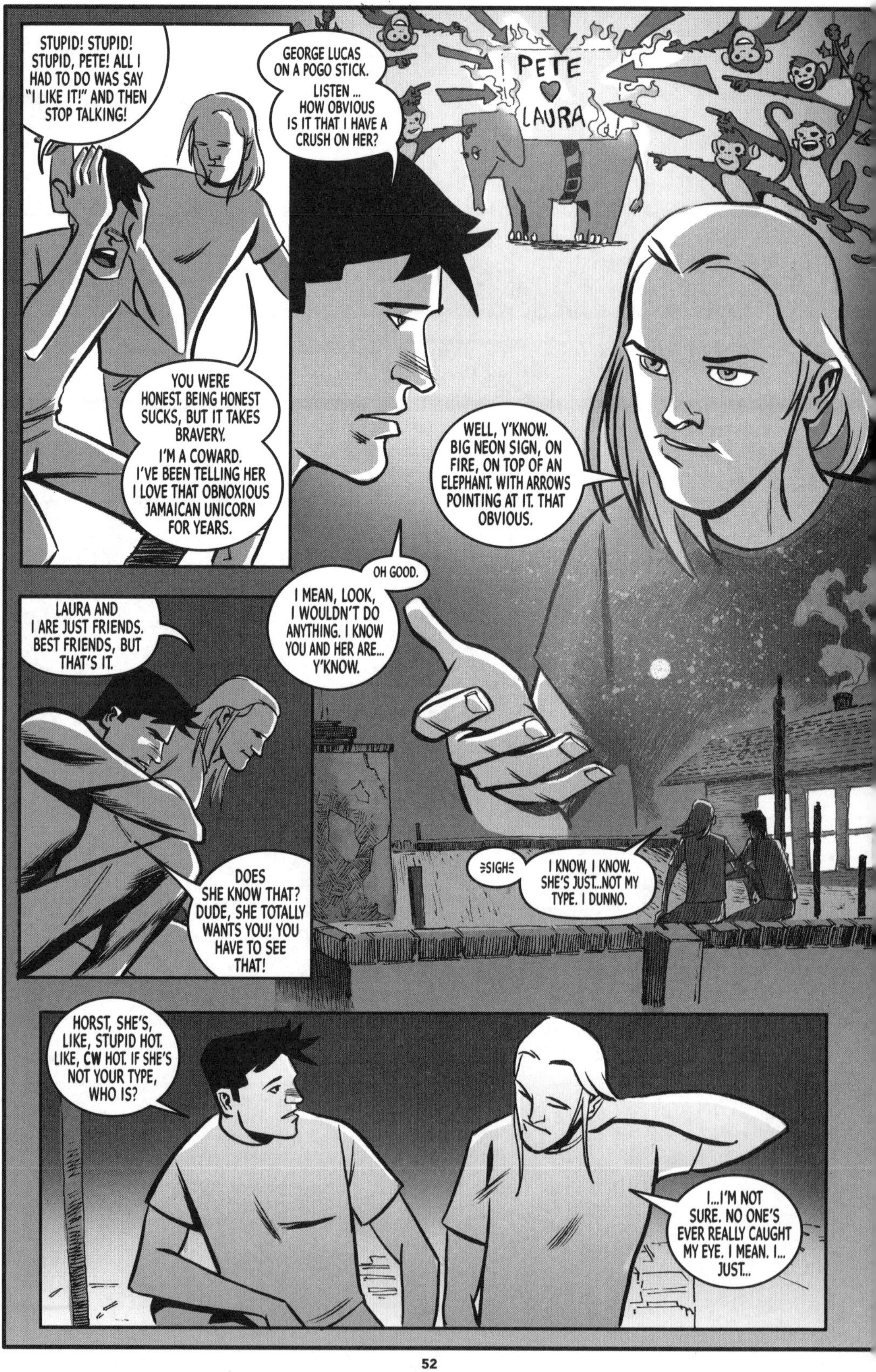
STUPID! STUPID! STUPID, PETE! ALL I HAD TO DO WAS SAY "I LIKE IT!" AND THEN STOP TALKING!
GEORGE LUCAS ON A POGO STICK.
LISTEN ... HOW OBVIOUS IS IT THAT I HAVE A CRUSH ON HER?
PETE
LAURA
YOU WERE HONEST. BEING HONEST SUCKS, BUT IT TAKES BRAVERY.
I'M A COWARD. I'VE BEEN TELLING HER I LOVE THAT OBNOXIOUS JAMAICAN UNICORN FOR YEARS.
WELL, Y'KNOW. BIG NEON SIGN, ON FIRE, ON TOP OF AN ELEPHANT. WITH ARROWS POINTING AT IT. THAT OBVIOUS.
OH GOOD.
I MEAN, LOOK, I WOULDN'T DO ANYTHING. I KNOW YOU AND HER ARE... Y'KNOW.
LAURA AND I ARE JUST FRIENDS. BEST FRIENDS, BUT THAT'S IT.
DOES SHE KNOW THAT? DUDE, SHE TOTALLY WANTS YOU! YOU HAVE TO SEE THAT!
SIGH
I KNOW, I KNOW. SHE'S JUST...NOT MY TYPE. I DUNNO.
HORST, SHE'S, LIKE, STUPID HOT. LIKE, CW HOT. IF SHE'S NOT YOUR TYPE, WHO IS?
I...I'M NOT SURE. NO ONE'S EVER REALLY CAUGHT MY EYE. I MEAN. I... JUST...

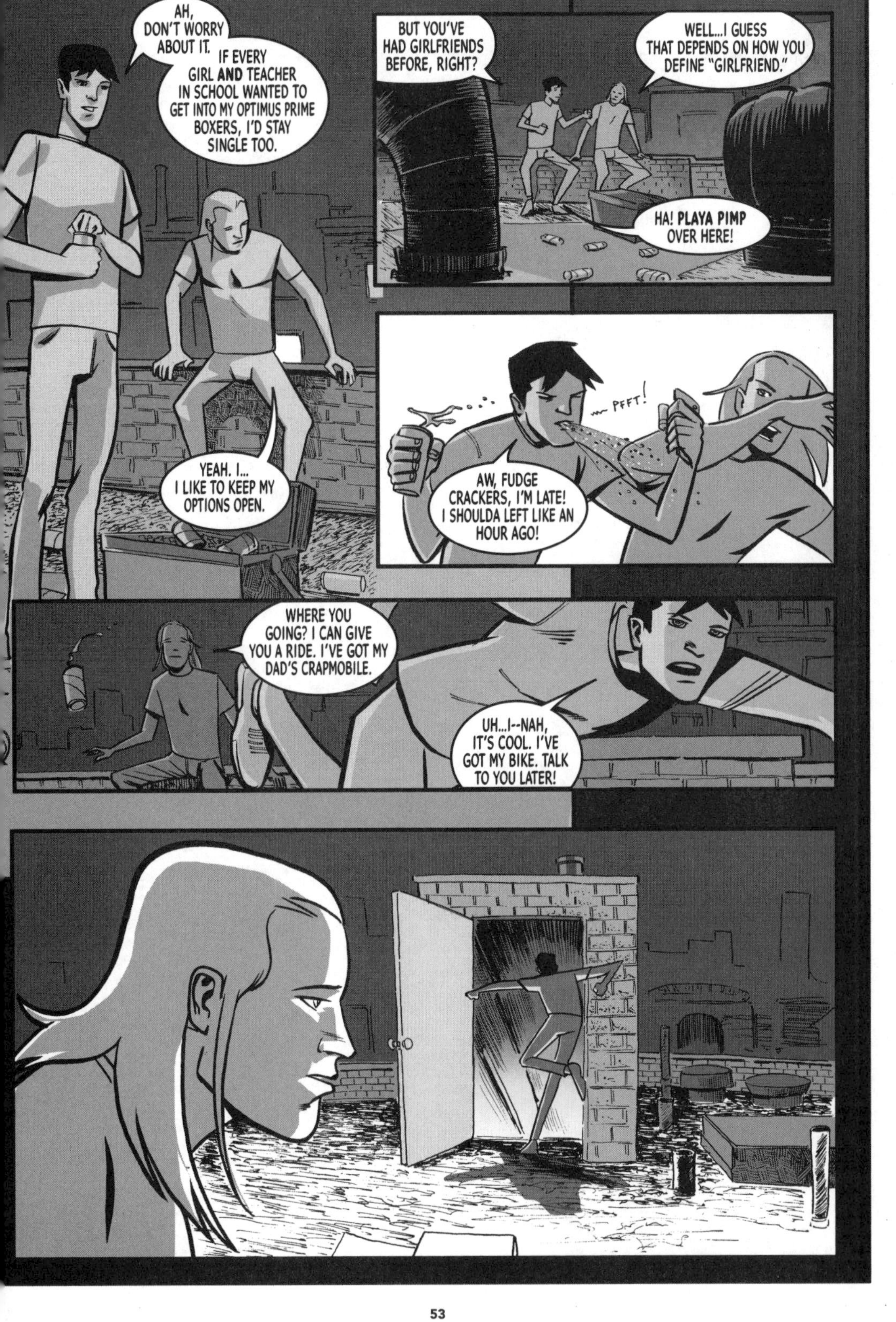
AH, DON'T WORRY ABOUT IT.
IF EVERY GIRL AND TEACHER IN SCHOOL WANTED TO GET INTO MY OPTIMUS PRIME BOXERS, I'D STAY SINGLE TOO.
YEAH. I... I LIKE TO KEEP MY OPTIONS OPEN.
BUT YOU'VE HAD GIRLFRIENDS BEFORE, RIGHT?
WELL...I GUESS THAT DEPENDS ON HOW YOU DEFINE "GIRLFRIEND."
HA! PLAYA PIMP OVER HERE!
PFFT!
AW, FUDGE CRACKERS, I'M LATE! I SHOULDA LEFT LIKE AN HOUR AGO!
WHERE YOU GOING? I CAN GIVE YOU A RIDE. I'VE GOT MY DAD'S CRAPMOBILE.
UH...I--NAH, IT'S COOL. I'VE GOT MY BIKE. TALK TO YOU LATER!

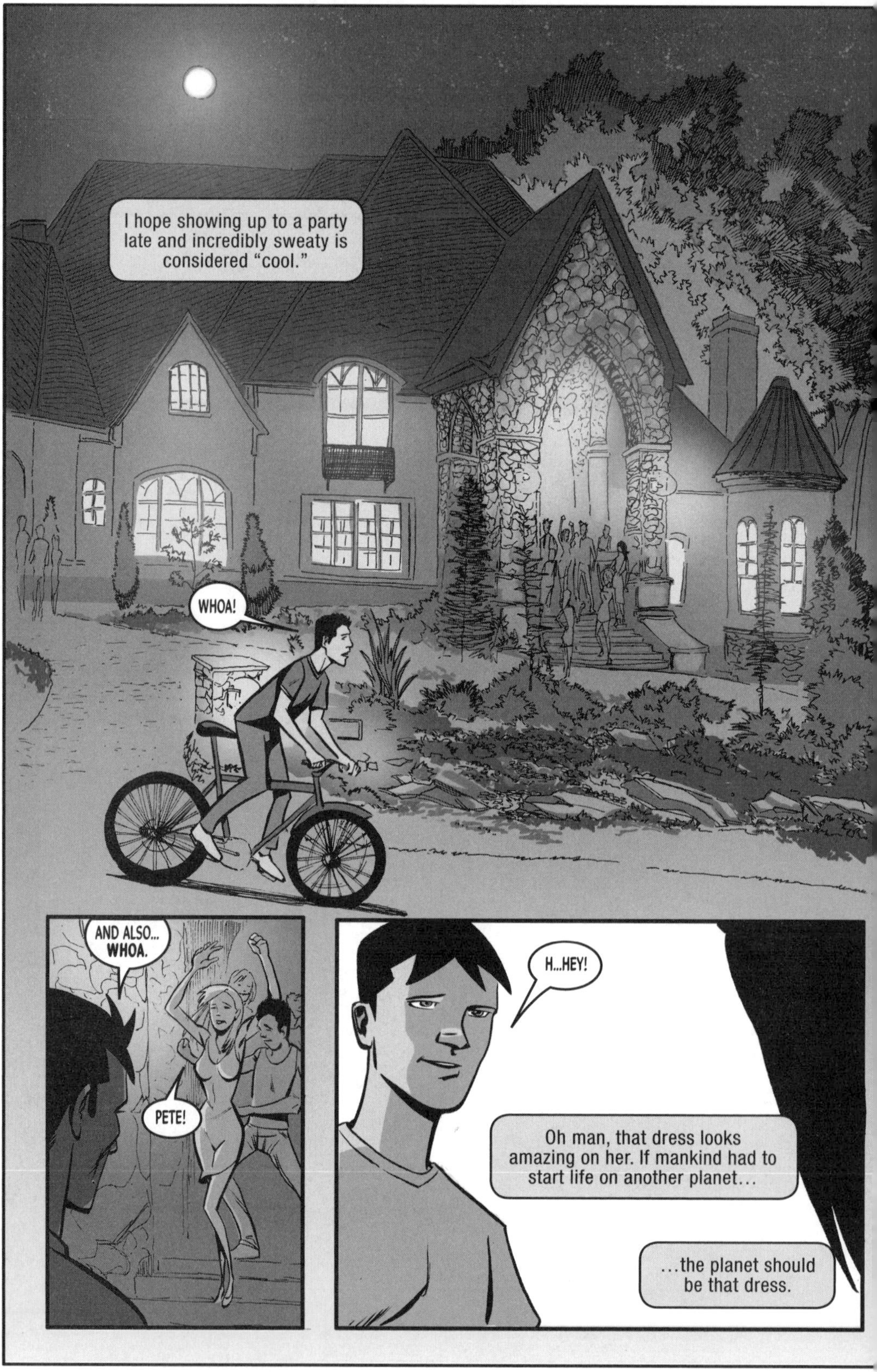

I hope showing up to a party late and incredibly sweaty is considered "cool."
WHOA!
AND ALSO... WHOA.
PETE!
H...HEY!
Oh man, that dress looks amazing on her. If mankind had to start life on another planet...
...the planet should be that dress.

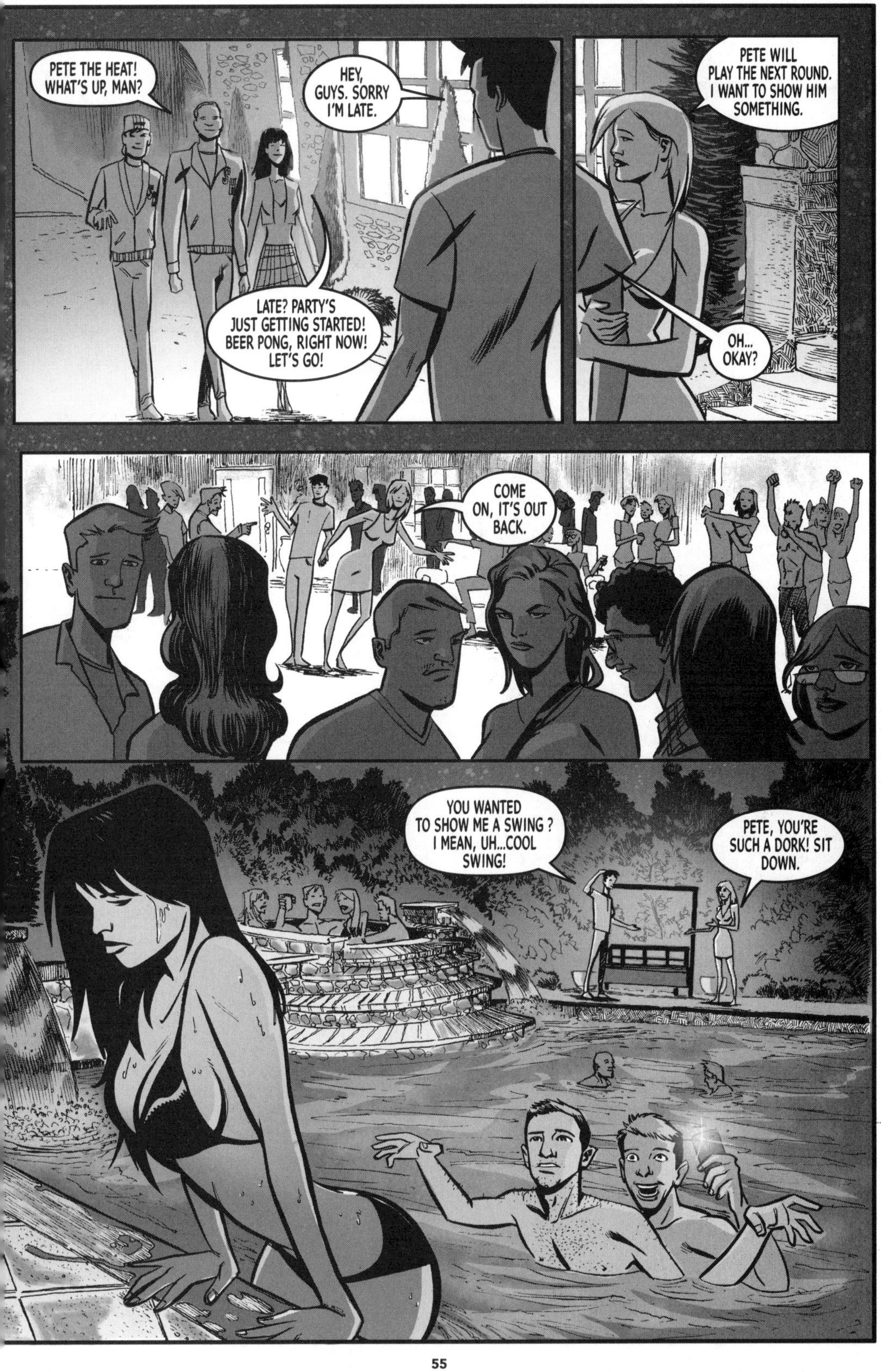
PETE THE HEAT! WHAT'S UP, MAN?
HEY, GUYS. SORRY I'M LATE.
LATE? PARTY'S JUST GETTING STARTED! BEER PONG, RIGHT NOW! LET'S GO!
PETE WILL PLAY THE NEXT ROUND. I WANT TO SHOW HIM SOMETHING.
OH... OKAY?
COME ON, IT'S OUT BACK.
YOU WANTED TO SHOW ME A SWING ? I MEAN, UH...COOL SWING!
PETE, YOU'RE SUCH A DORK! SIT DOWN.

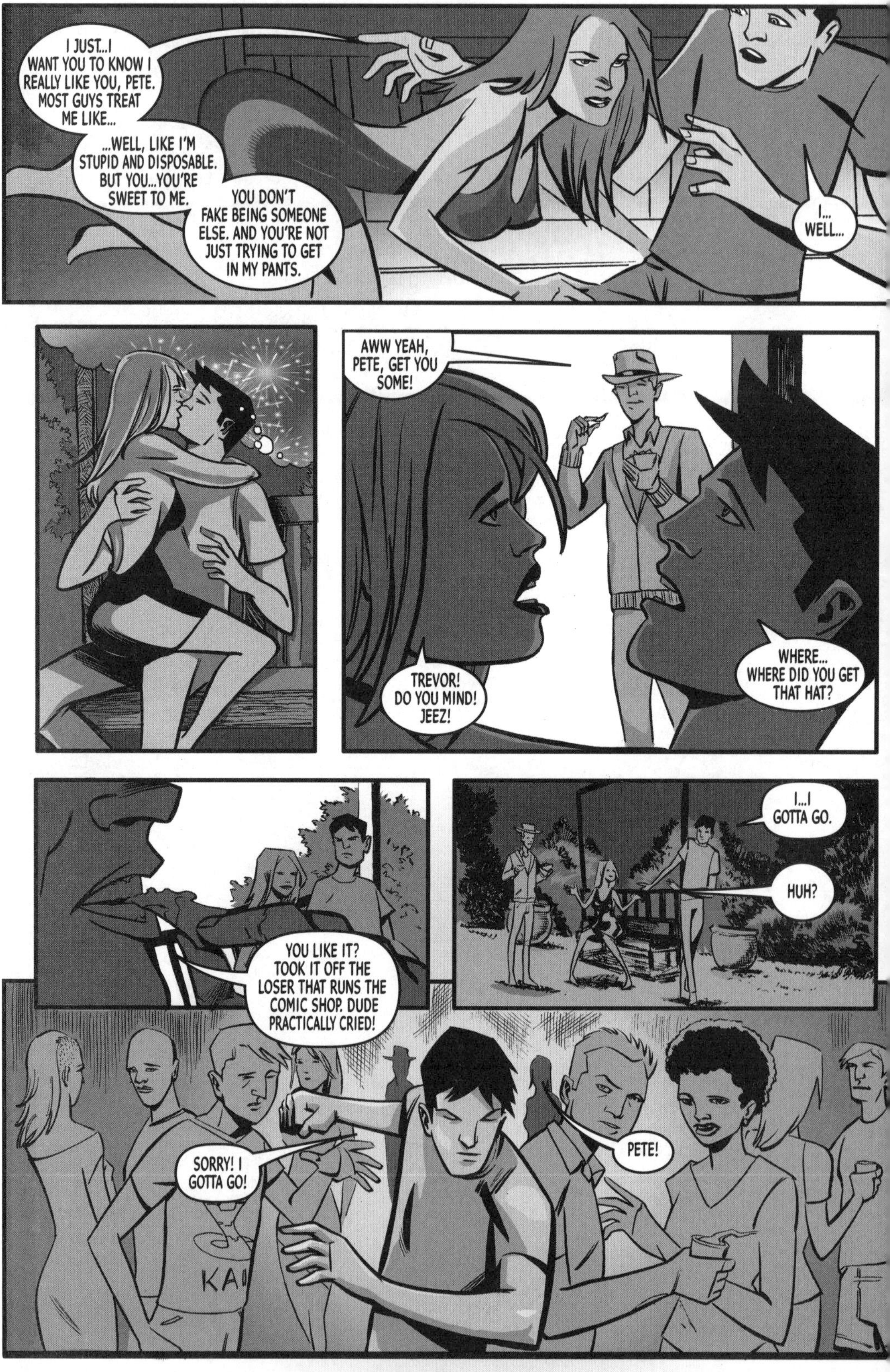
I JUST...I WANT YOU TO KNOW I REALLY LIKE YOU, PETE. MOST GUYS TREAT ME LIKE...
...WELL, LIKE I'M STUPID AND DISPOSABLE. BUT YOU...YOU'RE SWEET TO ME.
YOU DON'T FAKE BEING SOMEONE ELSE. AND YOU'RE NOT JUST TRYING TO GET IN MY PANTS.
I... WELL...
AWW YEAH, PETE, GET YOU SOME!
TREVOR! DO YOU MIND! JEEZ!
WHERE... WHERE DID YOU GET THAT HAT?
YOU LIKE IT? TOOK IT OFF THE LOSER THAT RUNS THE COMIC SHOP. DUDE PRACTICALLY CRIED!
I...I GOTTA GO.
HUH?
PETE!
SORRY! I GOTTA GO!
KAI

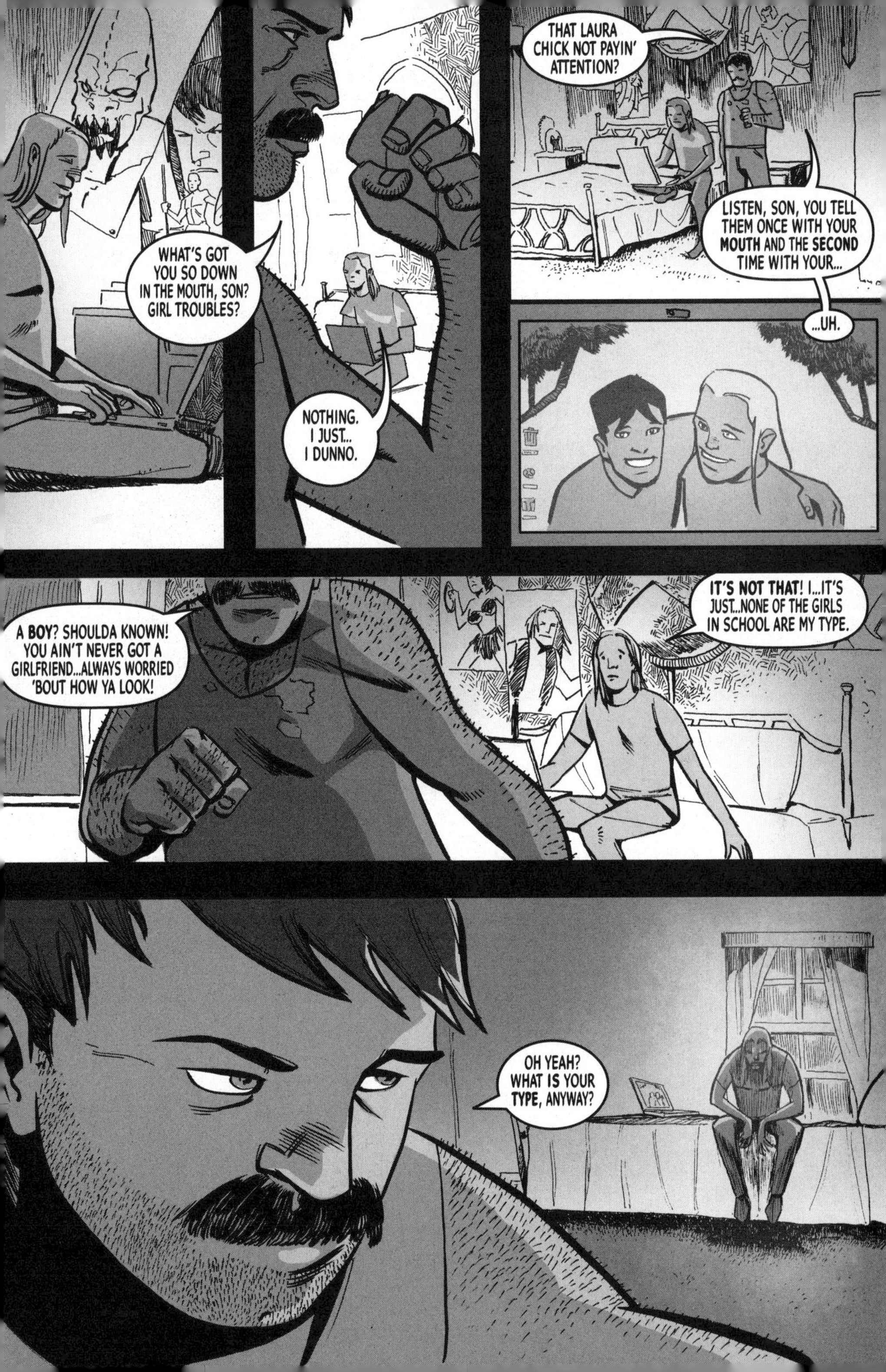
WHAT'S GOT YOU SO DOWN IN THE MOUTH, SON? GIRL TROUBLES?
NOTHING. I JUST... I DUNNO.
THAT LAURA CHICK NOT PAYIN' ATTENTION?
LISTEN, SON, YOU TELL THEM ONCE WITH YOUR MOUTH AND THE SECOND TIME WITH YOUR...
...UH.
A BOY? SHOULDA KNOWN! YOU AIN'T NEVER GOT A GIRLFRIEND...ALWAYS WORRIED 'BOUT HOW YA LOOK!
IT'S NOT THAT! I...IT'S JUST...NONE OF THE GIRLS IN SCHOOL ARE MY TYPE.
OH YEAH? WHAT IS YOUR TYPE, ANYWAY?

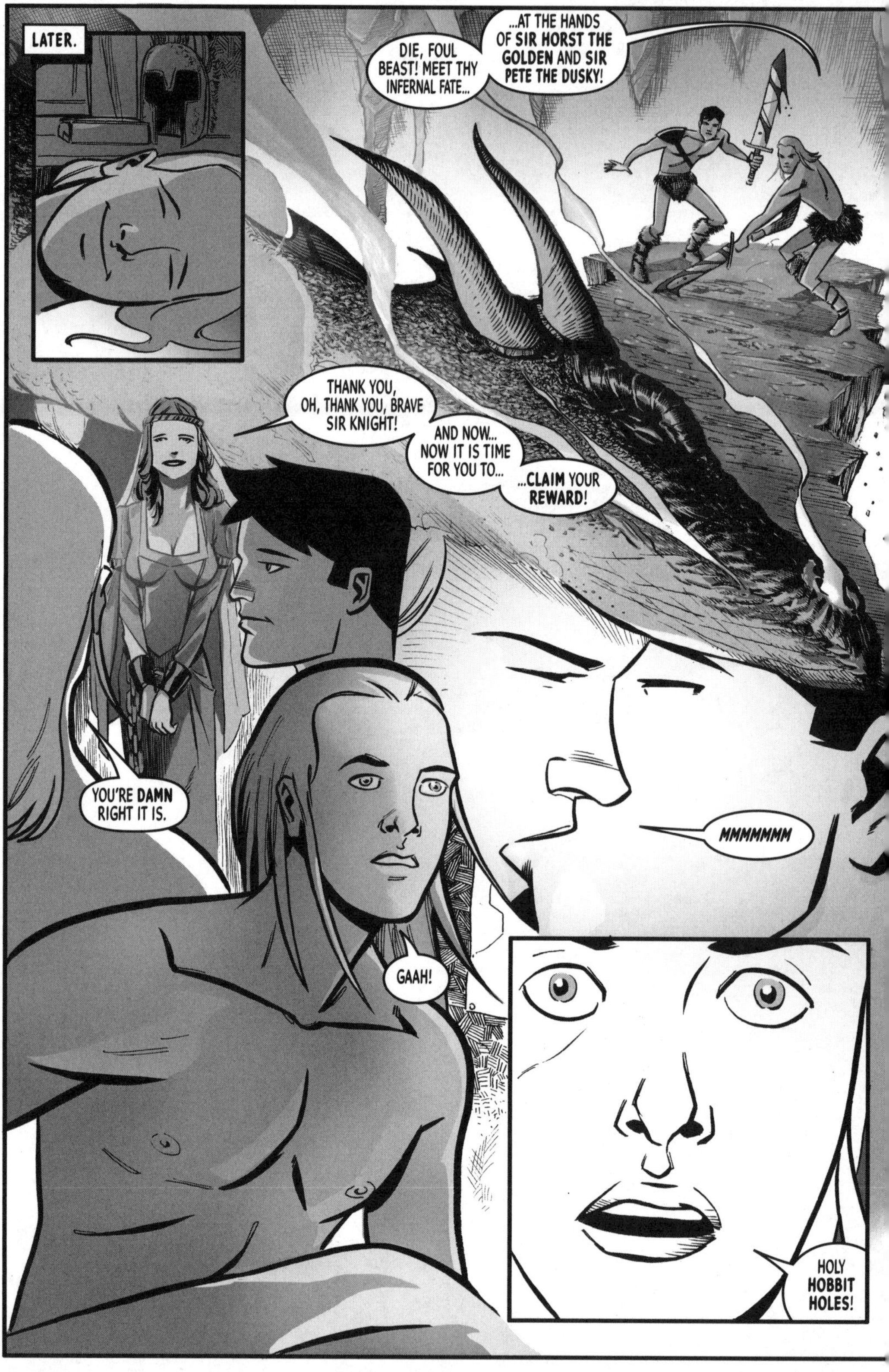
LATER.
DIE, FOUL BEAST! MEET THY INFERNAL FATE...
...AT THE HANDS OF SIR HORST THE GOLDEN AND SIR PETE THE DUSKY!
THANK YOU, OH, THANK YOU, BRAVE SIR KNIGHT!
AND NOW... NOW IT IS TIME FOR YOU TO...
...CLAIM YOUR REWARD!
YOU'RE DAMN RIGHT IT IS.
MMMMMMM
GAAH!
HOLY HOBBIT HOLES!

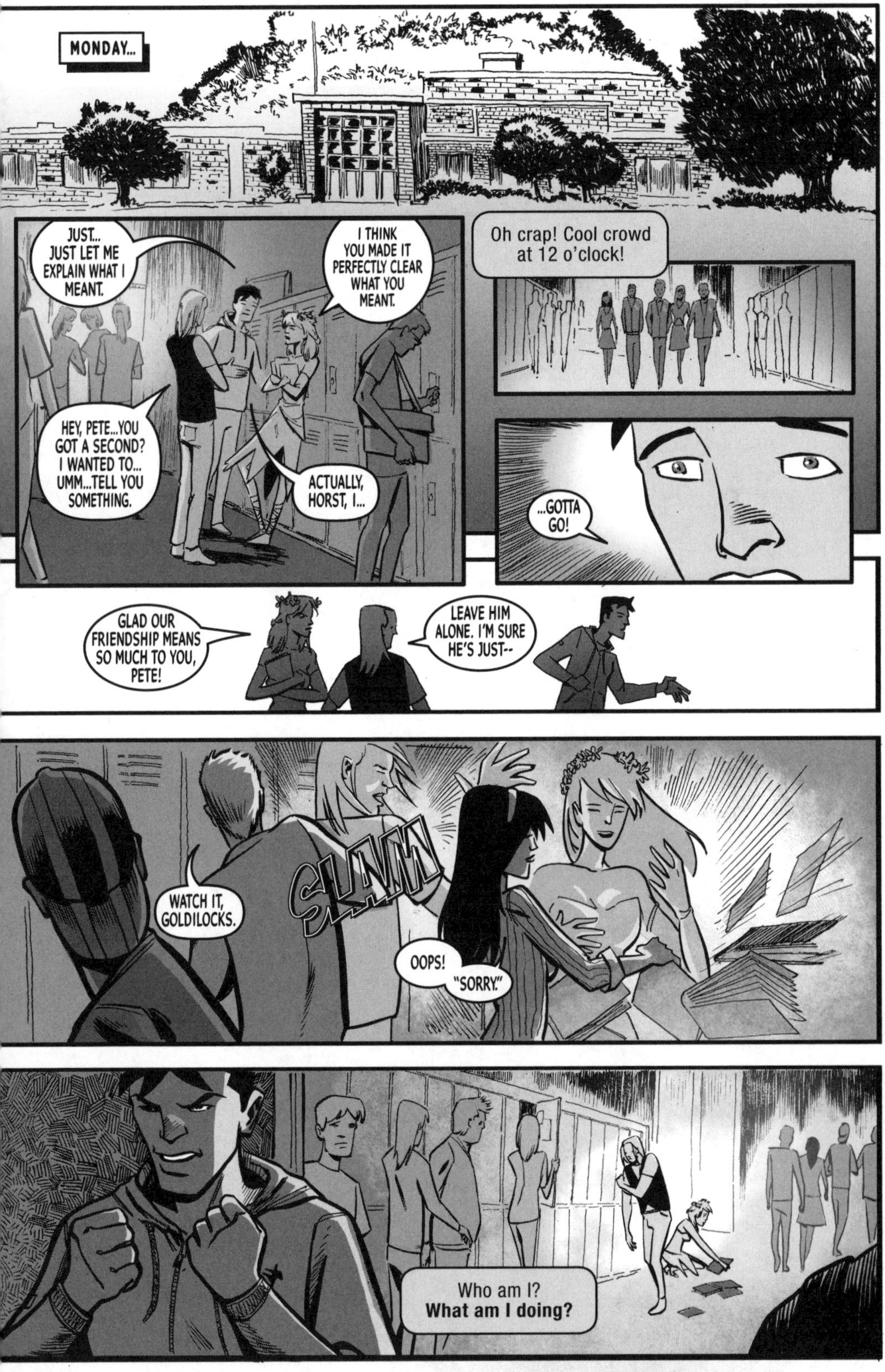
MONDAY...
JUST... JUST LET ME EXPLAIN WHAT I MEANT.
I THINK YOU MADE IT PERFECTLY CLEAR WHAT YOU MEANT.
HEY, PETE...YOU GOT A SECOND? I WANTED TO... UMM...TELL YOU SOMETHING.
ACTUALLY, HORST, I...
Oh crap! Cool crowd at 12 o'clock!
...GOTTA GO!
GLAD OUR FRIENDSHIP MEANS SO MUCH TO YOU, PETE!
LEAVE HIM ALONE. I'M SURE HE'S JUST--
WATCH IT, GOLDILOCKS.
SLAM
OOPS!
"SORRY."
Who am I?
What am I doing?

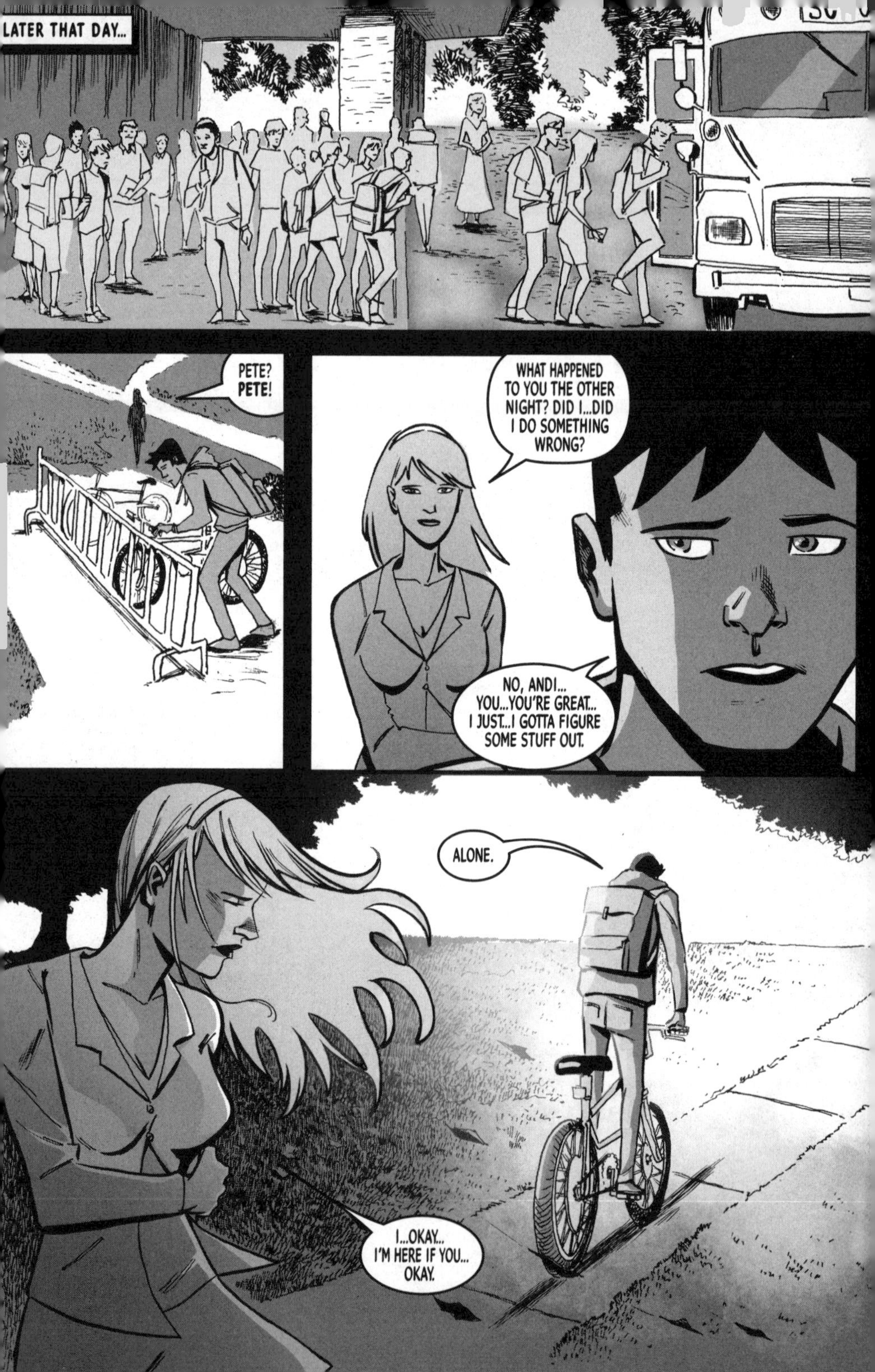
LATER THAT DAY...
PETE? PETE!
WHAT HAPPENED TO YOU THE OTHER NIGHT? DID I...DID I DO SOMETHING WRONG?
NO, ANDI... YOU...YOU'RE GREAT... I JUST...I GOTTA FIGURE SOME STUFF OUT.
ALONE.
I...OKAY... I'M HERE IF YOU... OKAY.

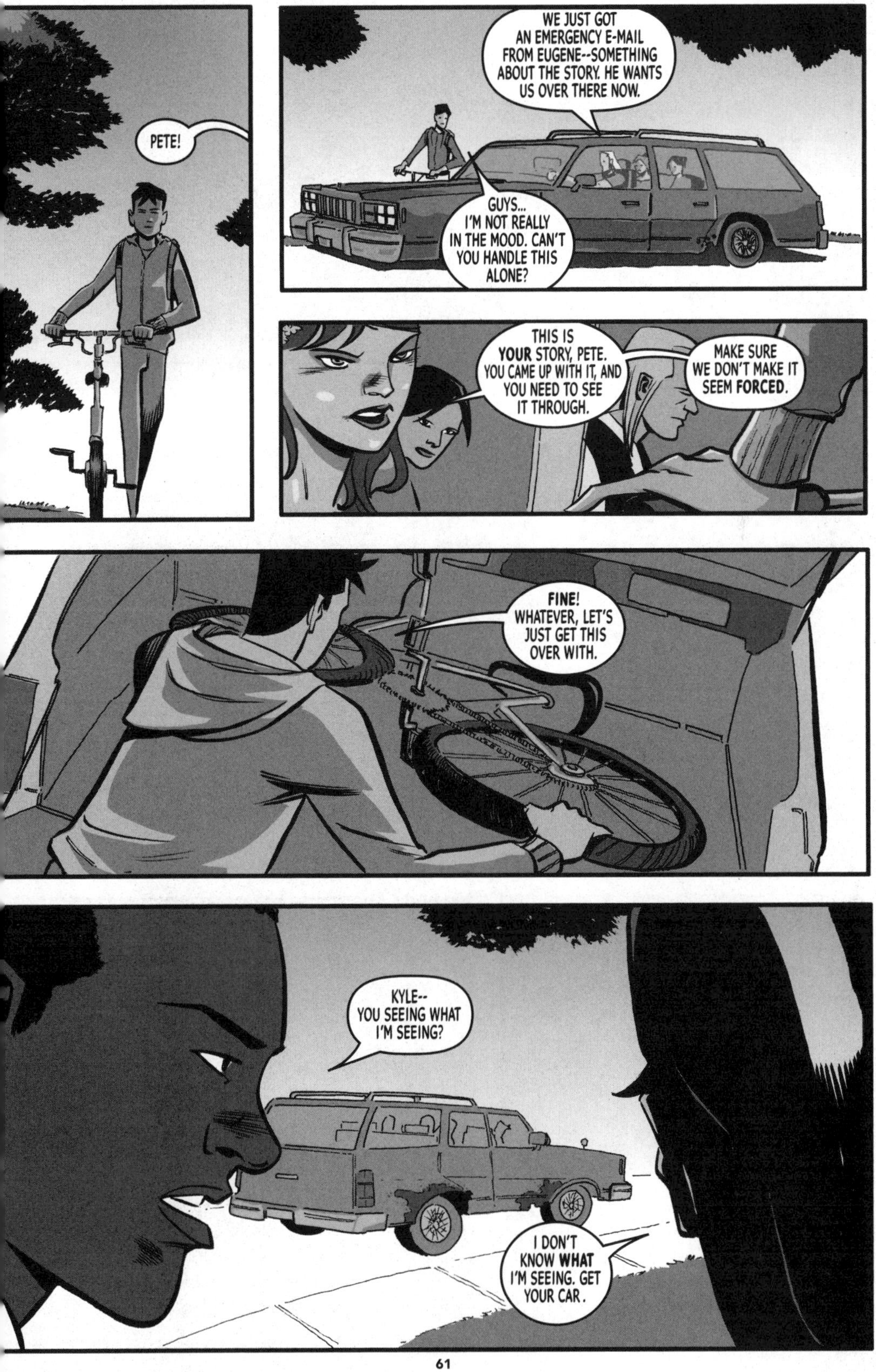
PETE!
WE JUST GOT AN EMERGENCY E-MAIL FROM EUGENE--SOMETHING ABOUT THE STORY. HE WANTS US OVER THERE NOW.
GUYS... I'M NOT REALLY IN THE MOOD. CAN'T YOU HANDLE THIS ALONE?
THIS IS YOUR STORY, PETE. YOU CAME UP WITH IT, AND YOU NEED TO SEE IT THROUGH.
MAKE SURE WE DON'T MAKE IT SEEM FORCED.
FINE! WHATEVER, LET'S JUST GET THIS OVER WITH.
KYLE-- YOU SEEING WHAT I'M SEEING?
I DON'T KNOW WHAT I'M SEEING. GET YOUR CAR.

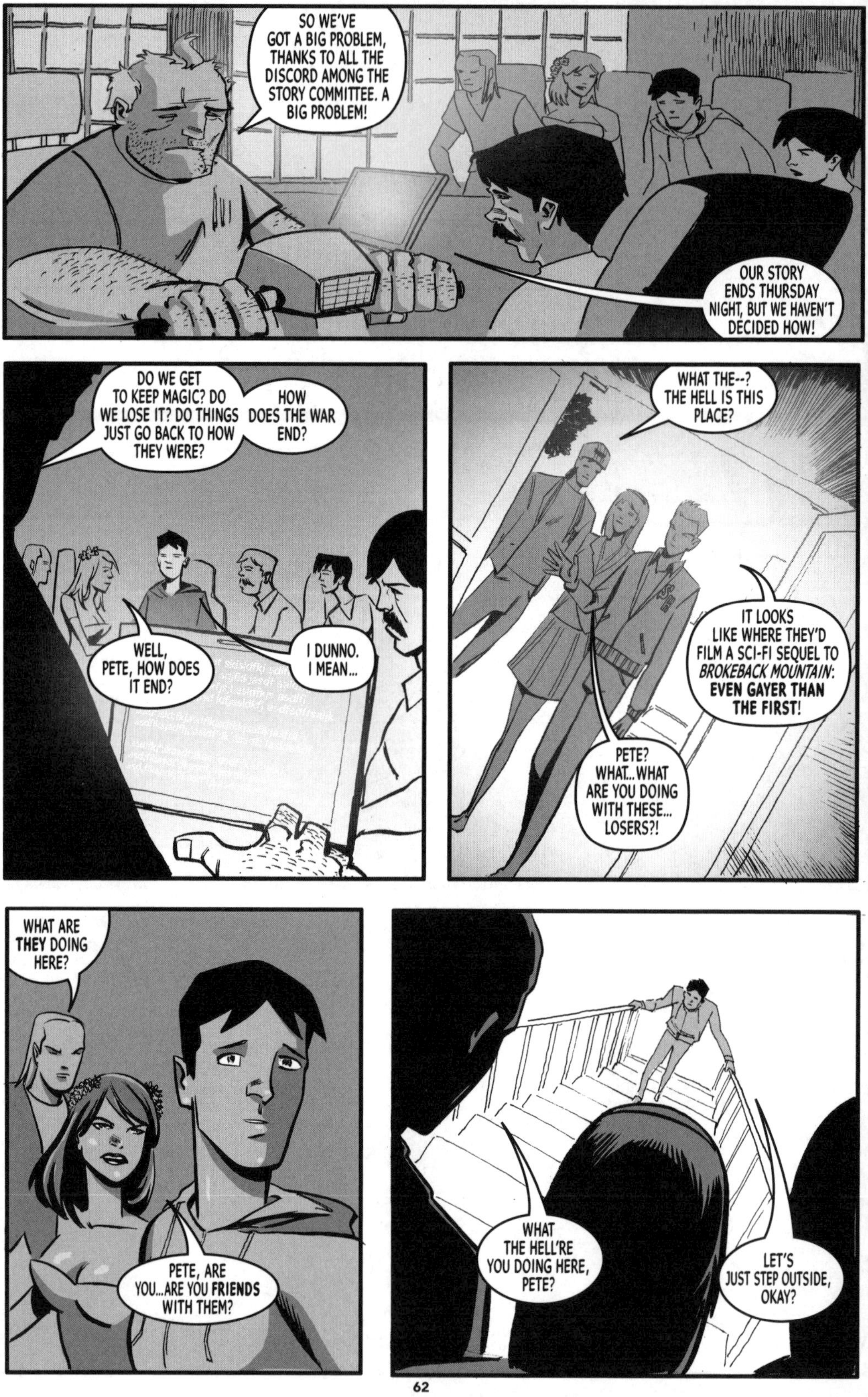
SO WE'VE GOT A BIG PROBLEM, THANKS TO ALL THE DISCORD AMONG THE STORY COMMITTEE. A BIG PROBLEM!
OUR STORY ENDS THURSDAY NIGHT, BUT WE HAVEN'T DECIDED HOW!
DO WE GET TO KEEP MAGIC? DO WE LOSE IT? DO THINGS JUST GO BACK TO HOW THEY WERE?
HOW DOES THE WAR END?
WELL, PETE, HOW DOES IT END?
I DUNNO. I MEAN...
WHAT THE--? THE HELL IS THIS PLACE?
IT LOOKS LIKE WHERE THEY'D FILM A SCI-FI SEQUEL TO *BROKEBACK MOUNTAIN*: **EVEN GAYER THAN THE FIRST**!
PETE? WHAT...WHAT ARE YOU DOING WITH THESE... LOSERS?!
WHAT ARE **THEY** DOING HERE?
PETE, ARE YOU...ARE YOU **FRIENDS** WITH THEM?
WHAT THE HELL'RE YOU DOING HERE, PETE?
LET'S JUST STEP OUTSIDE, OKAY?

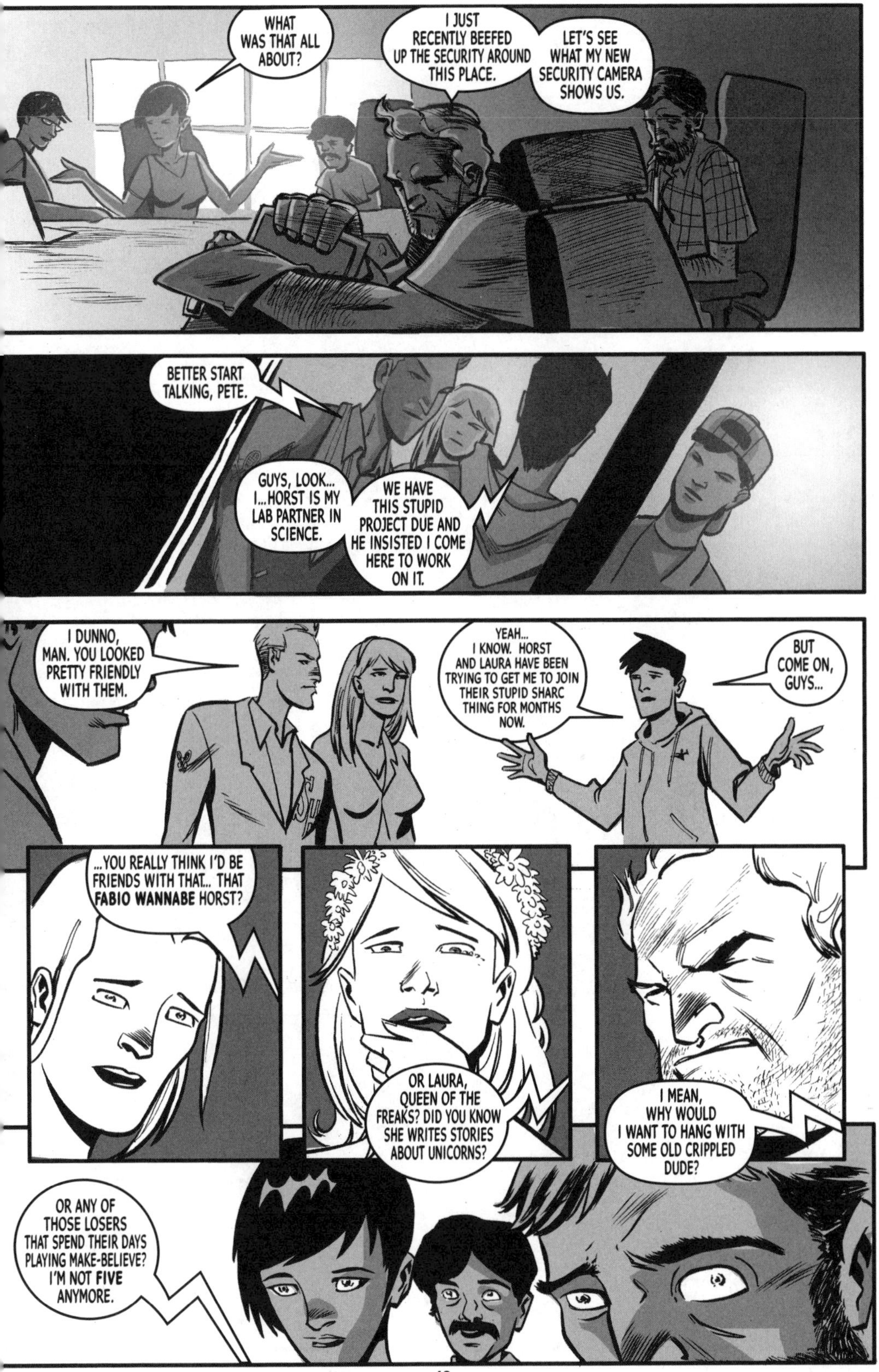
WHAT WAS THAT ALL ABOUT?
I JUST RECENTLY BEEFED UP THE SECURITY AROUND THIS PLACE.
LET'S SEE WHAT MY NEW SECURITY CAMERA SHOWS US.
BETTER START TALKING, PETE.
GUYS, LOOK... I...HORST IS MY LAB PARTNER IN SCIENCE.
WE HAVE THIS STUPID PROJECT DUE AND HE INSISTED I COME HERE TO WORK ON IT.
I DUNNO, MAN. YOU LOOKED PRETTY FRIENDLY WITH THEM.
YEAH... I KNOW. HORST AND LAURA HAVE BEEN TRYING TO GET ME TO JOIN THEIR STUPID SHARC THING FOR MONTHS NOW.
BUT COME ON, GUYS...
...YOU REALLY THINK I'D BE FRIENDS WITH THAT... THAT **FABIO WANNABE** HORST?
OR LAURA, QUEEN OF THE FREAKS? DID YOU KNOW SHE WRITES STORIES ABOUT UNICORNS?
I MEAN, WHY WOULD I WANT TO HANG WITH SOME OLD CRIPPLED DUDE?
OR ANY OF THOSE LOSERS THAT SPEND THEIR DAYS PLAYING MAKE-BELIEVE? I'M NOT **FIVE** ANYMORE.

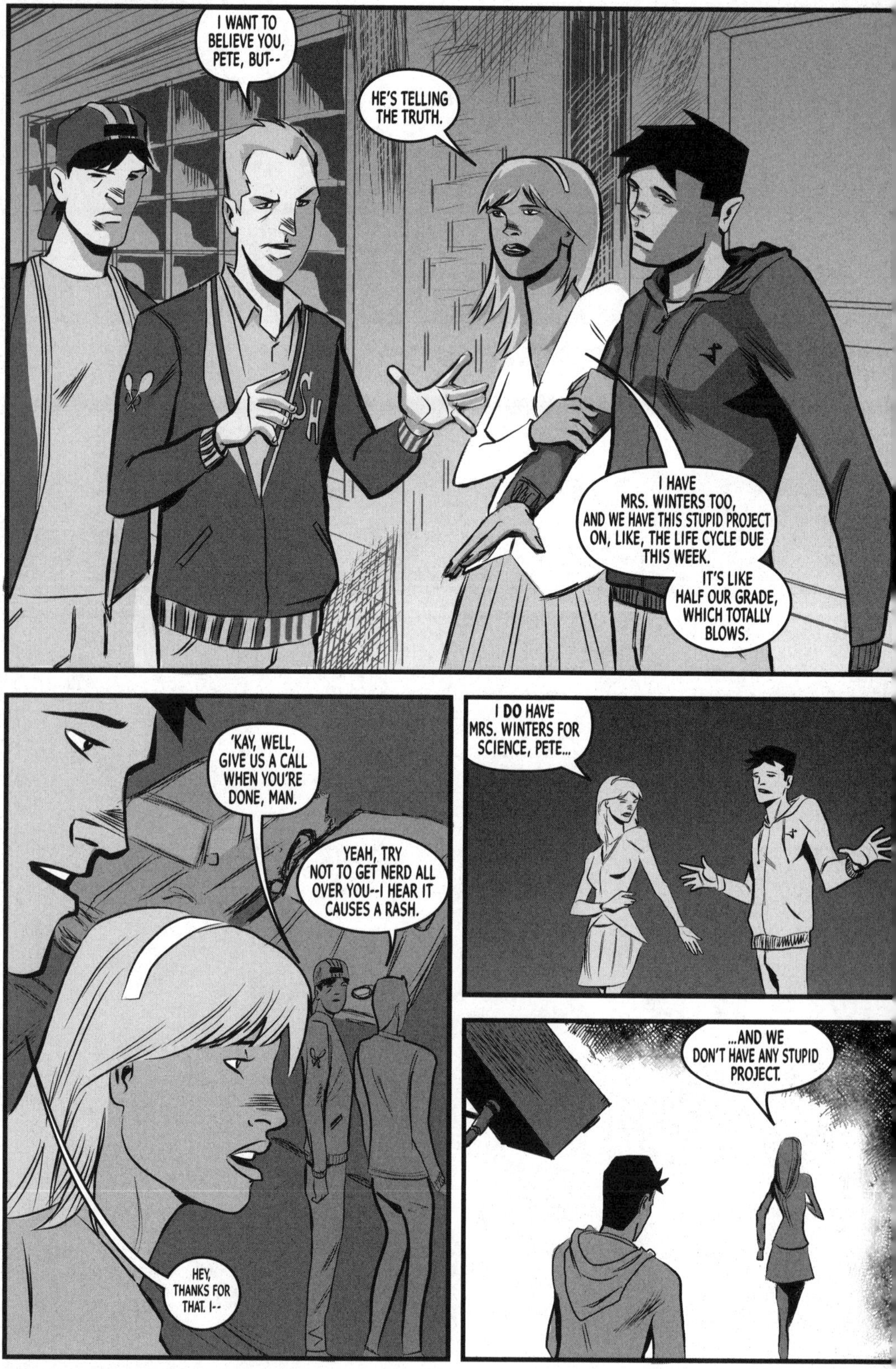
I WANT TO BELIEVE YOU, PETE, BUT--
HE'S TELLING THE TRUTH.
I HAVE MRS. WINTERS TOO, AND WE HAVE THIS STUPID PROJECT ON, LIKE, THE LIFE CYCLE DUE THIS WEEK.
IT'S LIKE HALF OUR GRADE, WHICH TOTALLY BLOWS.
'KAY, WELL, GIVE US A CALL WHEN YOU'RE DONE, MAN.
YEAH, TRY NOT TO GET NERD ALL OVER YOU--I HEAR IT CAUSES A RASH.
HEY, THANKS FOR THAT. I--
I DO HAVE MRS. WINTERS FOR SCIENCE, PETE...
...AND WE DON'T HAVE ANY STUPID PROJECT.

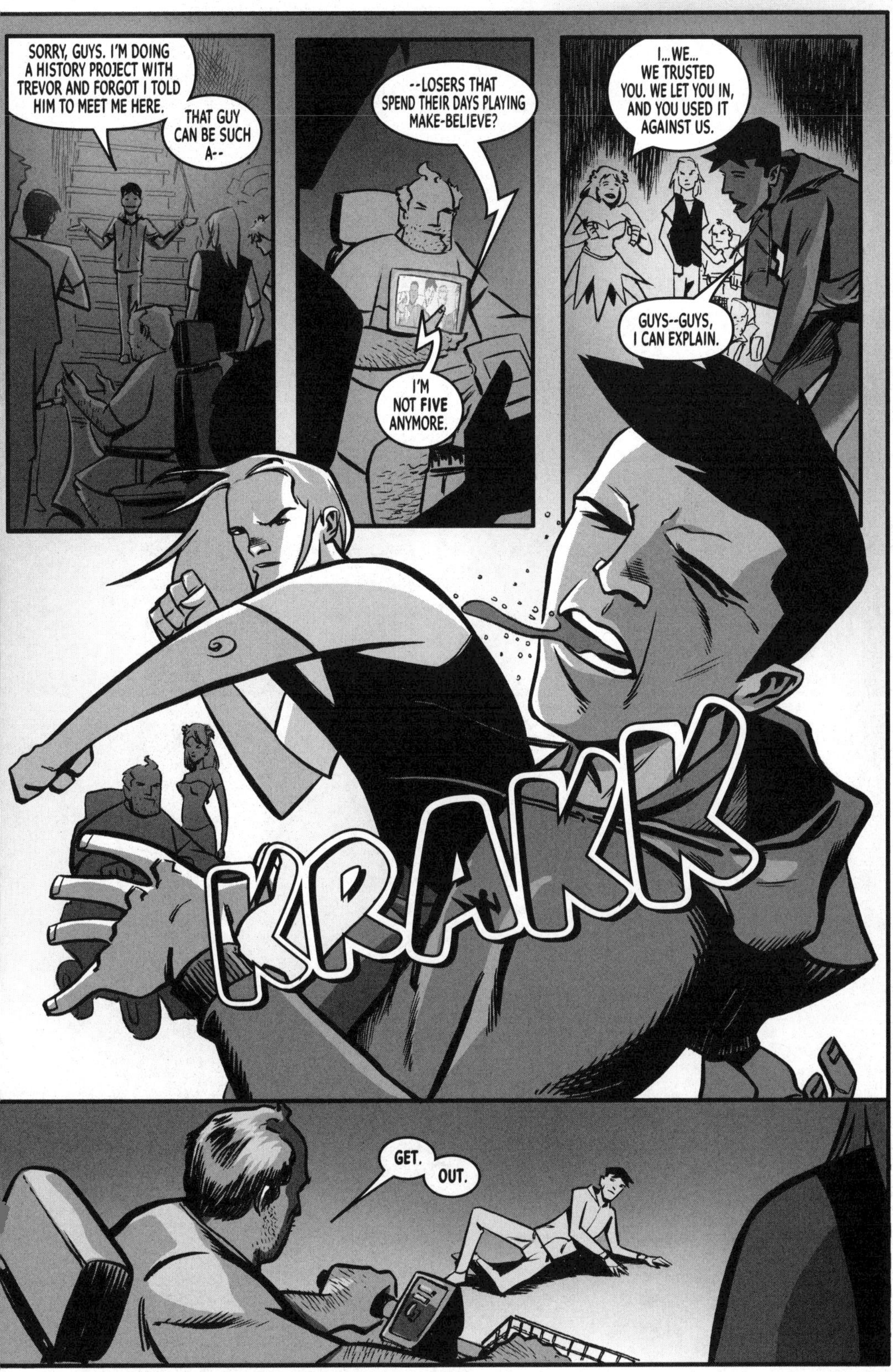
SORRY, GUYS. I'M DOING A HISTORY PROJECT WITH TREVOR AND FORGOT I TOLD HIM TO MEET ME HERE.
THAT GUY CAN BE SUCH A--
--LOSERS THAT SPEND THEIR DAYS PLAYING MAKE-BELIEVE?
I'M NOT FIVE ANYMORE.
I...WE... WE TRUSTED YOU. WE LET YOU IN, AND YOU USED IT AGAINST US.
GUYS--GUYS, I CAN EXPLAIN.
KRAKK
GET.
OUT.

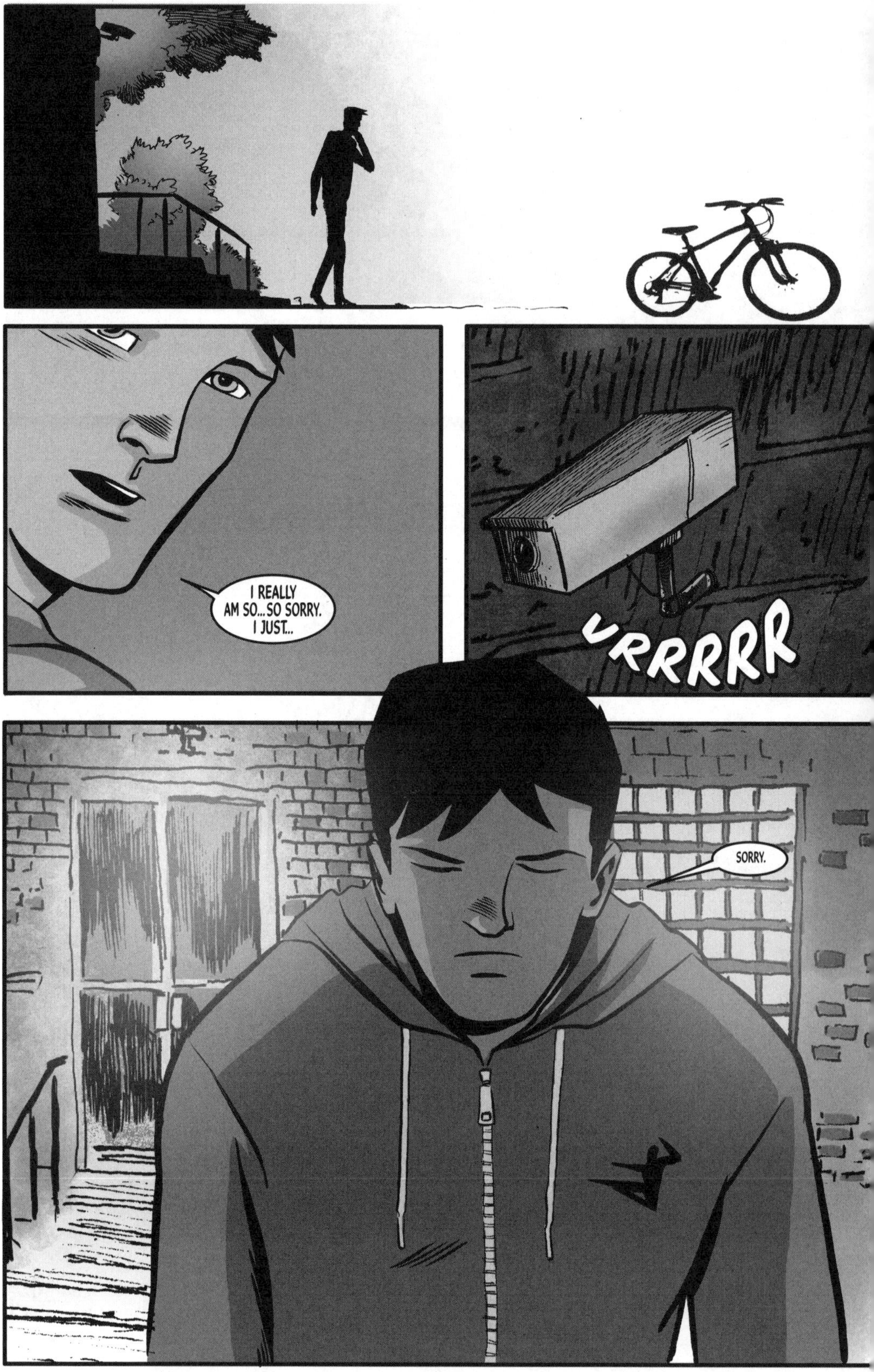
I REALLY AM SO...SO SORRY. I JUST...
URRRRR
SORRY.

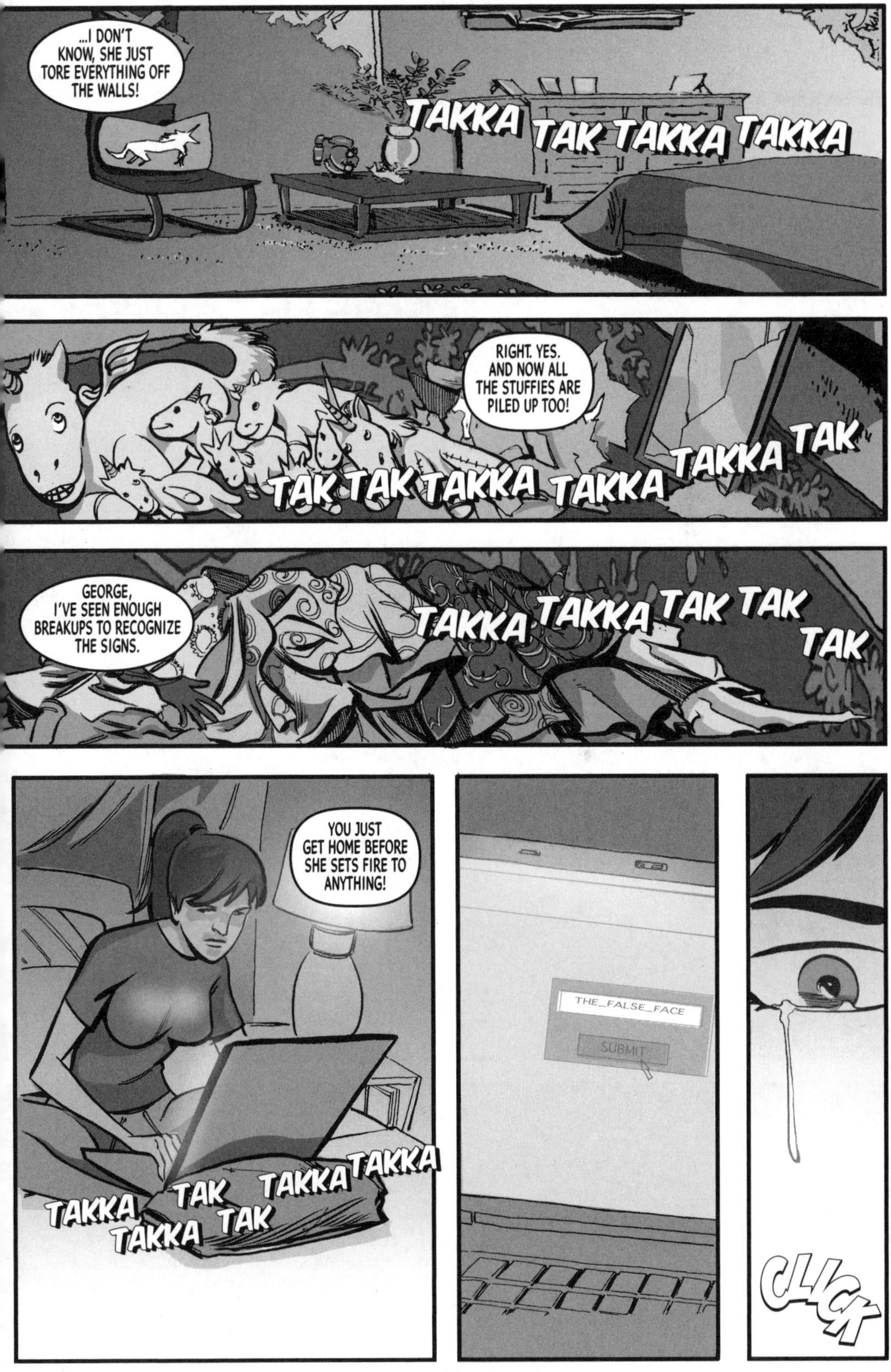
...I DON'T KNOW, SHE JUST TORE EVERYTHING OFF THE WALLS!
TAKKA TAK TAKKA TAKKA
RIGHT. YES. AND NOW ALL THE STUFFIES ARE PILED UP TOO!
TAK TAK TAKKA TAKKA TAKKA TAK
GEORGE, I'VE SEEN ENOUGH BREAKUPS TO RECOGNIZE THE SIGNS.
TAKKA TAKKA TAK TAK TAK
YOU JUST GET HOME BEFORE SHE SETS FIRE TO ANYTHING!
TAKKA TAKKA TAK TAK TAKKA TAKKA
THE_FALSE_FACE
SUBMIT
CLICK

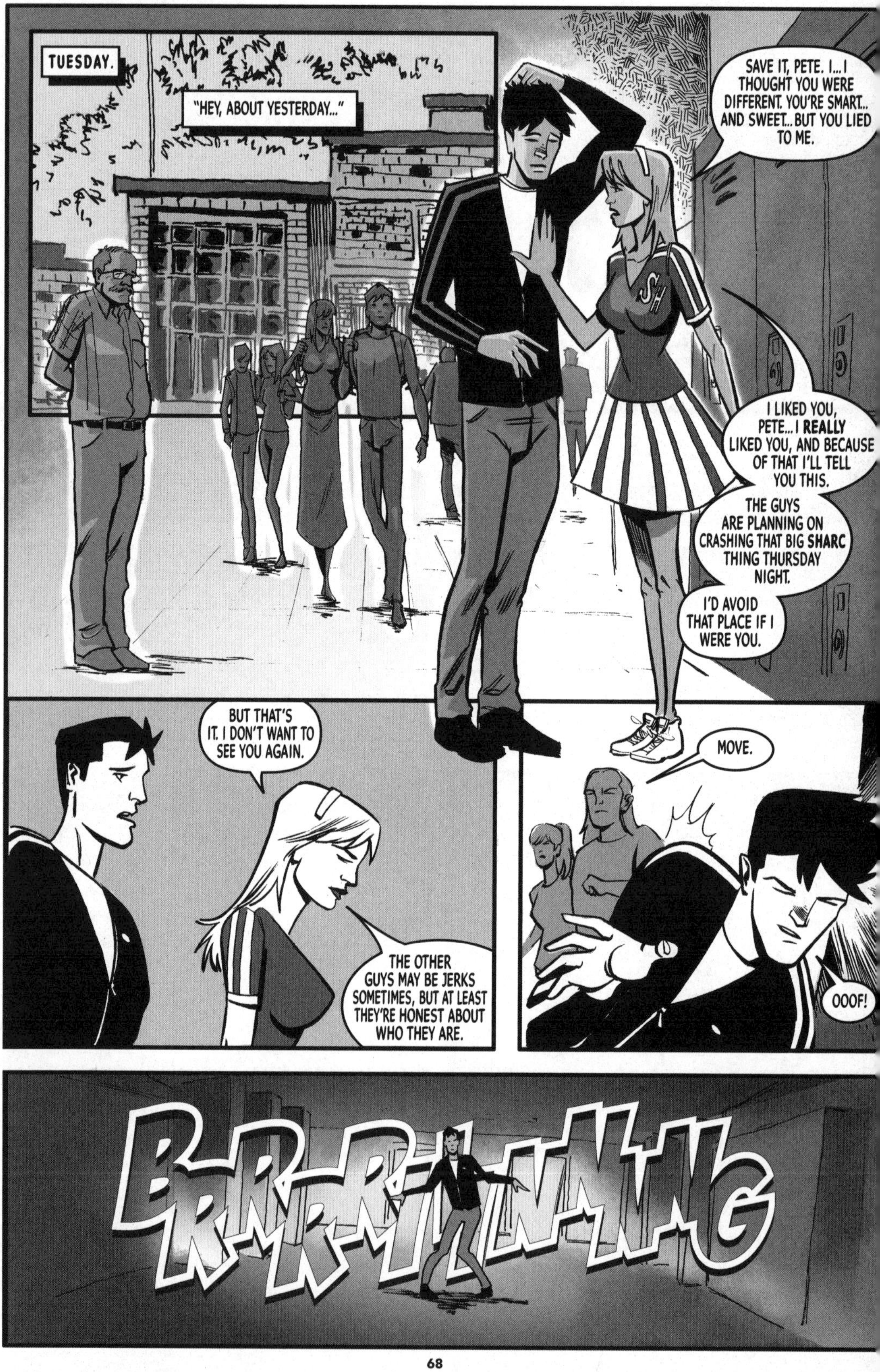
TUESDAY.
"HEY, ABOUT YESTERDAY..."
SAVE IT, PETE. I...I THOUGHT YOU WERE DIFFERENT. YOU'RE SMART... AND SWEET... BUT YOU LIED TO ME.
I LIKED YOU, PETE... I **REALLY** LIKED YOU, AND BECAUSE OF THAT I'LL TELL YOU THIS.
THE GUYS ARE PLANNING ON CRASHING THAT BIG **SHARC** THING THURSDAY NIGHT.
I'D AVOID THAT PLACE IF I WERE YOU.
BUT THAT'S IT. I DON'T WANT TO SEE YOU AGAIN.
THE OTHER GUYS MAY BE JERKS SOMETIMES, BUT AT LEAST THEY'RE HONEST ABOUT WHO THEY ARE.
MOVE.
OOOF!
BRRRRRIIINNNNG

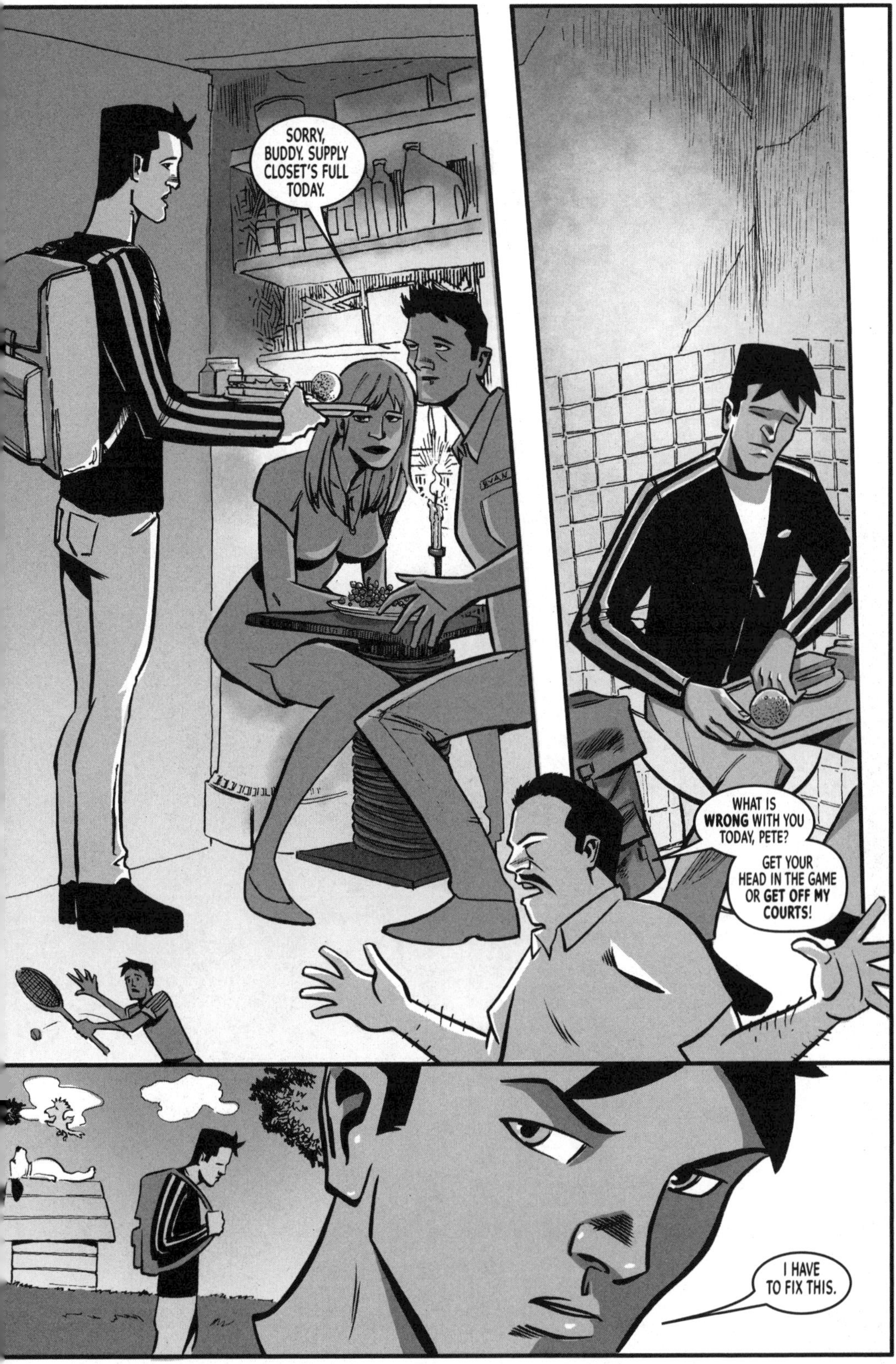
SORRY, BUDDY. SUPPLY CLOSET'S FULL TODAY.
EVAN
WHAT IS **WRONG** WITH YOU TODAY, PETE?
GET YOUR HEAD IN THE GAME OR **GET OFF MY COURTS!**
I HAVE TO FIX THIS.

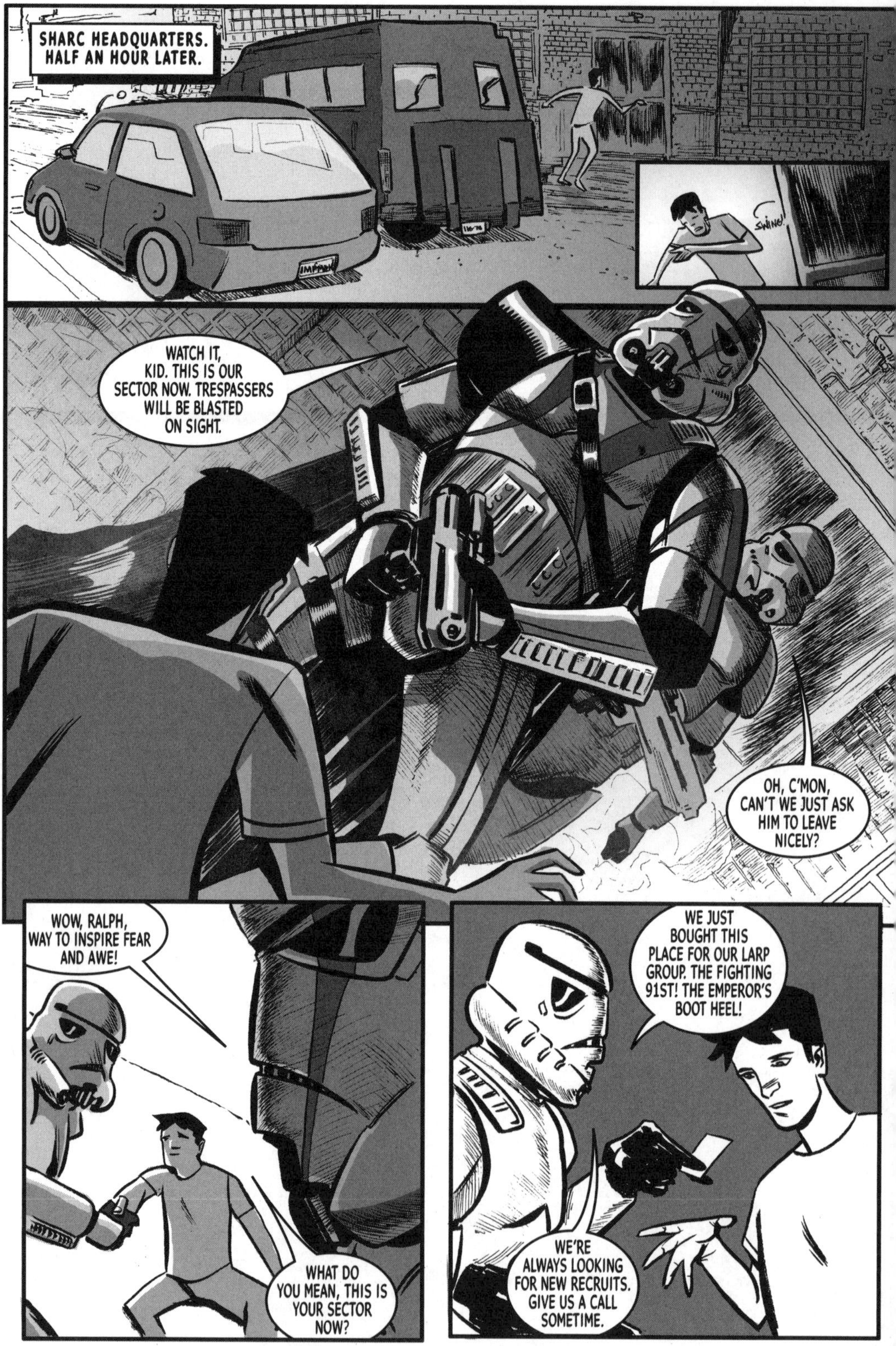
SHARC HEADQUARTERS. HALF AN HOUR LATER.
SWING!
WATCH IT, KID. THIS IS OUR SECTOR NOW. TRESPASSERS WILL BE BLASTED ON SIGHT.
OH, C'MON, CAN'T WE JUST ASK HIM TO LEAVE NICELY?
WOW, RALPH, WAY TO INSPIRE FEAR AND AWE!
WHAT DO YOU MEAN, THIS IS YOUR SECTOR NOW?
WE JUST BOUGHT THIS PLACE FOR OUR LARP GROUP. THE FIGHTING 91ST! THE EMPEROR'S BOOT HEEL!
WE'RE ALWAYS LOOKING FOR NEW RECRUITS. GIVE US A CALL SOMETIME.

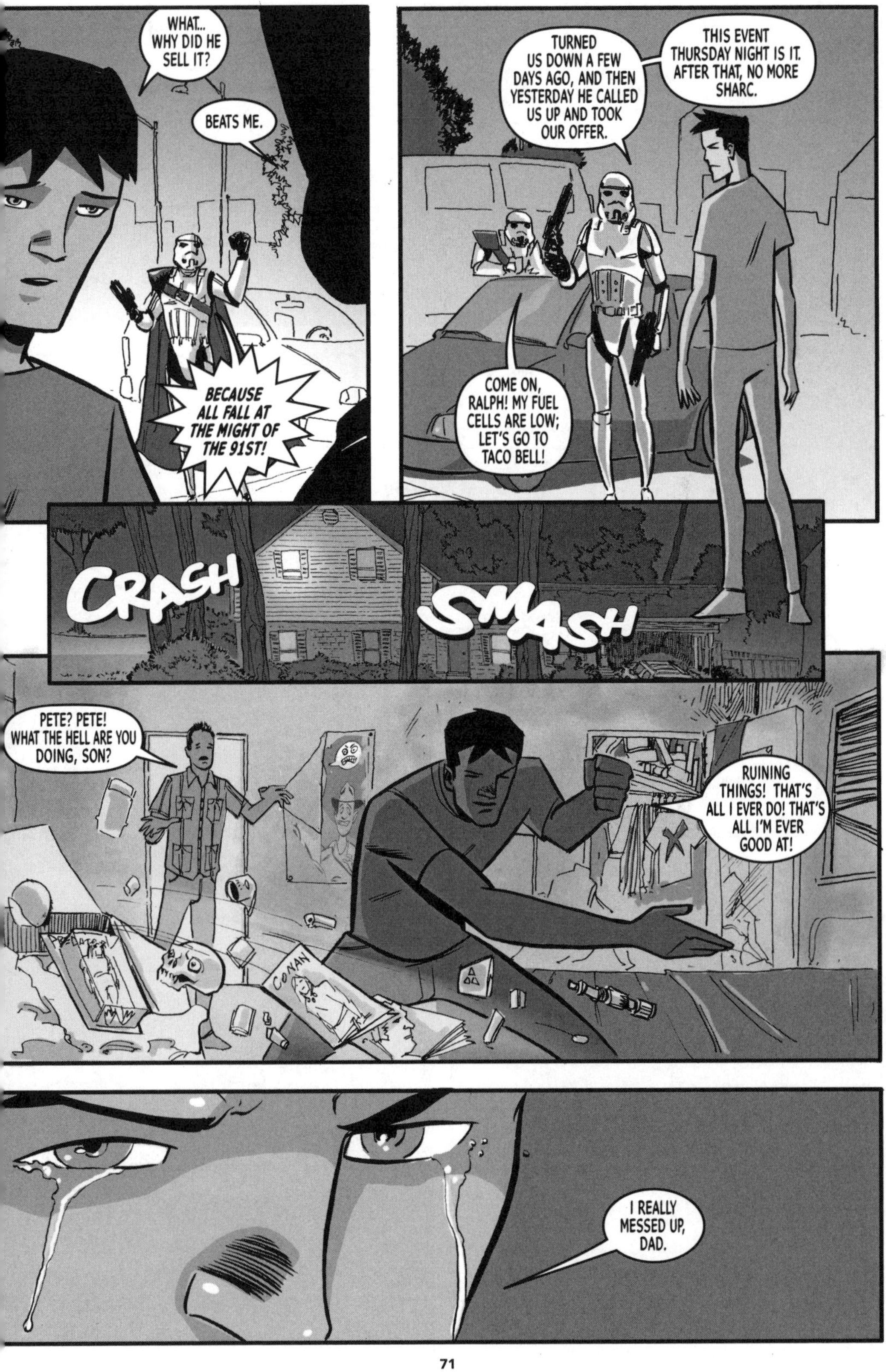
WHAT... WHY DID HE SELL IT?
BEATS ME.
BECAUSE ALL FALL AT THE MIGHT OF THE 91ST!
TURNED US DOWN A FEW DAYS AGO, AND THEN YESTERDAY HE CALLED US UP AND TOOK OUR OFFER.
THIS EVENT THURSDAY NIGHT IS IT. AFTER THAT, NO MORE SHARC.
COME ON, RALPH! MY FUEL CELLS ARE LOW; LET'S GO TO TACO BELL!
CRASH
SMASH
PETE? PETE! WHAT THE HELL ARE YOU DOING, SON?
RUINING THINGS! THAT'S ALL I EVER DO! THAT'S ALL I'M EVER GOOD AT!
CONAN
I REALLY MESSED UP, DAD.

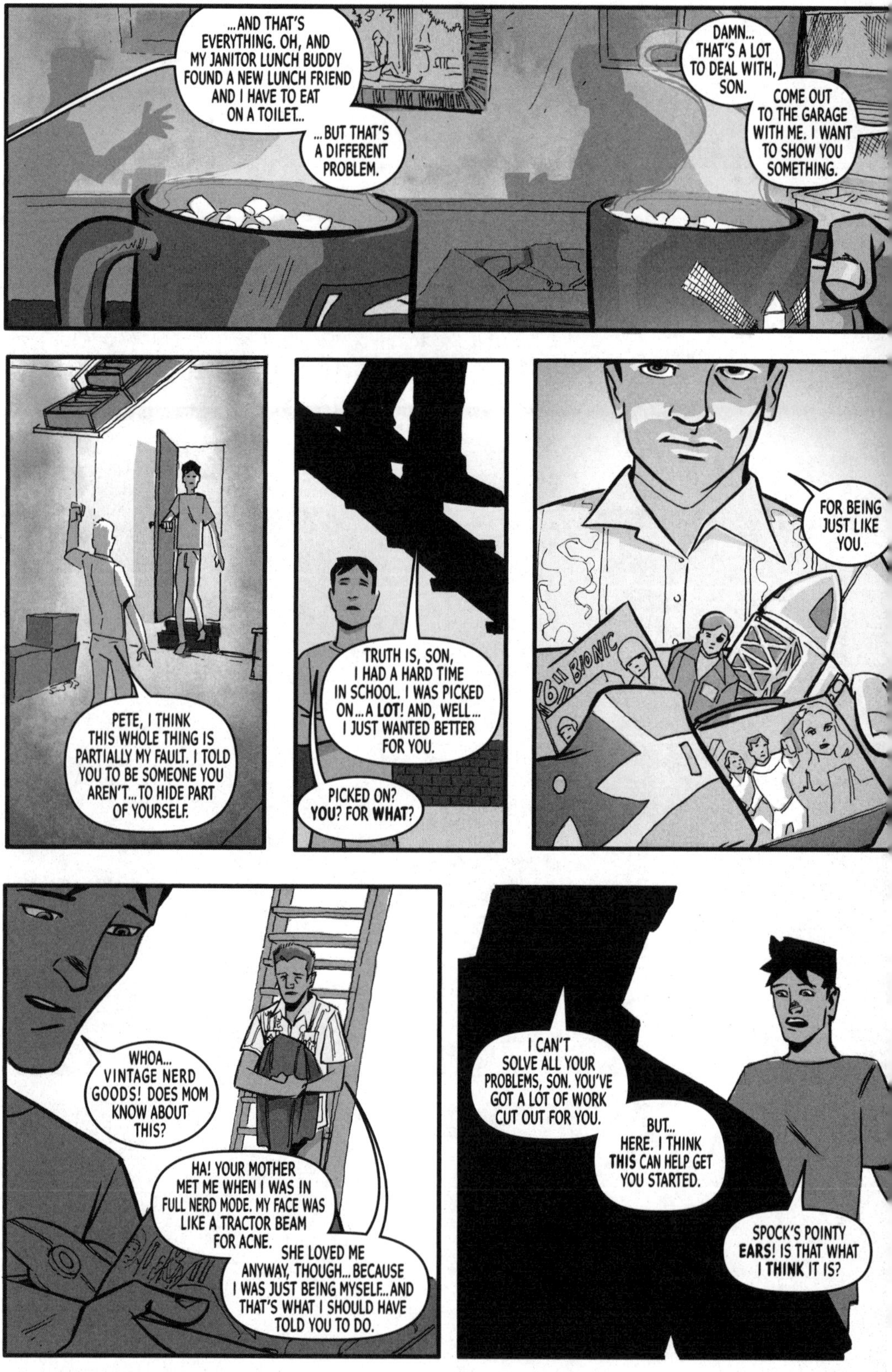
...AND THAT'S EVERYTHING. OH, AND MY JANITOR LUNCH BUDDY FOUND A NEW LUNCH FRIEND AND I HAVE TO EAT ON A TOILET...
...BUT THAT'S A DIFFERENT PROBLEM.
DAMN... THAT'S A LOT TO DEAL WITH, SON.
COME OUT TO THE GARAGE WITH ME. I WANT TO SHOW YOU SOMETHING.
PETE, I THINK THIS WHOLE THING IS PARTIALLY MY FAULT. I TOLD YOU TO BE SOMEONE YOU AREN'T...TO HIDE PART OF YOURSELF.
TRUTH IS, SON, I HAD A HARD TIME IN SCHOOL. I WAS PICKED ON...A LOT! AND, WELL... I JUST WANTED BETTER FOR YOU.
PICKED ON? YOU? FOR WHAT?
FOR BEING JUST LIKE YOU.
BIONIC
WHOA... VINTAGE NERD GOODS! DOES MOM KNOW ABOUT THIS?
HA! YOUR MOTHER MET ME WHEN I WAS IN FULL NERD MODE. MY FACE WAS LIKE A TRACTOR BEAM FOR ACNE.
SHE LOVED ME ANYWAY, THOUGH... BECAUSE I WAS JUST BEING MYSELF...AND THAT'S WHAT I SHOULD HAVE TOLD YOU TO DO.
I CAN'T SOLVE ALL YOUR PROBLEMS, SON. YOU'VE GOT A LOT OF WORK CUT OUT FOR YOU.
BUT... HERE. I THINK THIS CAN HELP GET YOU STARTED.
SPOCK'S POINTY EARS! IS THAT WHAT I THINK IT IS?

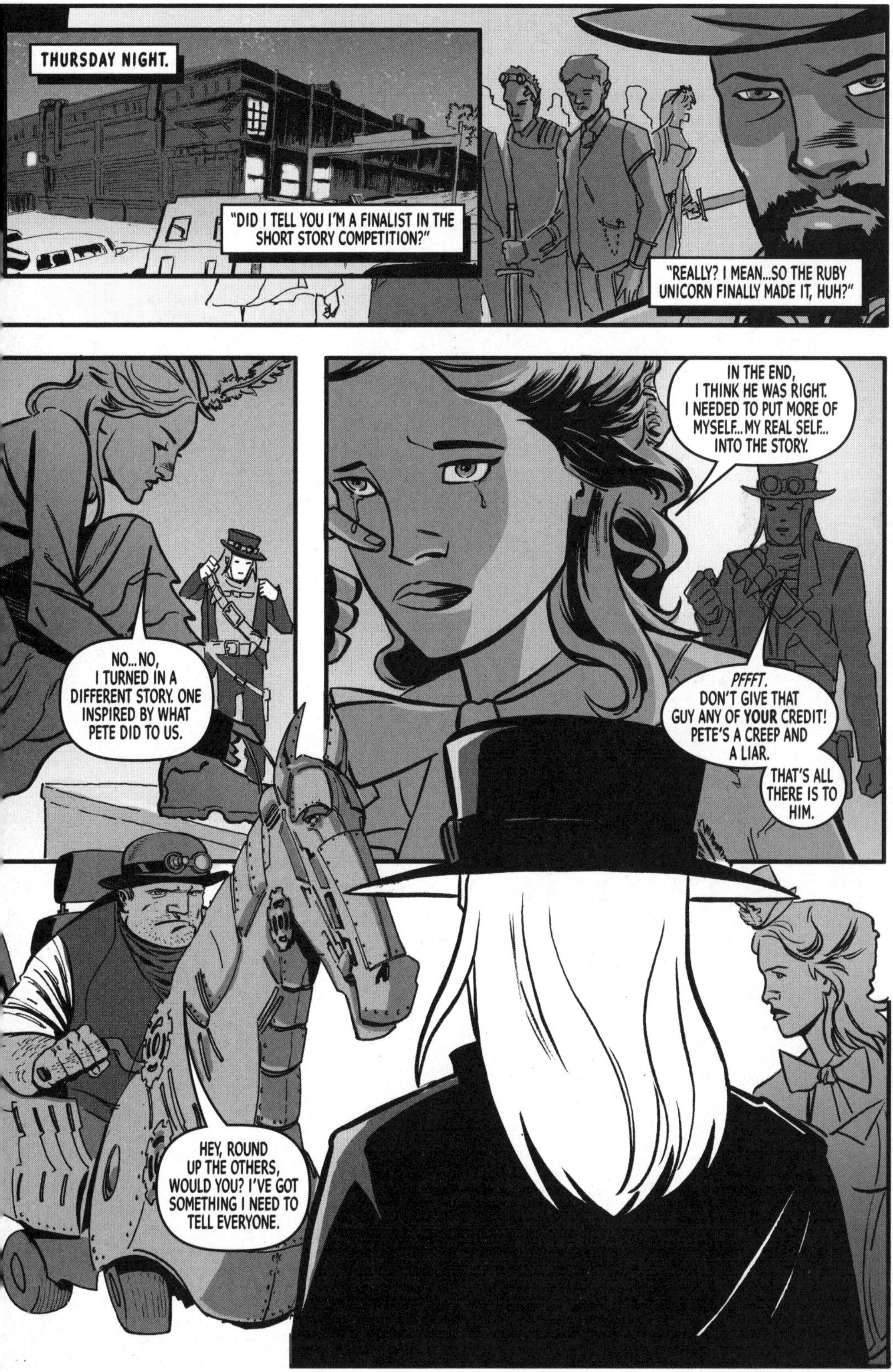
THURSDAY NIGHT.
"DID I TELL YOU I'M A FINALIST IN THE SHORT STORY COMPETITION?"
"REALLY? I MEAN...SO THE RUBY UNICORN FINALLY MADE IT, HUH?"
NO...NO, I TURNED IN A DIFFERENT STORY. ONE INSPIRED BY WHAT PETE DID TO US.
IN THE END, I THINK HE WAS RIGHT. I NEEDED TO PUT MORE OF MYSELF...MY REAL SELF... INTO THE STORY.
PFFFT. DON'T GIVE THAT GUY ANY OF **YOUR** CREDIT! PETE'S A CREEP AND A LIAR.
THAT'S ALL THERE IS TO HIM.
HEY, ROUND UP THE OTHERS, WOULD YOU? I'VE GOT SOMETHING I NEED TO TELL EVERYONE.

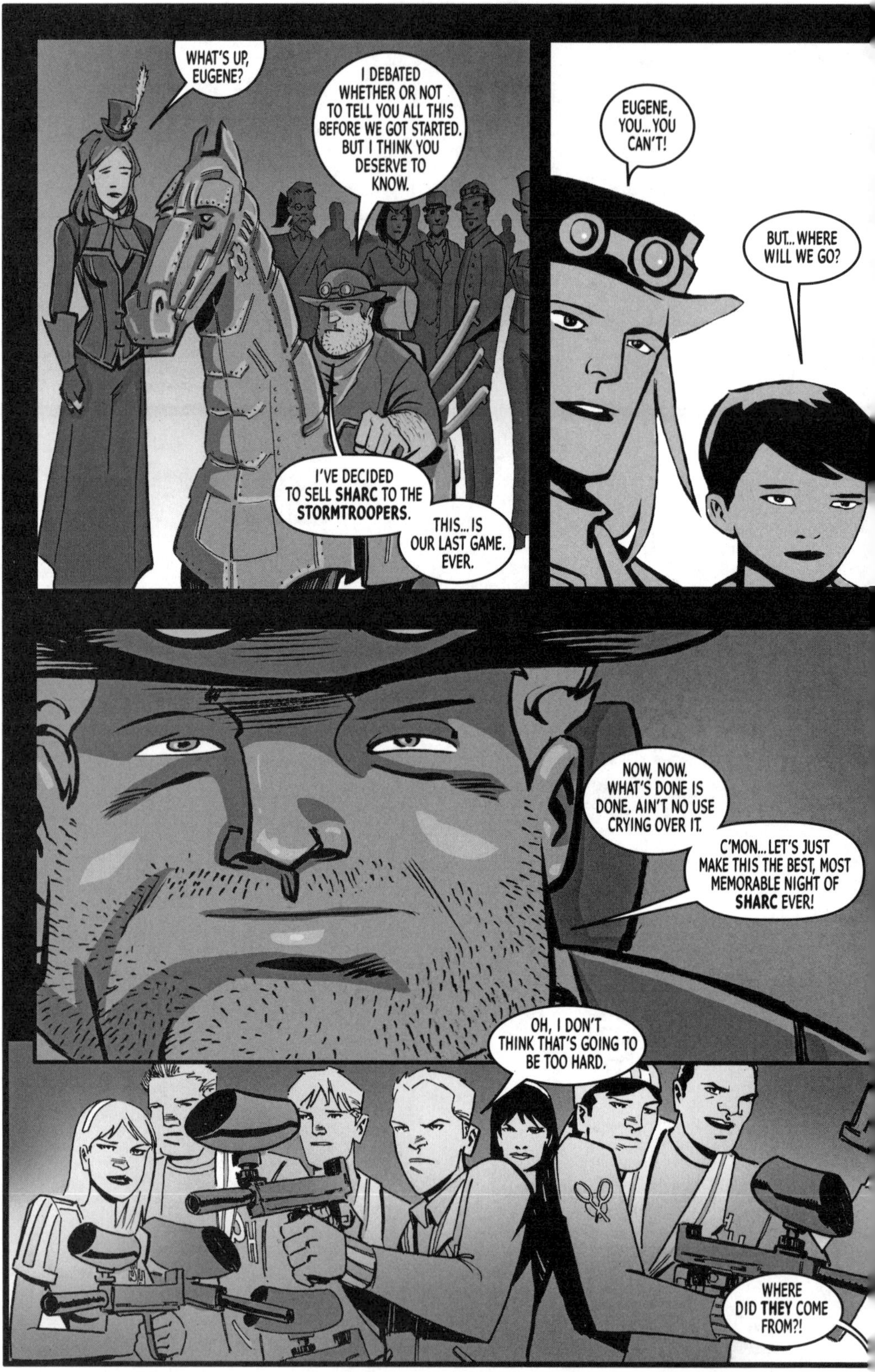
WHAT'S UP, EUGENE?
I DEBATED WHETHER OR NOT TO TELL YOU ALL THIS BEFORE WE GOT STARTED. BUT I THINK YOU DESERVE TO KNOW.
I'VE DECIDED TO SELL **SHARC** TO THE **STORMTROOPERS**.
THIS... IS OUR LAST GAME. EVER.
EUGENE, YOU... YOU CAN'T!
BUT... WHERE WILL WE GO?
NOW, NOW. WHAT'S DONE IS DONE. AIN'T NO USE CRYING OVER IT.
C'MON... LET'S JUST MAKE THIS THE BEST, MOST MEMORABLE NIGHT OF **SHARC** EVER!
OH, I DON'T THINK THAT'S GOING TO BE TOO HARD.
WHERE DID **THEY** COME FROM?!

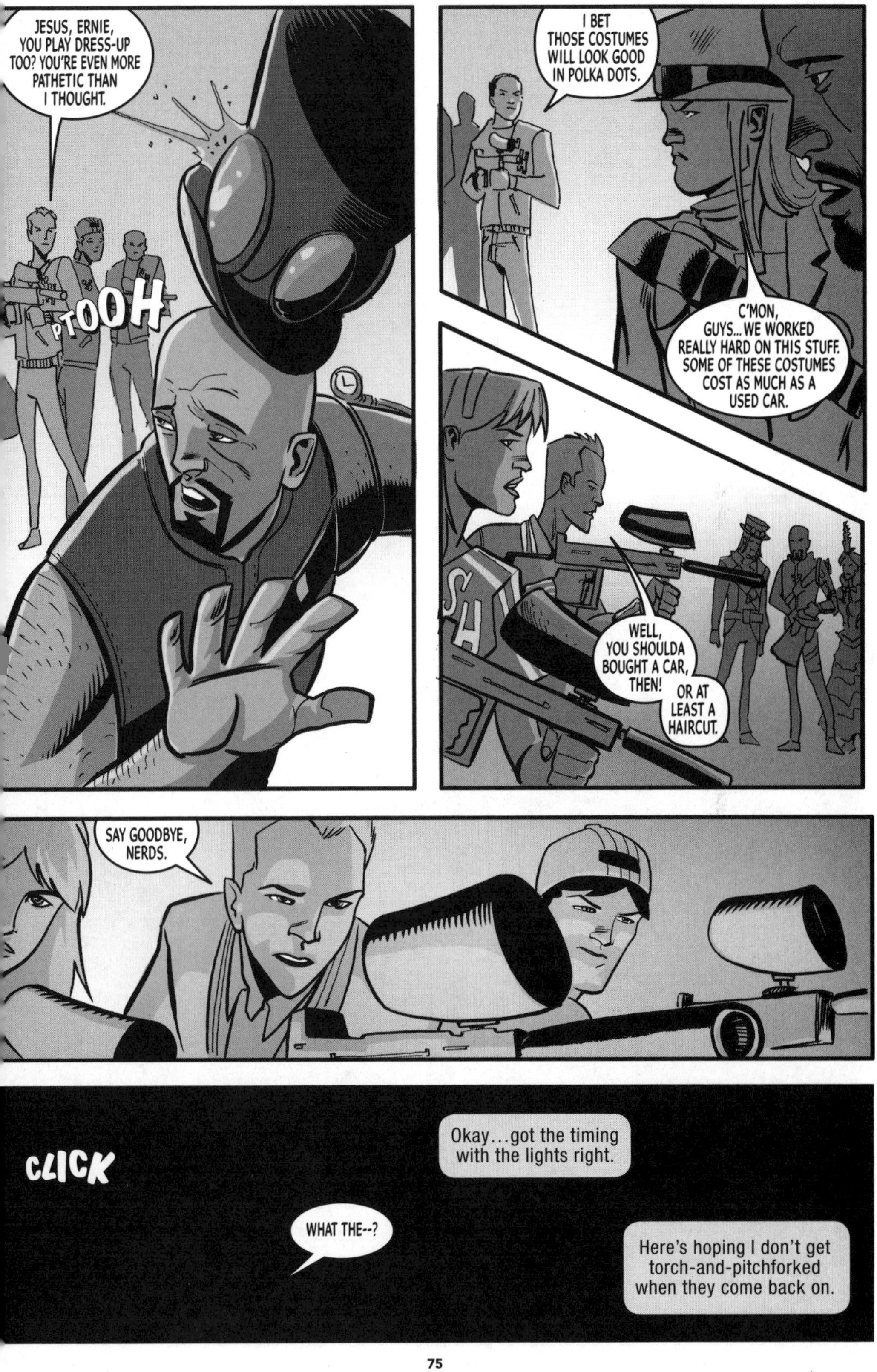
JESUS, ERNIE, YOU PLAY DRESS-UP TOO? YOU'RE EVEN MORE PATHETIC THAN I THOUGHT.
PTOOH
I BET THOSE COSTUMES WILL LOOK GOOD IN POLKA DOTS.
C'MON, GUYS...WE WORKED REALLY HARD ON THIS STUFF. SOME OF THESE COSTUMES COST AS MUCH AS A USED CAR.
WELL, YOU SHOULDA BOUGHT A CAR, THEN!
OR AT LEAST A HAIRCUT.
SAY GOODBYE, NERDS.
CLICK
Okay…got the timing with the lights right.
WHAT THE--?
Here's hoping I don't get torch-and-pitchforked when they come back on.

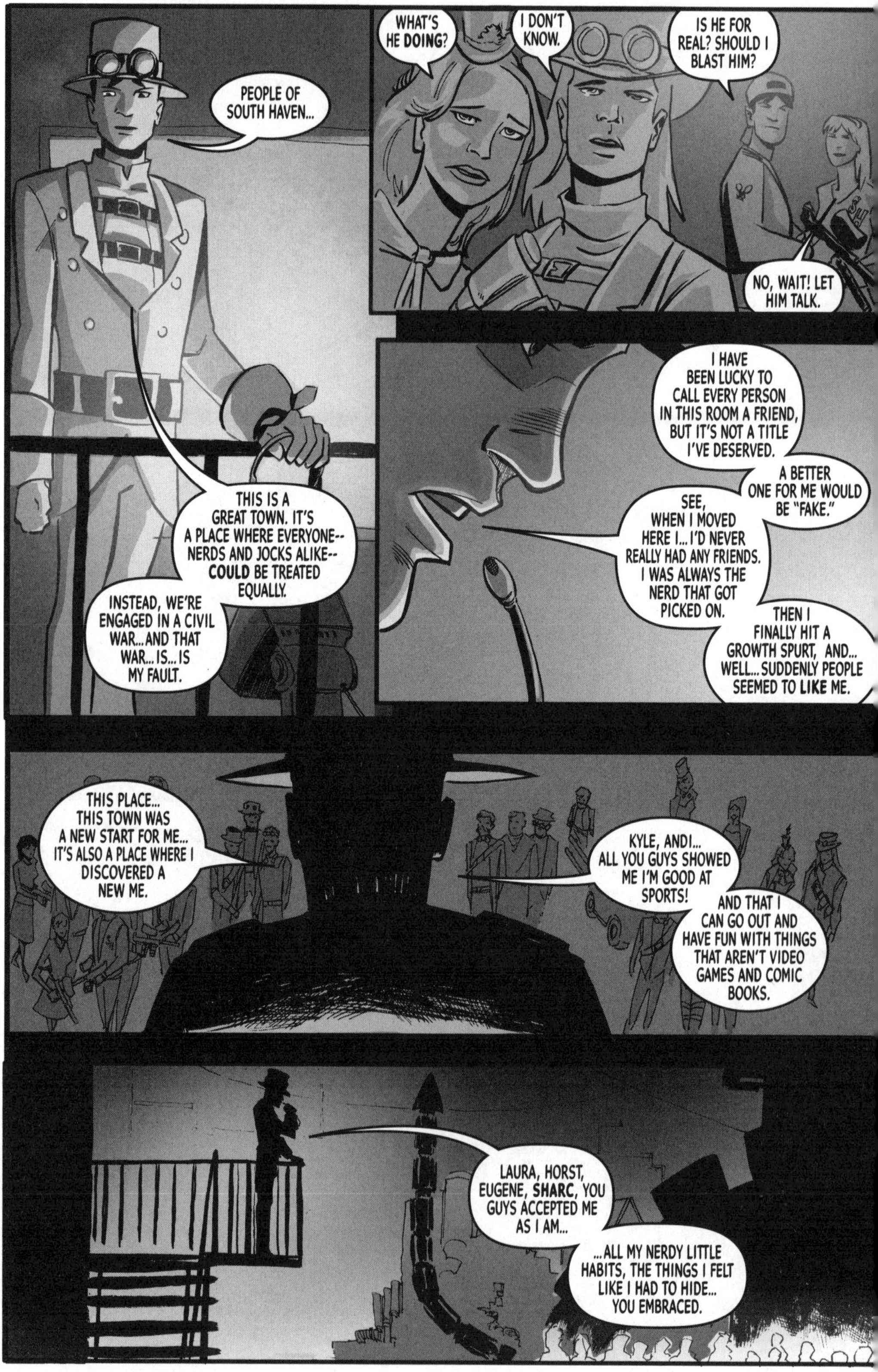
PEOPLE OF SOUTH HAVEN...
WHAT'S HE DOING?
I DON'T KNOW.
IS HE FOR REAL? SHOULD I BLAST HIM?
NO, WAIT! LET HIM TALK.
I HAVE BEEN LUCKY TO CALL EVERY PERSON IN THIS ROOM A FRIEND, BUT IT'S NOT A TITLE I'VE DESERVED.
A BETTER ONE FOR ME WOULD BE "FAKE."
SEE, WHEN I MOVED HERE I... I'D NEVER REALLY HAD ANY FRIENDS. I WAS ALWAYS THE NERD THAT GOT PICKED ON.
THEN I FINALLY HIT A GROWTH SPURT, AND... WELL... SUDDENLY PEOPLE SEEMED TO LIKE ME.
THIS IS A GREAT TOWN. IT'S A PLACE WHERE EVERYONE--NERDS AND JOCKS ALIKE--COULD BE TREATED EQUALLY.
INSTEAD, WE'RE ENGAGED IN A CIVIL WAR...AND THAT WAR...IS...IS MY FAULT.
THIS PLACE... THIS TOWN WAS A NEW START FOR ME... IT'S ALSO A PLACE WHERE I DISCOVERED A NEW ME.
KYLE, ANDI... ALL YOU GUYS SHOWED ME I'M GOOD AT SPORTS!
AND THAT I CAN GO OUT AND HAVE FUN WITH THINGS THAT AREN'T VIDEO GAMES AND COMIC BOOKS.
LAURA, HORST, EUGENE, SHARC, YOU GUYS ACCEPTED ME AS I AM...
...ALL MY NERDY LITTLE HABITS, THE THINGS I FELT LIKE I HAD TO HIDE... YOU EMBRACED.

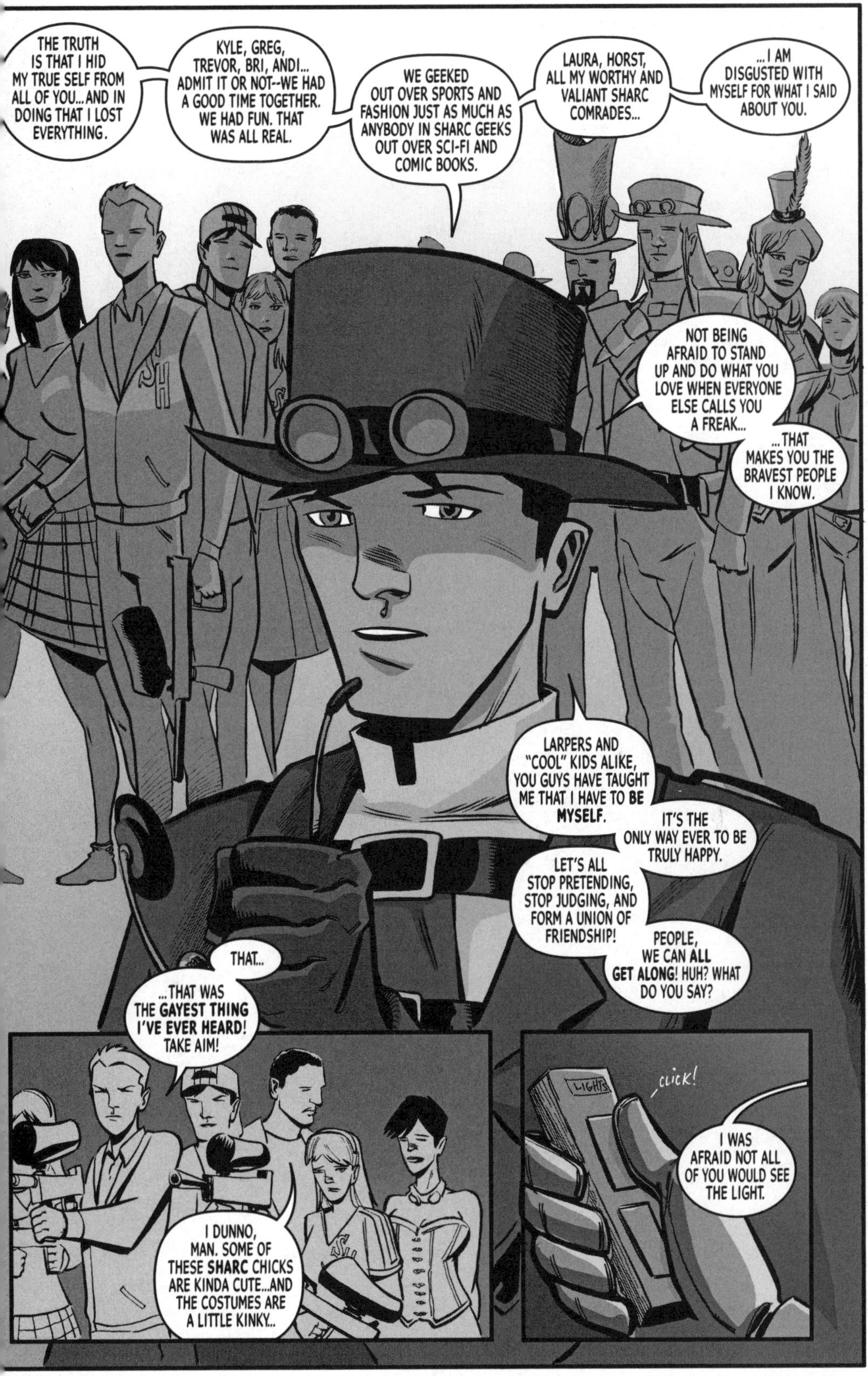
THE TRUTH IS THAT I HID MY TRUE SELF FROM ALL OF YOU...AND IN DOING THAT I LOST EVERYTHING.
KYLE, GREG, TREVOR, BRI, ANDI... ADMIT IT OR NOT--WE HAD A GOOD TIME TOGETHER. WE HAD FUN. THAT WAS ALL REAL.
WE GEEKED OUT OVER SPORTS AND FASHION JUST AS MUCH AS ANYBODY IN SHARC GEEKS OUT OVER SCI-FI AND COMIC BOOKS.
LAURA, HORST, ALL MY WORTHY AND VALIANT SHARC COMRADES...
...I AM DISGUSTED WITH MYSELF FOR WHAT I SAID ABOUT YOU.
NOT BEING AFRAID TO STAND UP AND DO WHAT YOU LOVE WHEN EVERYONE ELSE CALLS YOU A FREAK...
...THAT MAKES YOU THE BRAVEST PEOPLE I KNOW.
LARPERS AND "COOL" KIDS ALIKE, YOU GUYS HAVE TAUGHT ME THAT I HAVE TO **BE MYSELF**.
IT'S THE ONLY WAY EVER TO BE TRULY HAPPY.
LET'S ALL STOP PRETENDING, STOP JUDGING, AND FORM A UNION OF FRIENDSHIP!
PEOPLE, WE CAN **ALL GET ALONG**! HUH? WHAT DO YOU SAY?
THAT...
...THAT WAS THE **GAYEST THING I'VE EVER HEARD**! TAKE AIM!
I DUNNO, MAN. SOME OF THESE **SHARC** CHICKS ARE KINDA CUTE...AND THE COSTUMES ARE A LITTLE KINKY...
LIGHTS
CLICK!
I WAS AFRAID NOT ALL OF YOU WOULD SEE THE LIGHT.

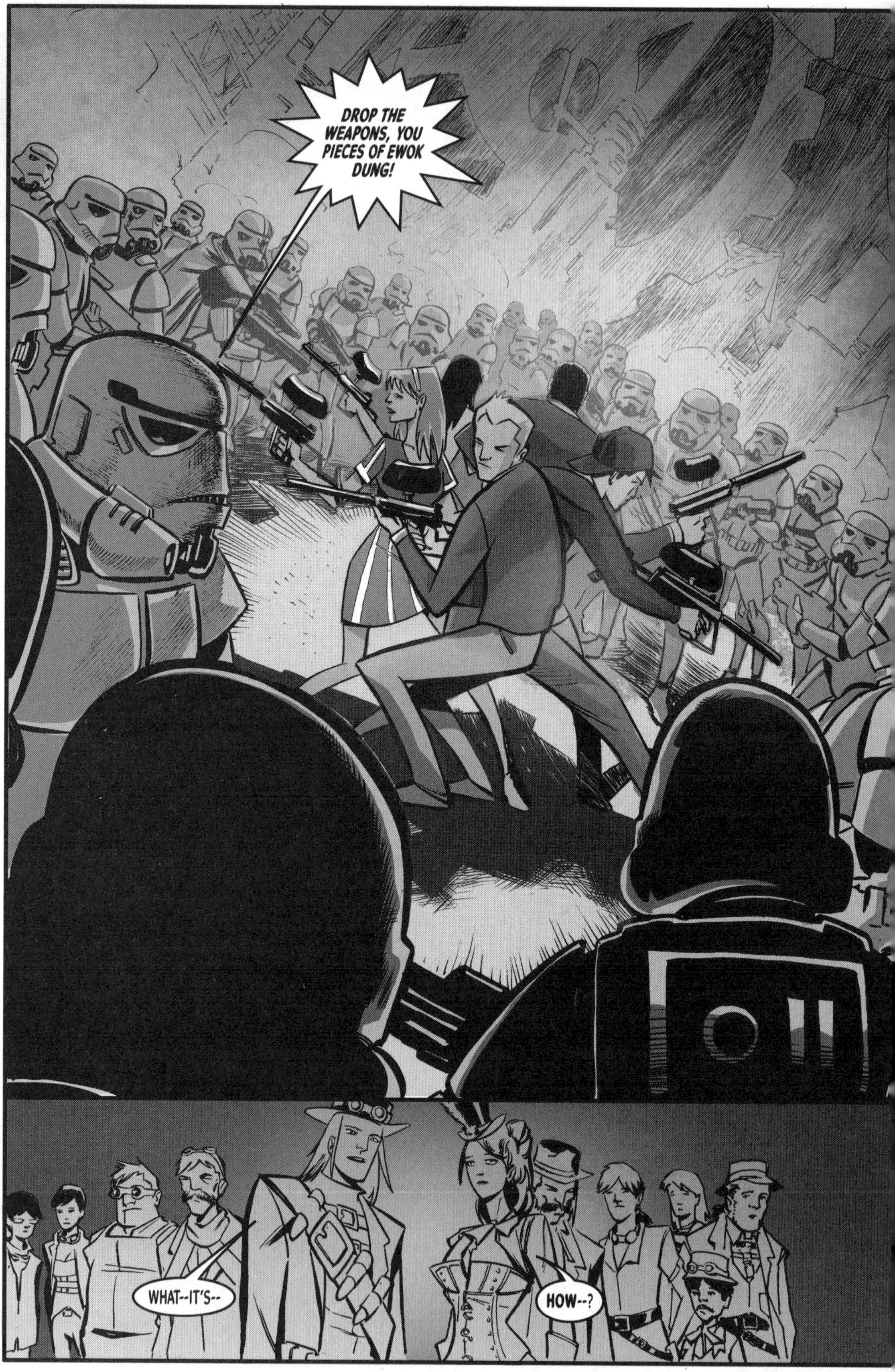
DROP THE WEAPONS, YOU PIECES OF EWOK DUNG!
WHAT--IT'S--
HOW--?

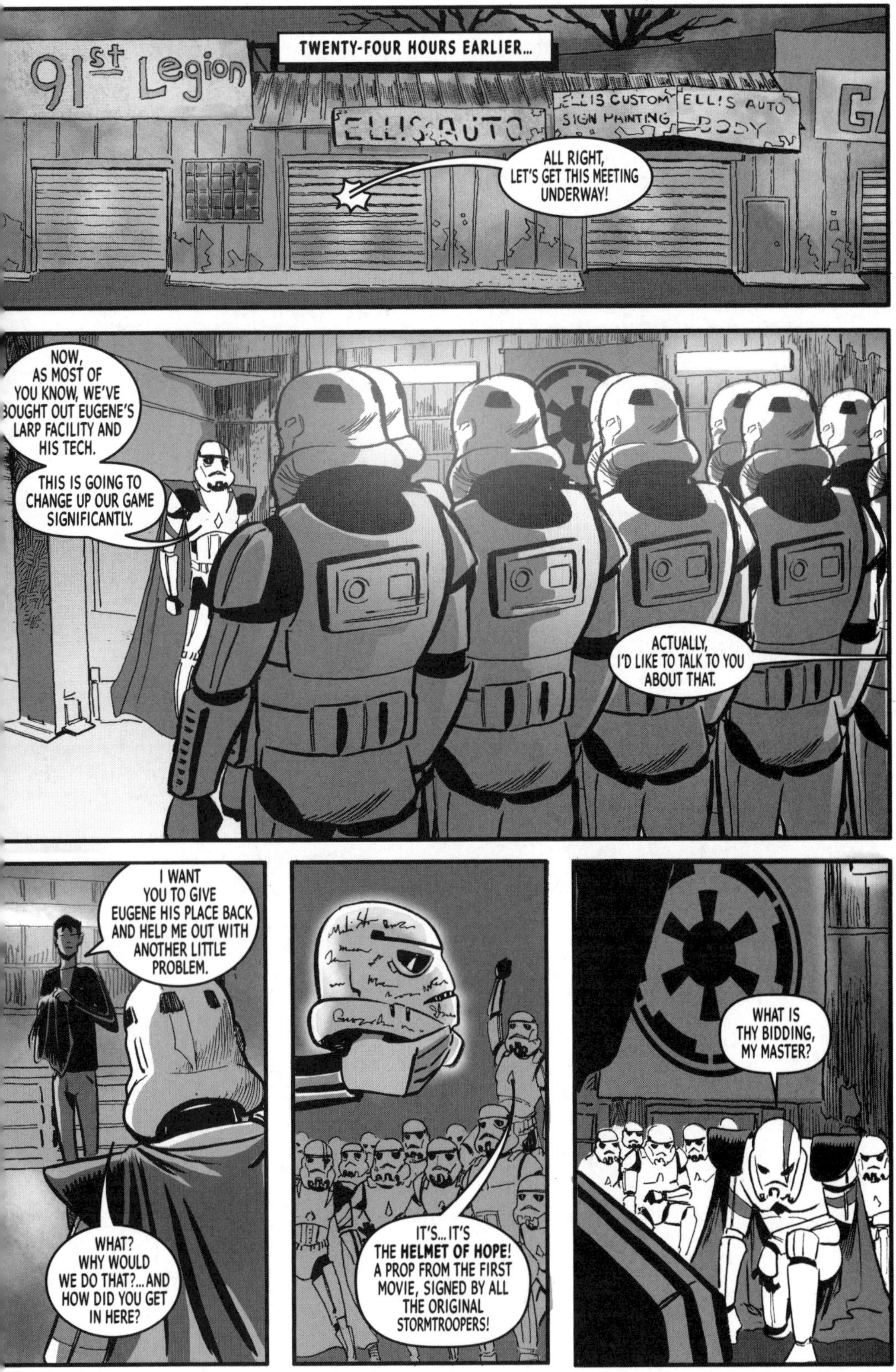

TWENTY-FOUR HOURS EARLIER...
91st Legion
ELLIS AUTO
ELLIS CUSTOM SIGN PAINTING
ELLIS AUTO BODY
ALL RIGHT, LET'S GET THIS MEETING UNDERWAY!
NOW, AS MOST OF YOU KNOW, WE'VE BOUGHT OUT EUGENE'S LARP FACILITY AND HIS TECH.
THIS IS GOING TO CHANGE UP OUR GAME SIGNIFICANTLY.
ACTUALLY, I'D LIKE TO TALK TO YOU ABOUT THAT.
I WANT YOU TO GIVE EUGENE HIS PLACE BACK AND HELP ME OUT WITH ANOTHER LITTLE PROBLEM.
WHAT? WHY WOULD WE DO THAT?...AND HOW DID YOU GET IN HERE?
IT'S...IT'S THE **HELMET OF HOPE**! A PROP FROM THE FIRST MOVIE, SIGNED BY ALL THE ORIGINAL STORMTROOPERS!
WHAT IS THY BIDDING, MY MASTER?

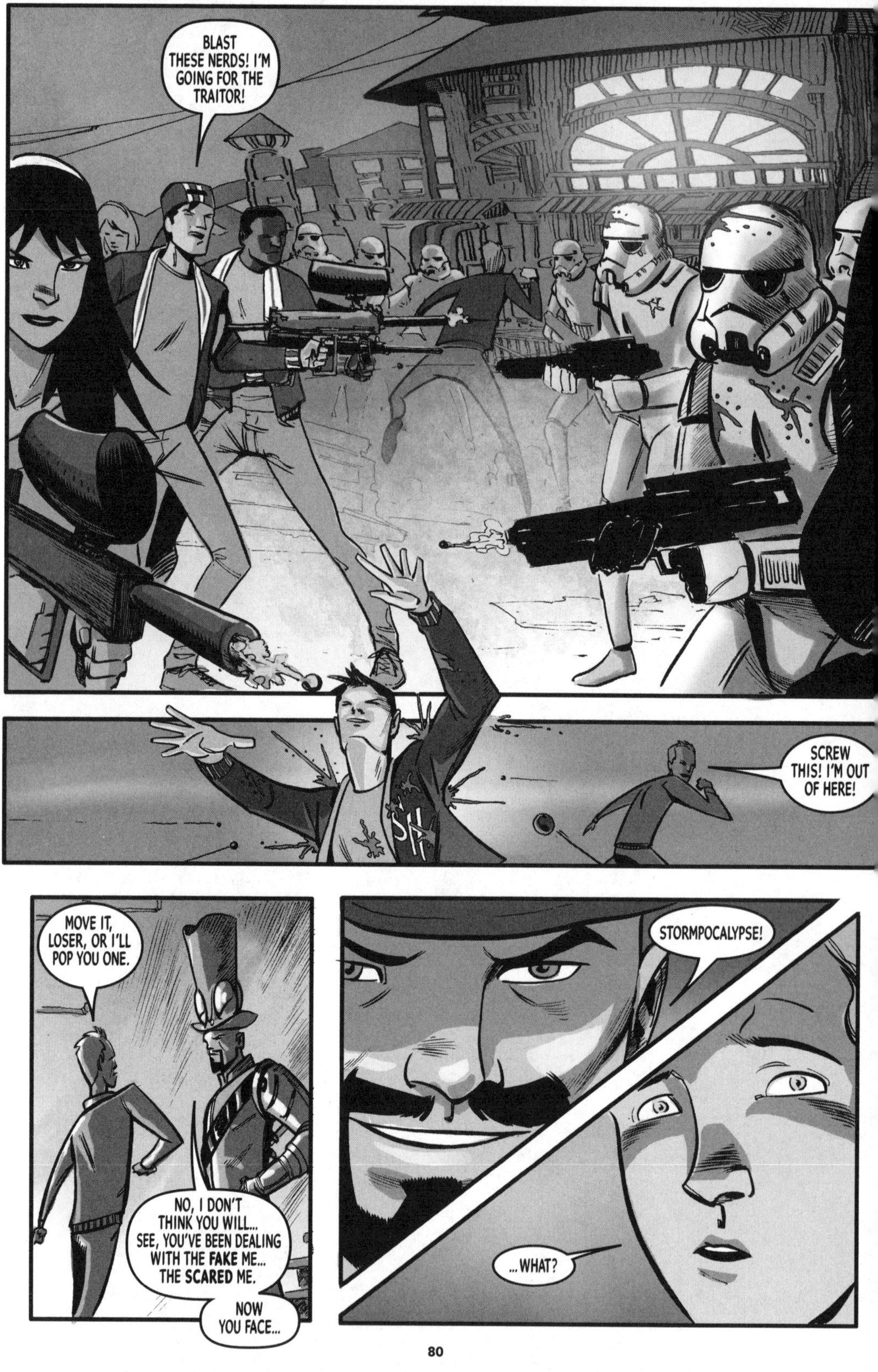
BLAST THESE NERDS! I'M GOING FOR THE TRAITOR!
SCREW THIS! I'M OUT OF HERE!
MOVE IT, LOSER, OR I'LL POP YOU ONE.
NO, I DON'T THINK YOU WILL... SEE, YOU'VE BEEN DEALING WITH THE FAKE ME... THE SCARED ME.
NOW YOU FACE...
STORMPOCALYPSE!
...WHAT?

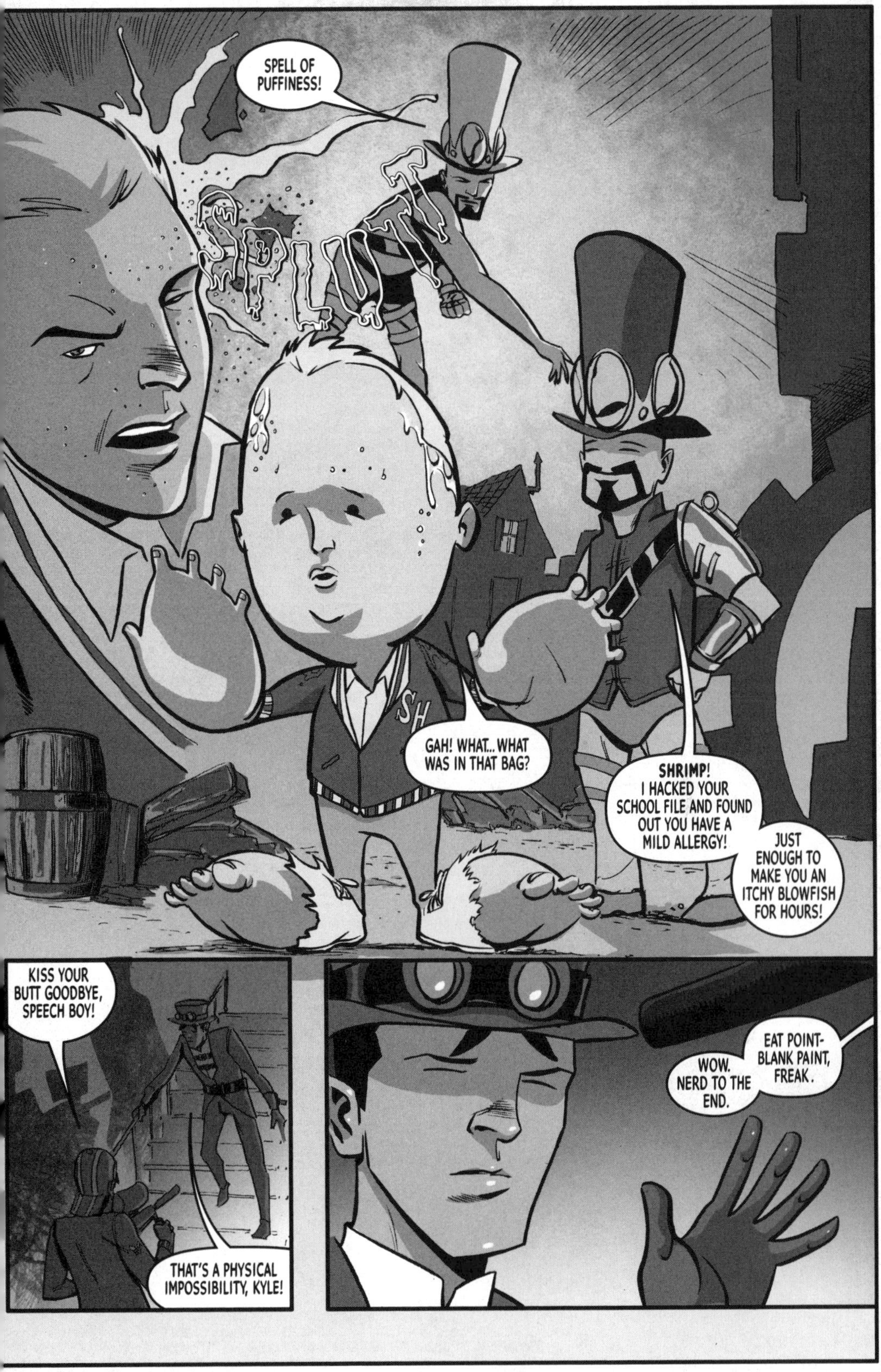
SPELL OF PUFFINESS!
SPLUT
GAH! WHAT... WHAT WAS IN THAT BAG?
SHRIMP! I HACKED YOUR SCHOOL FILE AND FOUND OUT YOU HAVE A MILD ALLERGY!
JUST ENOUGH TO MAKE YOU AN ITCHY BLOWFISH FOR HOURS!
KISS YOUR BUTT GOODBYE, SPEECH BOY!
THAT'S A PHYSICAL IMPOSSIBILITY, KYLE!
EAT POINT-BLANK PAINT, FREAK.
WOW. NERD TO THE END.

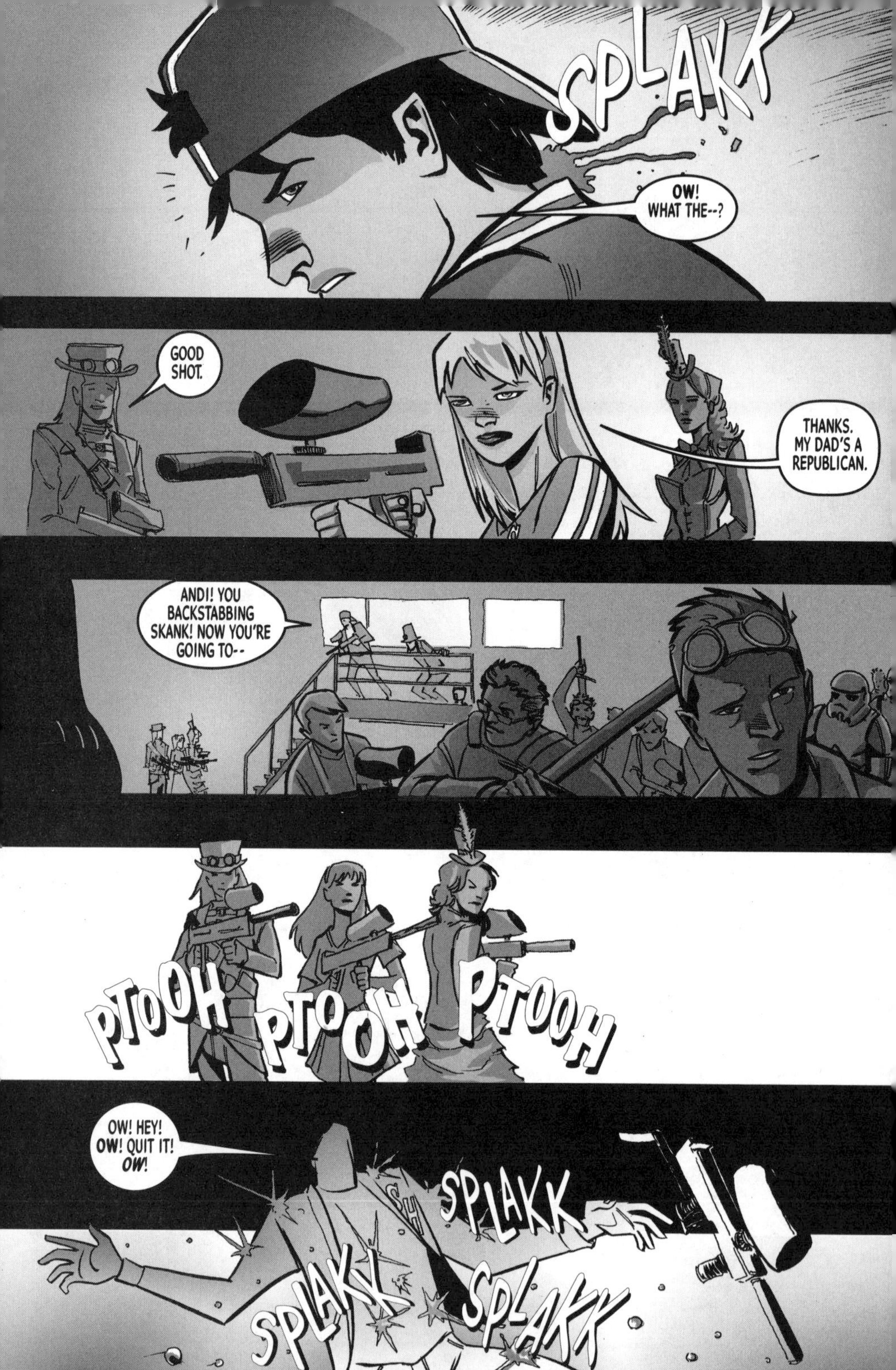
SPLAKK
OW! WHAT THE--?
GOOD SHOT.
THANKS. MY DAD'S A REPUBLICAN.
ANDI! YOU BACKSTABBING SKANK! NOW YOU'RE GOING TO--
PTOOH
PTOOH
PTOOH
OW! HEY! OW! QUIT IT! *OW!*
SPLAKK
SPLAKK
SPLAKK

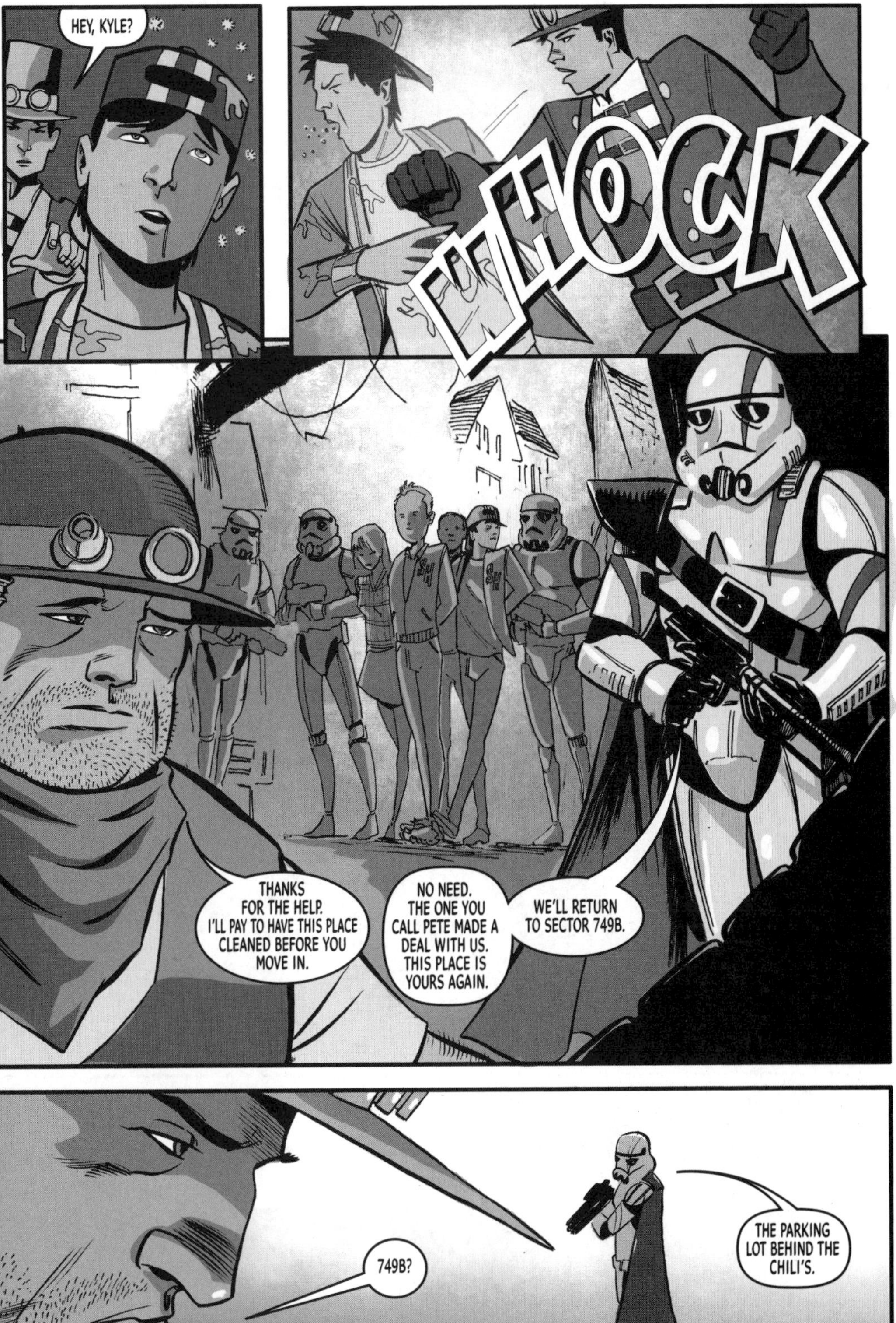
HEY, KYLE?
WHOCK
THANKS FOR THE HELP. I'LL PAY TO HAVE THIS PLACE CLEANED BEFORE YOU MOVE IN.
NO NEED. THE ONE YOU CALL PETE MADE A DEAL WITH US. THIS PLACE IS YOURS AGAIN.
WE'LL RETURN TO SECTOR 749B.
749B?
THE PARKING LOT BEHIND THE CHILI'S.

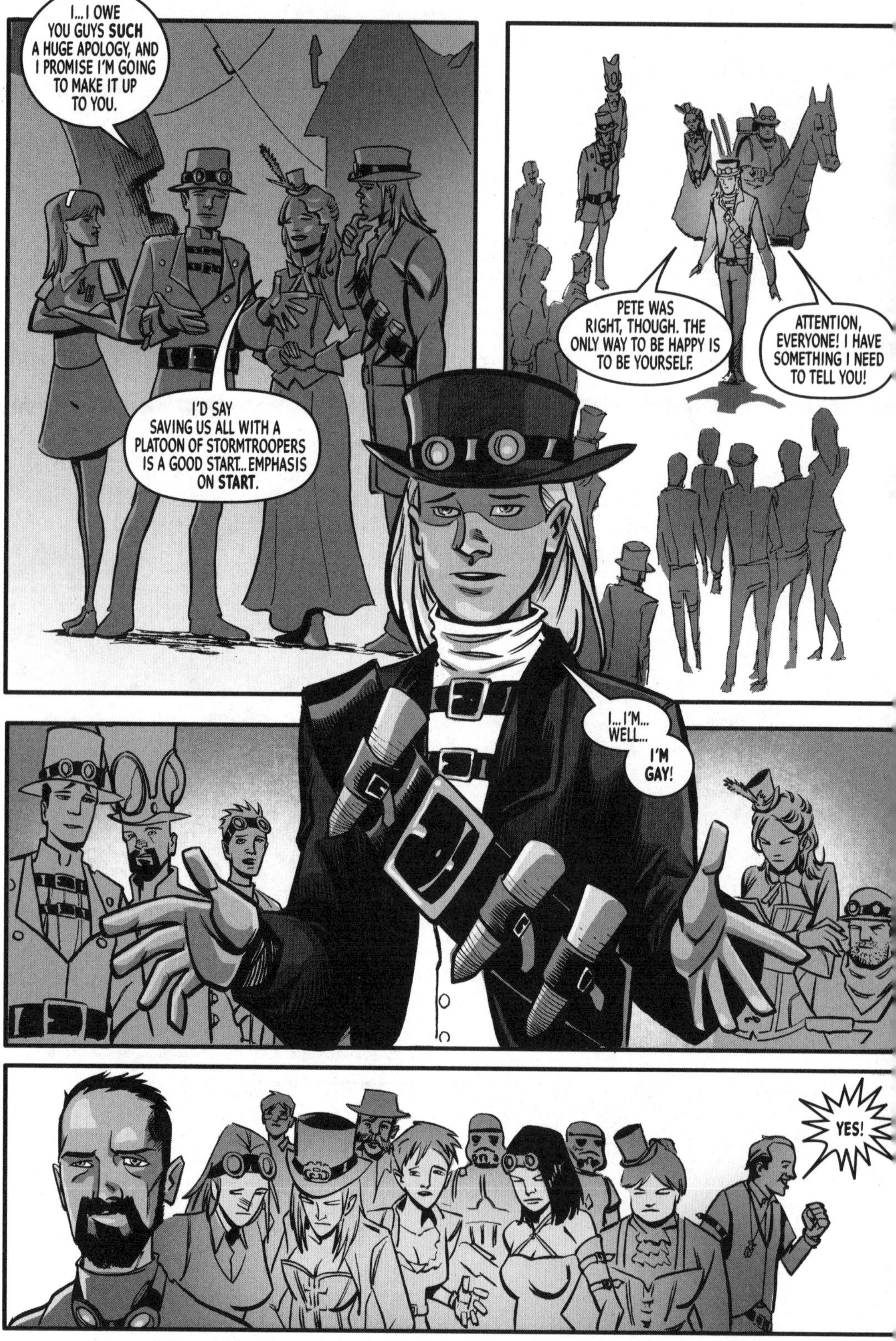

I...I OWE YOU GUYS SUCH A HUGE APOLOGY, AND I PROMISE I'M GOING TO MAKE IT UP TO YOU.
I'D SAY SAVING US ALL WITH A PLATOON OF STORMTROOPERS IS A GOOD START...EMPHASIS ON START.
ATTENTION, EVERYONE! I HAVE SOMETHING I NEED TO TELL YOU!
PETE WAS RIGHT, THOUGH. THE ONLY WAY TO BE HAPPY IS TO BE YOURSELF.
I...I'M... WELL...
I'M GAY!
YES!

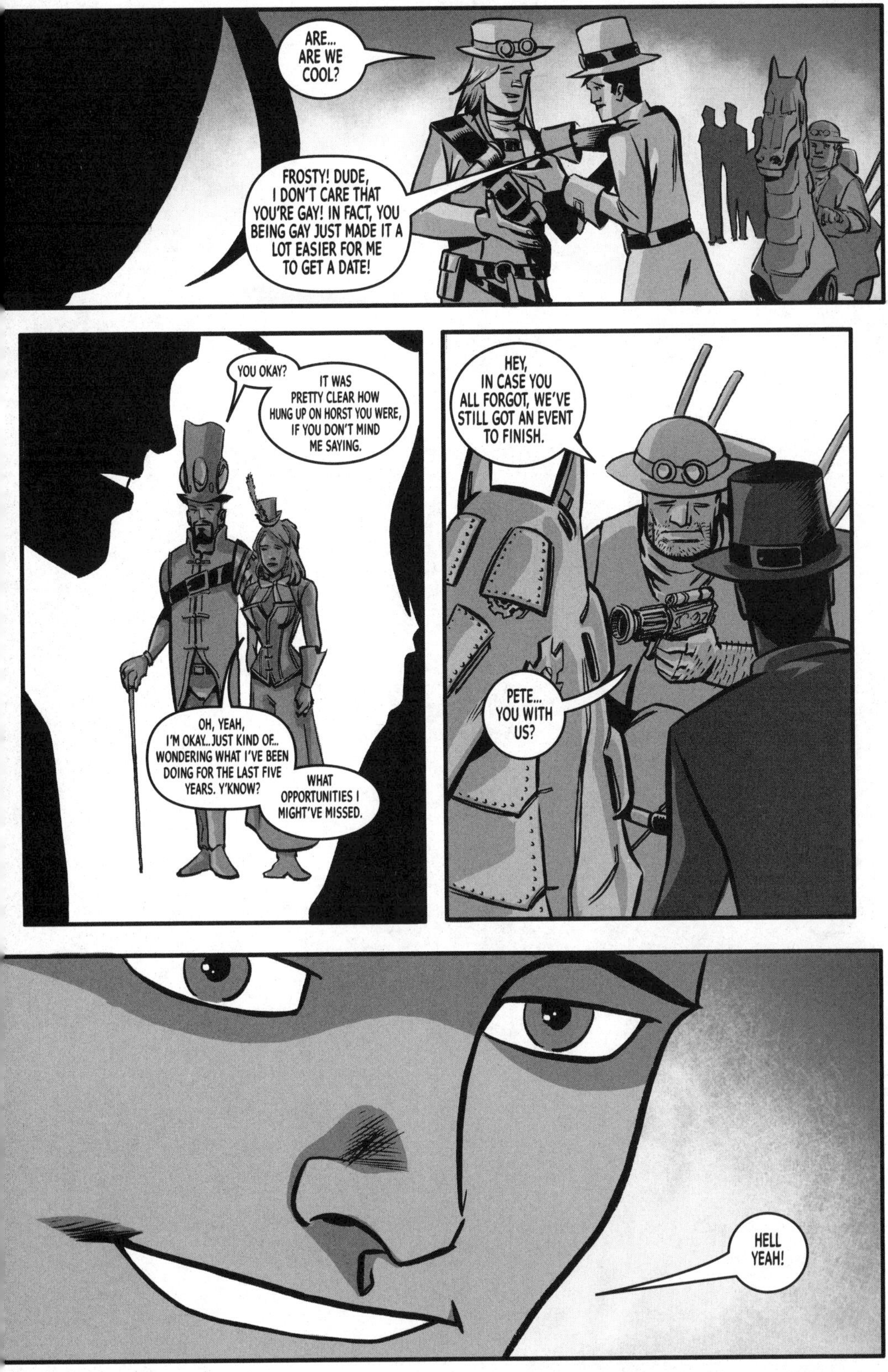

ARE... ARE WE COOL?
FROSTY! DUDE, I DON'T CARE THAT YOU'RE GAY! IN FACT, YOU BEING GAY JUST MADE IT A LOT EASIER FOR ME TO GET A DATE!
YOU OKAY?
IT WAS PRETTY CLEAR HOW HUNG UP ON HORST YOU WERE, IF YOU DON'T MIND ME SAYING.
OH, YEAH, I'M OKAY...JUST KIND OF... WONDERING WHAT I'VE BEEN DOING FOR THE LAST FIVE YEARS. Y'KNOW?
WHAT OPPORTUNITIES I MIGHT'VE MISSED.
HEY, IN CASE YOU ALL FORGOT, WE'VE STILL GOT AN EVENT TO FINISH.
PETE... YOU WITH US?
HELL YEAH!

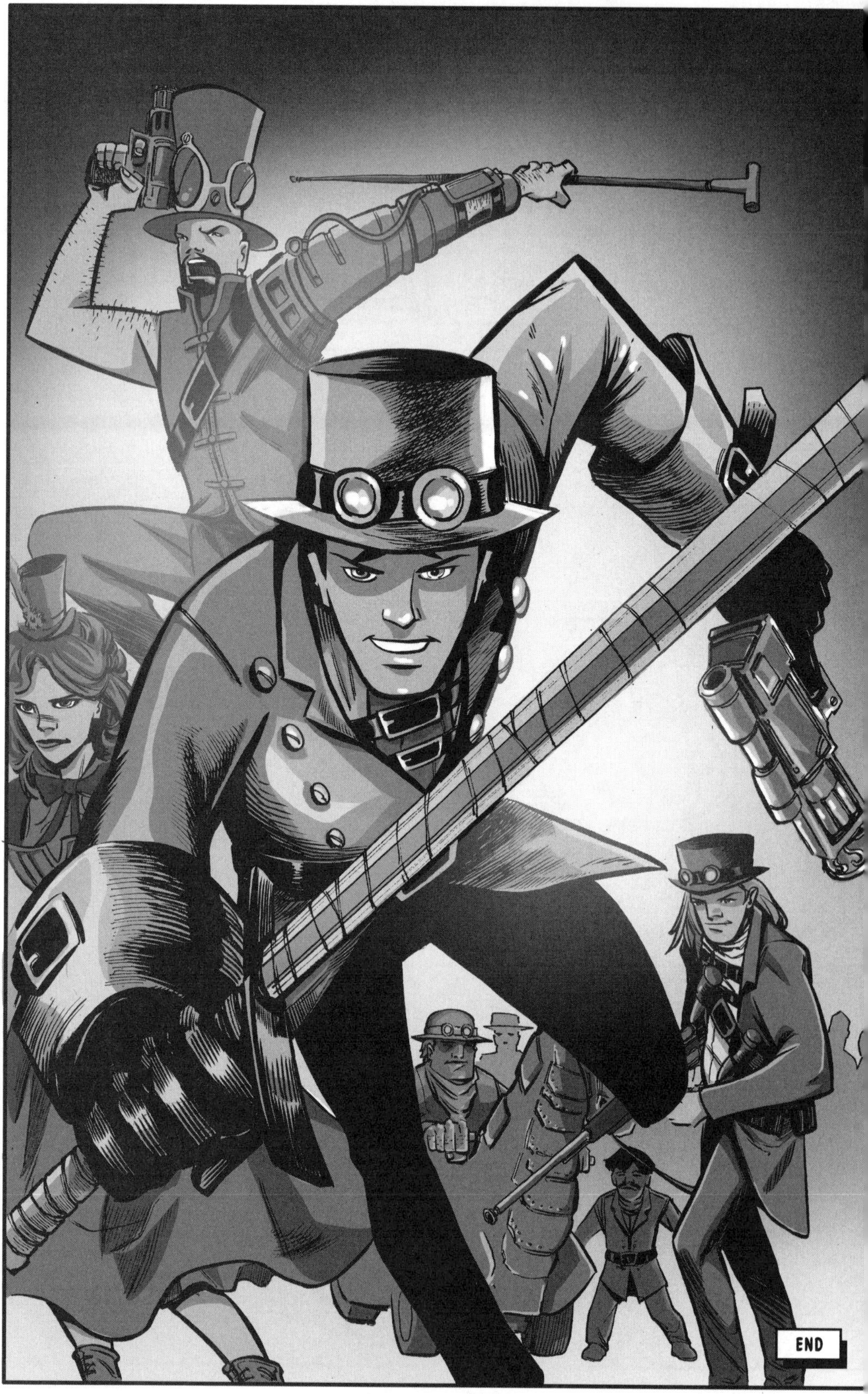
END

NEXT

THE COOL KIDS STRIKE BACK!

SHARC gets a surprising new member, Laura's literary ambitions grow, and the tennis squad vows revenge, in . . .

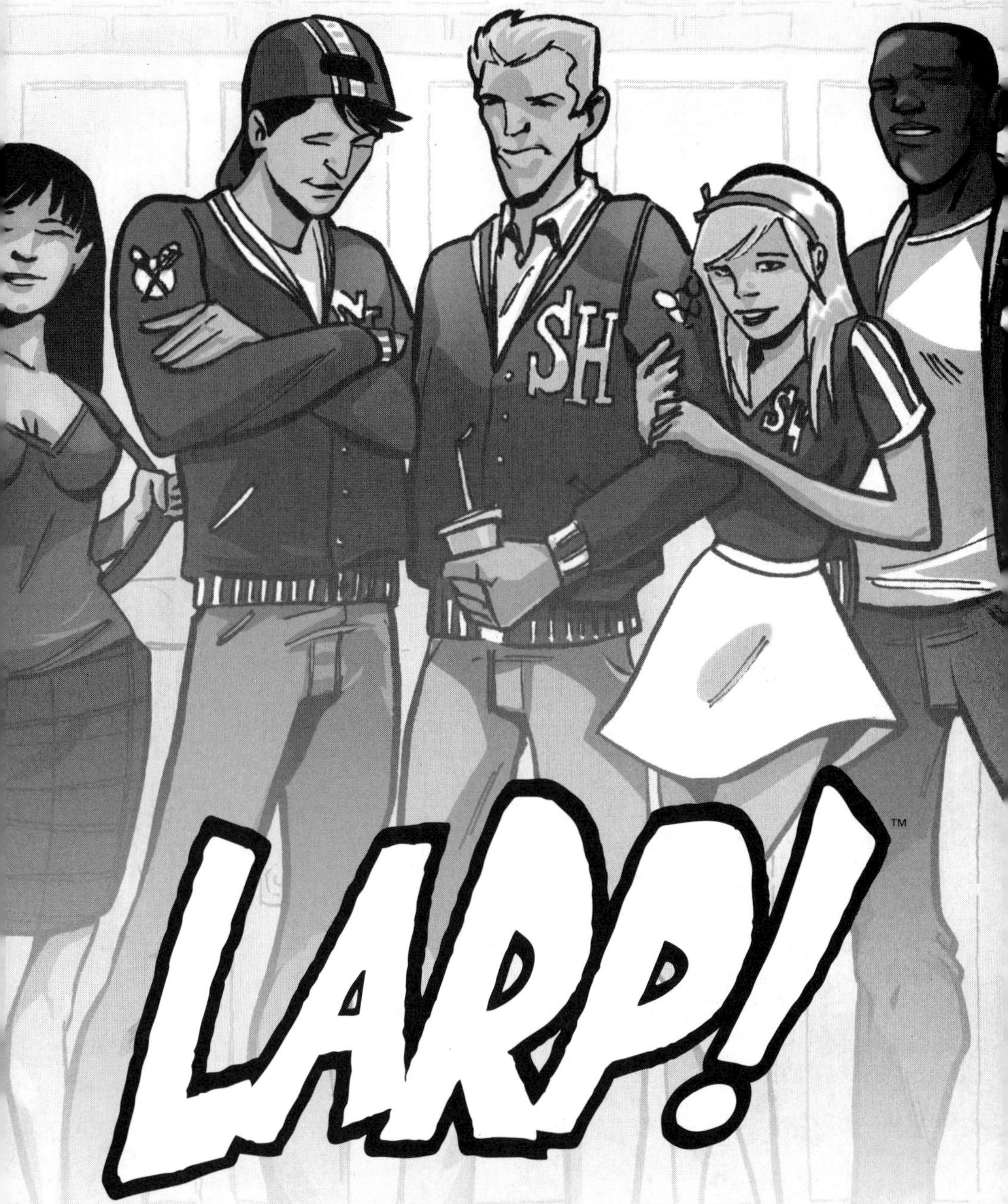
SH
LARP!™

BOOK 2

THE BIG CON!

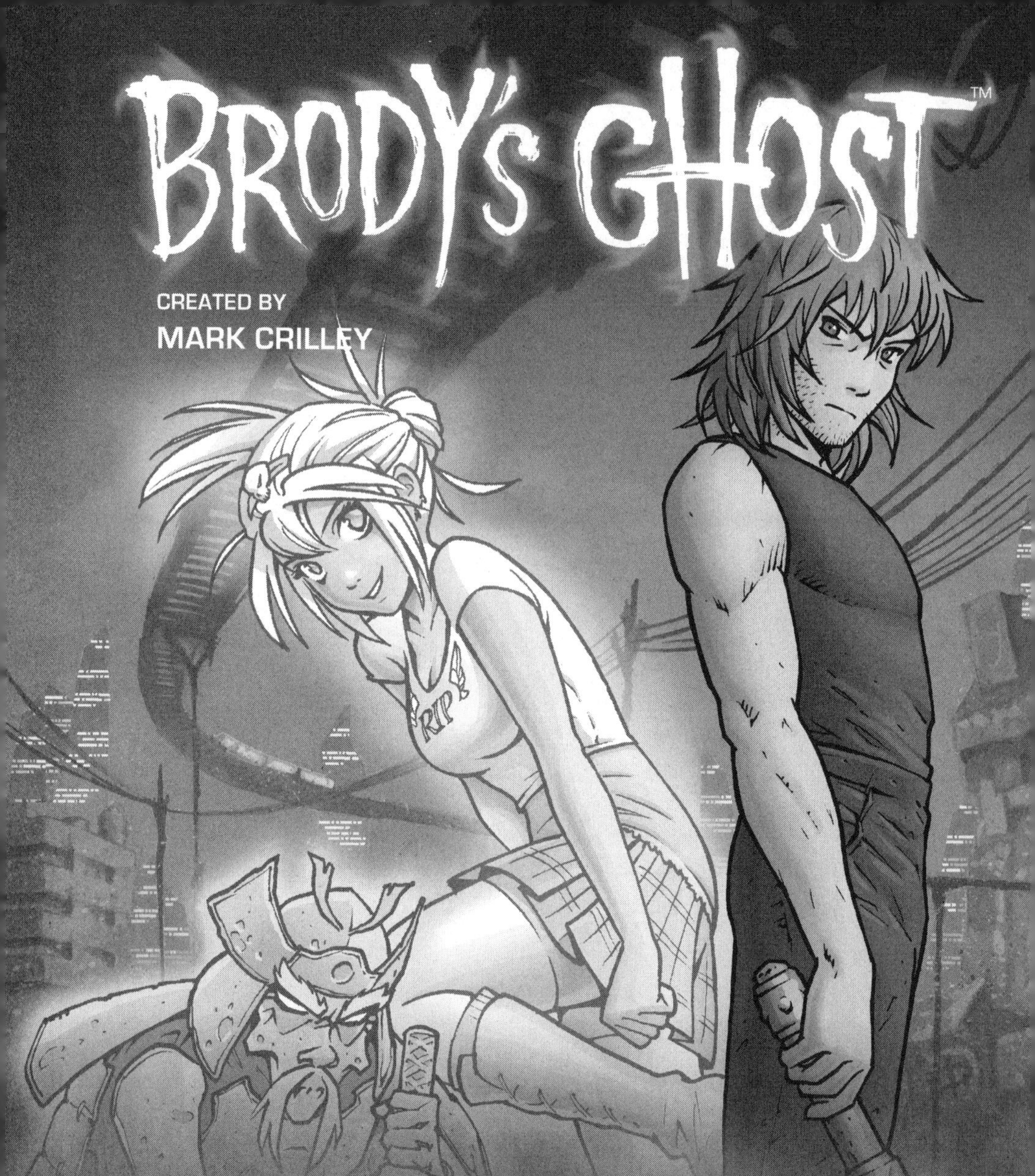
BRODY'S GHOST™
CREATED BY
MARK CRILLEY
RIP

Brody hoped it was just a hallucination. But the teenaged ghostly girl who'd come face to face with him in the middle of a busy city street was all too real. And now she was back, telling him she needed his help in hunting down a dangerous killer, and that he must undergo training from the spirit of a centuries-old samurai to unlock his hidden supernatural powers.

Thirteen-time Eisner Award nominee Mark Crilley creates his most original and action-packed saga to date!

BOOK 1	BOOK 2	BOOK 3	BOOK 4	BOOK 5	BOOK 6
978-1-59582-521-6	978-1-59582-665-7	978-1-59582-862-0	978-1-61655-129-2	978-1-61655-460-6	978-1-61655-461-3
$6.99	$6.99	$6.99	$6.99	$7.99	$7.99

AVAILABLE AT YOUR LOCAL COMICS SHOP OR BOOKSTORE To find a comics shop in your area, call 1-888-266-4226
For more information or to order direct: • On the web: DarkHorse.com
E-mail: mailorder@darkhorse.com • Phone: 1-800-862-0052 Mon.–Fri. 9 AM to 5 PM Pacific Time.

DARK HORSE BOOKS
DarkHorse.com